Also by Undra E. Biggs

When You Look At Me
0-9647635-6-7; June 2000

Other La Caille Nous titles

Separate but Equal
0-9718191-4-9; Sept. 2002

The Canon of Loose Canons
0-9718191-2-2; July 2002

When He Calls
0-9647635-9-1; June 2002

Father's Footsteps
0-9718191-1-4; June 2002

Bard From Par Taken
0-9718191-0-6; June 2002

Water in a Broken Glass
0-9647635-7-5; Sept. 2000

Temples
0-9647635-5-9; Feb. 1999

The Masks of Flipside
0-9647635-4-0; May 1998

Party Ain't Over Yet!
0-9647635-3-2; March 1997

The A# Blu's
0-9647635-2-4; Sept. 1996

My Baby's Father
0-9647635-8-3; April 2001 (revd.)

LoneWolf's Cry
0-9647635-0-8; Feb. 1996

BACKFIELD IN MOTION

BACKFIELD IN MOTION

Undra E. Biggs

La Caille Nous

Edited by Guichard Cadet

Cover Model: Donald McLeon
Cover Photo by Michael Washington
Cover Design by Shane Hudalla

Biggs, Undra E., 1966-
  Backfield in motion / Undra E. Biggs.
    p. cm.
  ISBN 0-9718191-3-0 (pbk.)
    1. African American football players—Fiction. 2. Triangles (Interpersonal relations)—Fiction. 3. African American families—Fiction. 4. Mothers and sons— Fiction. 5. Married people—Fiction. I. Title.

  PS3552.I435 B34 2002
  813'.6--dc21   2002024010

La Caille Nous Publishing Company, Inc.
PO Box 1004
Riverdale, MD 20738
www.lcnpub.com

Media & Distribution
328 Flatbush Avenue, Suite 240
Brooklyn, NY 11238
212-726-1293

DEDICATION

To the Angels who have come and gone swiftly across our paths,
And to the souls who are left to hold their memories dear.

If my pen can write
What my mind imagines
What my eyes see
And what my heart feels
Then let the experiences of my being
Be an Open Book

In hopes that HE will say "Well Done"

AKNOWLEDGMENTS

First and foremost GOD from Whom ALL BLESSINGS flow!!!

To my home town Trenton, New Jersey

Husband: Alvin R. Biggs, Sr., Children: Miya S. Jones-Biggs and Alvin R. Biggs, Jr. Parents: Charles and Dolly Clay; Family: William, Stella and Josephine Biggs; Kenneth, Brenda and Kenny McLeon; Ray and Keneisha Roberts; Linda, Tashara and Terron Edwards; and The Francis Family.

For their "STRONG" support of *When You Look At Me*: Mommy and Daddy; Jacqueline Clay; Aunt Anna Mae and Uncle Joe; HPP family; the American Standards Klocknor Rd. Gang; Baby Girl-Jennifer Leach, Joseph McLaurin; Valerie Rushmore; Andrea C. Seay; Donna Williams; Leslie Morris; Della Sutton; Brenda Brisbane; Sharrod J. Stewart; Tawanda White; Bonnie Reed; Jack Washington; Darrine Morris of Cream Magazine; ShaMecha Simms of City News Publishing; Carla Canty of SaywordTV; Feona S. Huff of The Black Rein newspaper; Ron Kavanaugh of Mosaic Literary Magazine; Mamu Rangel of Phenomenal Sistah; Imani Fuqa, Melissa Lee and ladies of Mind and Soul Bookstore; Learie Cunningham and Culture Plus Books; Maxine & Henry Page; Willie's Barbershop in Burlington; Foster's Military Lodge; Nubian News; Shonell Beacon of the Nubian Chronicles; Maxine Thompson of Black Butterfly Press; Tee C. Royal of R.A.W. Sistaz Book Club.

Joseph Lee; Doughtry Long; Yusuf Rastafari; Sibyl Moses, Ph.D.; Sandy Davis; Ernestine Counsel; Norma Kalibbala; John Wu; My OMB family; Cha Cha; Kamal; Tommi Vincent... Thank you all.

Organizations: Harvest Productions; African Americans In Publishing; Toastmasters International; Culture Plus Distributors.

My Football Squad: Peter John-Baptiste; David "Poppy" Sanderson; (*"Troy Vincent, Irving Fryar, Eddie George and Shannon Sharpe"* for sparking my imagination and being my blueprint!)

To my editor, Guichard Cadet, La Caille Nous Publishing Company... Thank you for the continued knowledge, guidance, and friendship. And for the opportunity to share my daydreams with the world! To my daughter Miya for all of the in-depth editorial analysis!!! To my son AJ- thanks for all of the hugs and kisses that make me feel so special.

Donald McLeon – model on cover… Thank you so much for coming through for your Lil Sis!

Special Thanks to all of my Harvest Productions, Love With Soul family members who have so positively supported and encouraged me from the inception of my writing career. To all of you who have read *When You Look At Me* and took the time to e-mail me with your heart warming stories. To all of you who went the extra mile to post reviews and spread the word about "this" new author and WYLAM… God Bless you ALL. I felt you, and you kept me inspired… What a BLESSING you all have been to me!

Hitman Assassinates Doubt on the Field

By Chuck Clay

SportzMan Magazine

It's hard to believe that only nine short months ago the Arizona Mavericks were heading off to training camp. Now after a lackluster 6—10 year their season has come to a merciful end. But through all of the rubbish, Running Back, Duane "The Hitman" Cummings has somehow remained focused, having had an exceptional year racking up yardage. The fourth leading rusher in the league, Cummings delivered a valiant effort in his sophomore Professional Football League (PFL) year.

Acquired by the Mavericks from West Virginia University as the second pick in the first round of the PFL draft, Cummings was signed to a four-year, 9 million dollar contract, with a 4.1 million dollar signing bonus. Although there were concerns about the large amount paid to Cummings, he has made a tremendous contribution of bringing the last place Mavericks to a somewhat respectable third place in the western conference.

Though he is accurately named "The Hitman" for his game execution skills, he is still no Superman, able to single-handedly carry the squad in a single bound and he should not be expected to. Football is a team sport, not a single effort on any one person's part as the Arizona Maverick's shoddy performances has implied.

Making his first appearance in Hawaii at the All-Pros game and being surrounded by the best players in the PFL, Cummings gave us a glimpse of his unrelenting talent. He demonstrated that if he had strong support from the Arizona offense that he could have easily been the number one rusher in the league.

For all those who grimaced when the Mavericks organization paid all those millions to acquire this young man, Cummings eradicated all doubt that he is anything less than a solid investment in the Arizona franchise's future. At six-feet-three, two hundred thirty-five pounds he is virtually unstoppable, possessing strength, agility and speed.

An All-American at Trenton High School, Cummings started his athletic career at the young age of eight when his mother encouraged him to study martial arts. Sylvia Cummings said, "Duane was into a little of everything. As a child he played basketball, baseball and soccer, as well as football. He was always a rough-and-tumble little boy, so sports gave him a constructive outlet for his energy and he loved it."

Sylvia Cummings also serves as her son's business manager, "It was important for me to oversee Duane's career. After all he's still young and it can be overwhelming for someone to call home from college asking for money one day and literally become a millionaire the next. My job is to make his transition as smooth as possible." When asked what type of duties being business manager entailed, Ms. Cummings replied, "First, making sure that Duane has the most qualified staff working in his best interest. After researching several offers, I selected a wonderful sports agent who is key in putting together deals and making negotiations on Duane's behalf. Through our contact with the agent we were able to find a financial advisor to help Duane invest and manage his money. These are two of the most important things that I handle so that my son is able to focus solely on becoming the best athlete he can be."

When reminded of the strained relationships, when parents are in authoritative professional roles over their young adult children in sports today, Ms. Cummings simply replied, "Duane and I are joined at the hip. Sure we are mother and son, but we are foremost friends. Duane and I have always had an open relationship where he can come and talk to me about any and everything. And as far as his professional life we have always had the same ambitions for his career. And that is for him to have a productive and successful career through dedicating himself to being the best player in the PFL. My son has a one-track mind just like his mother, and we are going to go all the way, together."

Duane "The Hitman" Cummings is home in Trenton, New Jersey, this off-season where he'll continue to workout in order to be ready for next season. And if he continues to work hard like he did this past year, it is sure to be an exciting season next year, indeed.

DINNER FOR TWO

It was early March, about quarter to seven in the evening and I was giving the condo a final inspection making sure that everything was in place. I made sure I changed the sheets on my bed and sprinkled some baby powder on there for the scent. Women like that kinda shit. Not saying that by the end of the evening we'd be between the sheets, but just in case we did, I wanted everything to be straight.

The potatoes were roasting in the oven and the chicken was frying in the pan. I had already showered and shaped up my spaghetti strap beard and lined up my goatee, and I was set. Truthfully, I was getting tired of all this dating bullshit. I mean after the high school sex, and the college sex, and being in the Professional Football League for two years, I was tired of fucking strays. Had had it with the meaningless conversations and the go nowhere relationships. I didn't want that anymore. What I did want was what my grandparents had…that *old fashioned* love!

Only problem was I hadn't come across anyone who was all the woman I needed her to be. A woman who wasn't afraid to take care of the kids I wanted her to have, and who wasn't afraid *to be happy* at home cooking and cleaning for me, *her* man. A woman who wasn't afraid of what her, upwardly mobile, working class girlfriends might say. That's what I wanted!

Say that to some women these days, they'll have your nuts in a vice grip talking 'bout, '*I make my own money, buy my own house and drive my own car! I am my own woman, thank you very much!*' Or on the other hand, there's Miss, give me the money and pay my bills, who I definitely wouldn't want influencing any kid of mine, let alone giving birth to them. And women say that good men are hard to find. Well good sistahs don't come a dime a dozen either.

But three weeks ago when I got into town for the off-season, me and my man went out to eat and I couldn't believe who I ran into. Asia Heartly!

When I was a kid I had the biggest crush on her. At the time I was eleven. She had to have been like seventeen and going into the twelfth grade. Every chance I could I dragged my friends down to the Quaker Bridge Mall just to see her. Me and the fellahs would jump on the bus and walk around to the different stores and to the arcade, but before we left I *had* to pass the theater where Asia worked. We'd go in and hustle her for free popcorn and candy...sometimes she'd give us the popcorn. And on days when there weren't many people around she'd let us catch a movie for free.

Thoughts of her faded with time, but every now and then she'd come to mind. I saw Asia at Maxine's Restaurant celebrating her thirtieth birthday. As I stood there talking to her all those old feeling and emotions came back just like when I was a kid and I knew I had to get her number. But when I asked she told me that it was good seeing me and all, but she wasn't into the dating thing.

I didn't ease up on her though. In fact, with my schedule and me living out of state if I didn't get her number that night, it could have been another thirteen years before we saw each other again. So getting her number had this urgency for me. Reluctantly she gave in and gave it to me.

Two nights later I called her and she had the sexiest phone voice. Sort of low and powdery smooth. Through our telephone conversations, she told me that she had gone through a failed marriage and within the last year gotten divorced. It had her head messed up pretty bad. And from what I picked up she was carrying a lot of baggage. Asia wouldn't elaborate on the details, she just kept things real general, not letting me in on the reason behind her pain or anything too personal about herself. Even though she told me she wasn't interested in having another man in her life something told me that I had to find out more about her.

Over the three weeks we spent talking on the phone she really intrigued me. She brought something new to the table. Asia was a quality woman who had values. Went to church, loved her parents, was a second grade school teacher for the past seven years and she had a good heart. So clearly I could see this woman in my life.

Only problem was when I tried to get into Asia's head and find out what was in her heart she had this way of emotionally detaching herself every time I asked her anything deep. Even with all the resistance I was getting from her, though, I just kept trying. But just getting her to agree to have dinner with me was a job in itself.

My boy Tompy, who I was staying with, had a business trip out of town, so I had the place all to myself and I really wanted to spend some face-to-face time with Asia. Tompy was my friend since childhood. Actually, he was more like my brother than a friend. We grew up on the same street and his mom and pop lived across the street from my grandparents. Mrs. Seagrams had nine kids, me and Tompy were the same age. He used to like to hang out at my house because all of his brothers and sisters were always around. And me being an only kid, I loved to hang out at his house because there *were* so many kids. Each of us envied the other's position, and over the years we stayed tight.

This year during my off-season I chose to stay at his place instead of staying at my mom's. She drove me crazy with her house rules last year. I'm a grown man and I work my ass off all pre-season and season long. So during my off time if I want to come home at four in the morning and sleep 'til noon…that's exactly what I'm gonna do!

Tompy had a real nice place. Two bedrooms, one-and-a-half baths, small kitchen and cozy little living room all on the third floor. The bedroom that I stayed in was his office slash second bedroom. It was a tight fit, but it had to do. Since I was only home three months out of a year it didn't make much since to get my own place.

By the end of our dinner tonight I was hoping that Asia would at least let her guard down far enough to realize that I had feelings for her. I moved the curtain to the side and looked out into the black March night and the winters in New Jersey were no joke. It was snowing outside and had been ever since I got into town. I sure missed the sixty-two degree Arizona winter that I just left.

At the sound of the bell, I buzzed her in then turned down the music. "Welcome," I said bowing to Asia. "It's an honor." I over exaggerated 'cause, damn, I had to do a whole lot of talking to get her over here. That was my first time seeing her since the night of her birthday, and the second time in thirteen years. Time had been real good to her.

A soft blush came across her lips, "I'm here."

"Yes you most certainly are. And looking good if I may say."

I gave her a light hug before I took her coat. Asia, was wearing a gray loose fitting pants suit, which made her look more like she was going to a business meeting rather than to chill out with an old friend. I was just coolin' in a pair of jeans and a blue ribbed short sleeve shirt.

"This is a nice place," Asia said walking around Tompy's condo.

"You want anything to drink. We got some sodas, beer, or something stronger if you like."

"No thank you, I'm fine." Sitting there on the couch, Asia looked uncomfortable.

"Suit yourself." I sat on the couch across from her.

Asia's eyes made contact with the SportzMan magazine that I had been reading. It just happened to be open to the page that my article was on. I didn't plan it like that, just forgot to put it away after I finished reading it. Tonight, I didn't want to be the topic of discussion.

"Nice picture." She said lifting the magazine so she could get a closer look. It was taken in Hawaii right after we won the All Pros game. That's the game made up with the best players from each team in the PFL. I was standing at the press podium holding up our championship trophy.

"Looking at that picture reminds me of everything I love about football." I shook my head reminiscing about the PFL training camp, "All the effort it took to get to that day. Asia, the PFL training camp was a trip. For five weeks, I played football like I had never played before. Those guys were bigger than anyone I'd ever played against. 'Hey Rook! Hey Rook!' was all I heard for those first few weeks."

"Rook?"

I laughed, "Yeah, as in rookie. The veterans on the team had us do their laundry, run errands, buy their snacks. We even had to entertain them *on demand*. They'd say 'Hey Rook sing us a song and make it a rap song'. So I'd break out and free-style, which luckily for me I had a little skill at that too. Then they'd say, 'We want to hear some jokes' and I'd break out my best Chris Tucker impression...*And you know this man!"*

Asia laughed at me trying to sound like Chris Tucker, "Oh I don't think I could handle the hazing."

"It was all in fun," I told her. "Just a way for the veterans to test our temperament and find out what we were made of. But it didn't take long for the pranks to turn into golden advice, though." I felt myself getting pumped just thinking about it. "Once the old-heads saw that I wasn't there just to make a spot on the squad, but to make some big plays, they really started respecting my game. And the bigger the plays the more respect I earned. *And I loved it!* Being passed the ball by the quarterback and running down the field with a man on by back, one on my arm and dragging another on my leg *still* racking up yardage!"

It was obvious that Asia didn't know the first thing about football, so I was really digging how she was taking an interest in what I did. With anyone else, I could have talked about it for the rest of the night. But with Asia I didn't want to go there. I didn't want to be the focus of conversation, I wanted to get to know her better and I wanted her to know *me*.

Asia looked at my picture in the magazine like she was impressed, "Well look at you, Mr. Hitman. Now that must be exciting. We've talked about so many things, but you never really talk about how you like being a celebrity."

Taking the magazine from her, I closed it and placed it on the coffee table. "I ain't gonna lie. It's one great big party. One blast after another. I travel all across the United States getting crazy paid for doing something I've always wanted to do. How do you think it feels?..." Asia was all ears. See the funny thing is when people ask that question they only want to know that being a millionaire athlete is wonderful. People want to believe that money makes you happy, but what they fail to understand is that although it makes certain situations convenient, money doesn't make you any less *human*. I experience the same ups and downs like everyone else. Some people think that as soon as you cash your first check, you become lifted from reality into never-never land. But these days I've been feeling *real human* and in need of some stability around me.

Ever since I was in high school I couldn't wait to turn pro because of the reputation of the life the player's lived. I jumped in, *head* first. Girls, girl, girls! Once I turned pro I couldn't walk down the street without having some girl pushing her phone number in my face. Even when we went out of town, as soon as the bus pulled up...girls. Go up to the hotel room and somehow there would be girls waiting in the hallway standing by the room door. And drugs were like candy. Go to some parties and there would be white lines, pills, alcohol and whatever else was your pleasure sitting out like refreshments.

At first the fast life was fun. Made me feel like a big man, then once the newness wore off it started feeling wrong cause that kind of life was never in me. I think what woke me up was one morning finding myself with a fucking migraine, butt naked next to this female I didn't know. Didn't even know her name and...she didn't know *me*. All she knew was *of* me. Then I had to ask myself what was I doing 'cause I sure wasn't raised like that. Now, as far as I was concerned, the fast life had nothing I wanted. I was looking for that special someone to take into the next phase of my life 'cause I was feeling empty on the inside, "But let me ask you this..." I told her, "...What happens to a man who fills up on sweets if he has no substance?"

She looked at me puzzled, "I'm not following you."

Shit, my chicken! I saw smoke easing its way from the kitchen into the living room. "Think about it." I got up to go check out the food.

Asia waited a few seconds then cornered me in the kitchen as I turned the chicken in the black iron pan. "You just gonna leave me hangin' trying to solve your riddle?"

"Excuse me?" I quizzed. My mind had shifted to trying to salvage dinner and I wasn't sure what she was talking about.

"You know, that stuff about sweets with no substance. I'm still trying to figure that one out." she folded her arms.

"Oh you like to analyze?"

"No." Asia said slowly, "But I'm a teacher, not a mind reader. We were having a conversation then you made a comment that I don't understand. I would just appreciate you clearing it up, that's all."

Hunching my shoulders I looked at her, "I was just saying, seeing is not always believing." I knew I wasn't making much sense, "Don't mind me, I'm going through some changes." Asia had a puzzled gaze on her face, so I tried to further explain my thoughts, "At first turning pro was all that. It still is, don't get me wrong, just something's missing."

Asia leaned up against the counter finally understanding what I was trying to say to her. "Oh I can relate so very well."

"You, naw? As fine as you are? You don't look like anything's bothering you." I bit into a chicken wing then wiped the hot juice off my mouth with a napkin.

"True." she laughed, "But you just said seeing is not always believing. All my life I wanted to be a teacher. I love my career, but aside from working for a complete jerk, I feel like something is missing in my life too. You maybe unsure of your feelings, but I know exactly what my problem is."

I just had to ask, " Well, what is it?"

"I'm getting old, man!" Asia faked like she was crying.

"Old? Girl get out of here, I'm twenty-four. You're only a few years older than me, and I damn sure don't consider myself anywhere near old." I said munching that piece of chicken that I had seasoned to perfection.

"Actually I'm six years older than you but that's not the point. I just thought I'd have my career *and my family* by now."

Sounded like I heard opportunity knocking, "If I were you I wouldn't let that bother me. Your man could be standing right in your face."

"Oh really," Asia dismissed my comment. "Well if he is I sure can't see him."

I wondered if it was intentional or if she just didn't get the invitation. "You ever see your ex around?"

"In passing," she looked at me like she didn't expect that question.

"Where's he at now?" I needed to know 'cause the last thing I wanted was to get hooked up with her if she was still feeling for her ex.

"In Camden with the woman he left me for. Look, I really don't keep tabs on him." Asia snapped.

Caught off-guard by her attitude, I stopped what I was doing and looked her square in the eyes. "Hey, sorry. I didn't mean to get all up in your business so you don't have to get on the defensive with me, alright?"

"Look Duane, I'm sorry if I'm giving off bad vibes. It's just that..." she paused, "...forget it." Taking a deep breath, Asia refolded her arms and leaned up against the counter. She got real quiet and had this *what am I doing here* look on her face.

"Hey," I called to get her attention. "Stop looking so serious. We're suppose to be having fun, remember?"

She gave me a half smile.

After I fixed our plates, I brought them into the living room and turned off the overhead ceiling light. The room was lit by a dim lamp, next to the couch and made the atmosphere nice and cozy. Sitting on the couch next to Asia with the plate in my hand, I looked down at the dinner and hoped I could pull the night off, because there was something special about her. Maybe it was still that school boy crush I had on her when I was eleven and she worked at the mall. Maybe it was the way she carried herself like royalty - so mature and everything in the right place. As I thought, I began to get nervous cause I knew this queen deserved a lobster dinner with the best bottle of wine that my money could buy instead of the fried chicken, home made potato wedges and strawberry milk shake shit I threw together. If I messed this up, I'd never forgive myself. But instead of sweating it out, I chilled and acted like everything was alright.

"Very interesting meal." Asia said biting into the chicken.

"You making fun of my dinner, Woman?" I teased.

Asia laughed, "No. I guess I was expecting some 'I got to impress her' kind of meal. This is just different than what I'd expected."

"What? You mean you ain't impressed with my frying skills?" I stared down at her.

Asia laughed, "Oh *very* impressed Mr. Cummings. Actually, you did a better job on this chicken than I ever could."

As she dug in, I just didn't feel right inside, "I gotta fess up to you, Asia. I know you're better than this. I didn't think you were gonna show so I didn't really prepare. Usually, I would have had some lobster tails, fettuccine, and a bottle of *Cristal*. Baby, I know you better, than this."

Asia took a sip of the homemade strawberry shake I made her then placed the glass back on the coaster, "Yeah, and like I was suppose to walk in here wearing a *red* tight-fitting dress, stiletto heels, a long weave and chewing gum then, right?"

"Wait, wait, you lost me. What does that mean?" She threw me with that statement.

"Duane, this is not a Keith Sweat video, okay. I am not interested in getting to know your ego. If anything, I want to know you… who you are past all the hype. That lobster dinner would have gone in and come out the same way as this delicious fried chicken."

I stared at her puzzled because I never heard that before. Not what she said, but what she meant. I was "The Hitman" and women expected me to *pay and perform*. My mind wandered back to when I was a kid and used to be called 'that black *ugly* boy' because of my dark complexion. It wasn't until my junior high school paper ran an article about me being multi-gifted in sports that females even noticed me. That used to hurt at the time, but then I just stopped caring. Long as I was getting mine. Then when I turned pro, it really got crazy. Meeting people and not being able to figure them out. Everybody wanting something from me. Smiling all up in my face. Why? Cause they were trying to get what *I* worked for. Wanting to shine all up in my sunlight, get some glory from *my* spot.

But staring at Asia as she dug in, I knew she meant what she said and it was a serious reality check for me. It was like I had just discovered something about myself that I knew, but never took stock of. Here I was thinking it was all about me, but I always had to try so damned hard at it. Sure, I could pull the girls, but once they were with me I always wondered why? Were they there for me, the person I was on the inside or were they there for the free ride? Making me no more significant to them than damn Santa Claus, the fucking Easter Bunny or some sugar daddy. My revelation made me think about that old Harold Melvin and the Blue Notes song that my gramps use to play to death. When the lead singer, Teddy Pendergrass, sang about all the friends he had when the money was plenty, but when the money was gone so were the so-called friends. It felt so much like my life. I placed the plate down on the coffee table. Leaned back against the couch thinking where in the hell all this introspective coming from.

From the edge of the couch where she sat, Asia looked back over her shoulder at me. "What's wrong?"

"Just watching you tear that food up, that's all. You must have been hungry girl. Ain't no shame to your game. No salads for you, huh?" I teased.

Putting the napkin up to her mouth, Asia started laughing then playfully punched me in the arm. "Ooh Duane, no you didn't."

"If you hurt me I'll tell my coach on you. This is a valuable arm brought and paid for by the Mavericks you know?" I drew myself back like she was going to hurt me then started laughing. "You know I'm just kidding."

"What were you thinking about?" she asked.

I wanted to look deep into her eyes and ask her what she saw when she looked at me. I wanted to look in her eyes and have her soul reveal everything there was to know about her, all of her dreams, and fears. I wanted to touch her brown skin with my fingers, and tell her I was tired. Tired of being alone, frontin' like everything was alright, that I needed someone who wanted *me*, that black ugly boy before he turned into the junior high athlete, then the multi-million dollar Hitman. "Everything's fine, I'm just glad you're here," I said instead. Picking up my plate, I joined her in eating.

We both were cracking up watching the movie, Good Burger. It was some old Nickelodeon flick I found in Tompy's wall unit. It must have belonged to one of his nieces or nephews. They stayed over a lot. Asia was laughing so hard, tears were rolling down her eyes.

"See, I told you Good Burger was the deal. My boy said the chicken says, mooo." I imitated the character Ed by flapping my arms like wings.

Asia wiped the tears of laughter from her eyes as she gathered up the dirty dishes taking them into the kitchen and I put in another videotape.

The next movie was a suspense. She came out and sat close to me totally relaxed and her perfume was smelling good. We talked through the entire second movie. Asia asked me about my horseshoe brand on my left arm, and how it was to pledge Omega Psi Phi. She asked how I *found time* to pledge, play football and graduate with a major in Physical Education, and a minor in Nutrition. I laughed and told her not to worry, that I actually *did study* and took *my own* tests too. I was feeling real strong about how the night was turning out.

Asia looked at the clock and it was past midnight, "Thanks Duane, I really needed this night. Now I can live off of this high for the rest of the week."

"The rest of the week? Don't make it sound that bad." Running my hand over Asia's medium length corkscrew curls, I pulled one out and I watched as it sprung back into position next to her face. She had a natural texture to her hair and with the exception of berry colored lipstick, her face was just as natural.

"You just don't know. I don't go out that much."

I wondered if she knew the things she'd been saying to me all night long. Putting all the pieces together it sounded to me like she was sending out a SOS. Like she was saying to me, 'save me from this loneliness'. I wanted to be her lifeguard, the man who would save her from the long lonely days and empty nights. And I wanted her to do the same for me.

"Duane, what is it? You've been looking at me strangely all night."

I couldn't keep my fingers out of her hair, "I dig you Asia, I was just wondering what it would be like if you were mine."

She looked at me like I had just insulted her mother. "If *I* were *yours*? Ahh no no. See, I knew it."

"You knew what?"

"Duane, please," Asia said agitated. "I thought this was supposed to be an evening between old friends, as you put it."

Her mood swings were wearing me thin, "Asia, I honestly dig you, I wanna be with you. What so wrong with that?" I frowned.

"You know, I knew this was a bad idea. I better leave." She sat on the edge of the couch, "But since we're being *honest* and everything, I'm not about getting played. I'm thirty years old and that's too old to be playing this kind of game. If you thought you were gonna run that *'I dig you shit'* on me, and that was gonna make me lay on my back for you, well then you were sadly mistaken, weren't you?" She was hot, and it was tripping me out to see her go from being relaxed like she was, only seconds ago, to being that fired up. It was like she was just waiting for something to go wrong so she could jump on it. Asia stood up glaring down at me, "Damn, Duane, why did you have to go there?"

"You wait a minute." Still seated, I reached up and grabbed her by the arm before she could walk off, "Asia, I'm not running no game on you. Why would I do that?" I looked at her with my eyebrows bunched. "I had a nice time with you tonight, and I *do* dig you. I always dug you, from way back." Releasing her arm I gritted my teeth and paused, then spoke softly to her, "Believe me Asia, this ain't no head game."

She wouldn't look at me, "Duane, I don't appreciate this," her voice cracked.

"Talk to me, babe." I stood up close to her, wondering what could have possibly hurt her so much in her past that she couldn't let her guard down for me.

"I'm not ready for this." She shook her head, "I just got divorced, I'm older than you are, and besides, Duane, you're still young. You're probably still running after anything with a hole."

"*Damn!*" I said in frustration. "Where is all this coming from? All I said was I dig you." The whole evening had begun to unravel leaving me to wonder if I should have just left her well enough alone.

Asia put her hands up to her face acting overwhelmed, "See this is a perfect example of what I'm talking about. Just say that you're on the up-and-up..."

"I *am* on the up-and-up." I stressed.

"Okay, you are. Neither my head nor my heart is in the right place right now. Apparently I'm still bitter from all of the mess I went through with Bryant. I don't want to carry that into another relationship. I'm sorry Duane, but I still have to find myself."

Flippantly, I pointed to the mirror on the wall, "There you go." I stood there with my arms folded looking at her.

Asia looked at her reflection in the mirror, then back at me, "Are you always this simple?"

"Naw, it's just that all that stuff you're talking about is bullshit."

She gasped "Wha...bullshit?"

"That's right. You don't need to find yourself. You ain't lost, you just got dogged that's all. And if you don't start trusting somebody now, *a man*, you ain't never gonna trust nobody. That's how you living?" I spouted.

Asia got quiet, then she turned the guns on me, "Can you *honestly* tell me that you're not seeing anyone right now? I mean with all you have going on for yourself, there just has to be a woman around somewhere."

She caught me off-guard with that and I wasn't sure if I should have just said no and lied about Missy, my woman back in Arizona because we were on the outs anyway. But I had the feeling that Asia would have been able to read me like a book, so I swallowed down hard and told her the truth, "There's someone in Arizona, but it's over."

"It's over? Just like that?" She eyed me, "Does *she* know it's over?"

"What kind of question is that?"

Asia was relentless, "One that I want an answer to."

"Have I told her I don't want to see her again?" I sighed, then answered my own question, "No, but she knows I'm not happy with the relationship. She's a good person and everything, but we just aren't seeing eye-to-eye on things. So yeah, she knows it's over just like I do. I guess neither one of us wanted to be the one to call it off." Looking deep into Asia's eyes I said, "I'm telling you the truth, Asia."

And it was the truth. Missy and I had been going through relationship drama for almost the whole year that we had been together. For one thing she was a Mavericks cheerleader and players dating cheerleaders wasn't allowed, so right there we were starting out on the down-low. But the biggest problem was we wanted different things from life. She was a med student and real serious about one day having her own pediatrics practice. Having a family like I wanted was the farthest thing on that girl's mind. I told her I was about ready to settle down and I wanted my wife to stay at home to raise our kids. She told me that I was tripping. Then when I told her that that was a real problem between us, she told me things between us was fine. Fine to her was the ability to make me bust a nut. Missy had this beautiful body and her shit was *good*. And like Asia, she was a step above all the riff raff. I knew Missy loved *me*, but I wanted more than just to be her man. That just wasn't enough for me anymore so it was time for me to move on.

"Don't you think you should completely close one door before trying to open another?"

"You're right, but I didn't know I would see you, or feel the way you making me feel."

"Oh, so I'm making you feel?" Asia mocked.

I was definitely feeling something, "Yeah, baby you are." *I* couldn't even understand it. In a crowded room of women, if I didn't know her, Asia *would not* be the one who would catch my eye. She had some real nice features like these dreamy ass bedroom eyes. She had pretty cocoa brown skin and she *seemed* to have a nice looking body. That is from what I could tell, because her style of dress was more concealing than revealing. If I were to guess, Asia had to have been around five-eight, a hundred-fifty pounds. She was attractive, don't get me wrong, but I've had some *real fine* women up in my face! What I felt for Asia was more like a chemical reaction. Like I *needed* her.

Smiling, Asia pointed at me. "You need to slow down."

"I know what I want. And it's not like we don't know each other," With my finger I traced her arm.

She looked into my eyes then asked slow and deliberately, "What do you want Duane... *from me?*"

Leaning so close to her ear that my lips brushed across it, I whispered, "A chance."

Asia closed her eyes like she caught a chill then walked away from me, "How long are you going to be in town?" She asked getting her coat and purse off of the chair where I had left it.

"I haven't thought about it. During the off season, I go and come as I please." To keep my body in shape, I had a trainer here in Trenton so I didn't have to attend any of the optional mini camps held back in Arizona. I helped Asia with her coat.

"Walk me to my car."

I unlocked the front door, and without a coat, I walked her out into the moonlit frosty March night. It had stopped snowing. We didn't quite know what to say to each other. Asia opened up the door to an older model white Pontiac Grand Am and got in as I stood in the doorway, "You okay?"

"I'm fine. I'm sorry if I messed up your evening."

Squatting down to make eye contact, I cupped Asia's chin in the palm of my hand, "I know you been through a lot of stuff, and true, I still have some business that I have to clean up, back in Arizona." I dropped my head cause I really wasn't sure what to say to her, then I looked up, "Asia, I don't have no fancy words... nothing like that. I just want you in my life. I believe you'll be good for me, and *I believe* I'll be good for you. All I want is a chance." I kissed her lightly above her brow, "Let me let you get out of this cold. Lock up these doors and call me when you get in, alright? We don't have to talk, just let the phone ring so I'll know you got in safely. You want me to follow you home in my car?"

Asia smiled, "No Duane, I'll be fine. I'll call you. And thanks again."

Twelve minutes later the phone rang and Asia's number came up on the

Caller ID. On the third ring the answering machine picked up and Asia left a message that she was home. Although I could have picked up the phone, I didn't... I just sat there on the couch.

BEAUTY WITH ATTITUDE

"Keneisha, girl, you know you can work some magic on this head." Holding up the mirror, I checked out the back of my hair as she removed the pink drape from around my shoulders. I'm one for experimenting and I've done everything from weaves to braids. I even tried dreads but had them cut out after six and a half months because they just weren't for me. But today I felt like wearing my own hair. I had Keneisha perm me up and cut it into a short little something. And most definitely I had her touch up the grays 'cause at forty, I was too damn young for that nonsense. Maybe when I'm sixty, but definitely not now!

After I paid Keneisha and made my appointment for two-weeks from today, I went upstairs in the salon to have my nails filled and repolished. As I walked into the nail area of *Something Mighty Wonderful Spa and Salon*, all of the manicure booths were occupied. The women, waiting to be serviced, read magazines while bobbing their heads to the music of WMSJ fm. My nail technician, Fancy, was waiting for me. Keneisha had called upstairs fifteen minutes before she finished my hair to let her know I was on the way up.

As I approached her table all eyes fell on me and I loved being on *this* end of the attention.

"Hey Sylvia."

"How are you today?" I asked and kept stepping, not waiting for her response. When I looked back over my shoulder, she was whispering to the woman whose nails she was filing. Then she pointed to the poster-sized picture of my son in his Arizona Maverick's uniform that was hanging up behind Fancy's chair. The lady's eyes got big, then she looked at me with this dazed grin on her face. I smiled back then sat down at Fancy's table and rested my purse on my lap.

"Did you get the pictures developed?" Fancy squealed. She once told me that she was my son's biggest fan and I'm starting to believe it.

"Yes I did." Digging them out of my pocketbook for the second time today, I proudly handed her the pictures of the Mavericks Awards dinner taken when I was in Arizona with Duane.

"Oh Miss Sylvia, he is *so* fine!" Fancy clutched the pictures to her heart with her eyes closed like she was feeling something. As she thumbed through the pictures, three other technicians ran over behind her, leaving their customers unattended as they drooled over my boy. I got up and went over to the wall covered with colorful bottles of nail polish to make my selection. And since I was due to pick up my *brand new,* white Mercedes in less than two hours, I decided to go with a French Manicure with the white tips to match my new car.

The girls were going crazy over my son. I watched, thinking how they reminded me of myself when I was their age. I have to admit though, that ever since I was twelve I was a lot to deal with. At an early age I got the call to be a woman. Sassy? Yes! Cute? Most definitely. So when I got my first job at sixteen, working at Rider College in the cafeteria for the summer, I had no problem with introducing myself to Jericho Austin.

Lord, he was the finest thing I had ever laid eyes on. He was tipping the charts at six-four, his skin was that same black and just as desirable as a cup of fresh brewed coffee, and he had deep curly hair. Through the grapevine I learned that he was a senior majoring in Architectural Landscaping, and would be graduating after the summer session was over. And even though I had just finished the tenth grade, I told him that I was eighteen and would be starting Rider in the fall.

I can't say that I knew Jericho long enough to be in-love with him, but I did feel something. But to see him all decked out in his graduation suit being escorted down the hall in handcuffs after my dad made me take him and the cops to his dorm room, I thought I was going to die. At eight weeks pregnant, it was more than I could stand. I was scared for both Jericho and myself. Felt guilty as all hell for the trouble I had caused him, and humiliated for how my parents were going off the deep end. I loved both my mother and father, but their way of dealing with my new baby was to throw him in the mix and act like nothing even happened. They were still the parents, but instead of two kids, they now had three.

For the first five months of my son's life, Duane slept in the room with my parents. A crib that I had bought him was set up in my room, but they kept him in a bassinet with them and I hated it. At first they said, "You just came home from the hospital. You need your rest." Then they said, "You don't know how to take care of no baby. Let him stay in here with us." Then it was, "You have school in the morning. You don't need the baby keeping you up all night." It wasn't until my baby got too big to sleep in the bassinet that he was even allowed to sleep with me in my room.

My parents went on with life as usual alright, only I had been reduced to a sister role in my own son's life. When my baby began to talk he called my dad, Dada, and all the ladies in the house: my mom, my sister Terry and I, Mama. Then as his language began to mature, my parents would say things to him like, 'tell Aunt Terry this', and 'tell Sylvia that'. They never said tell your mother. They always referred to me as Sylvia.

When Duane was five I remember freaking out on everyone about it. I was not that boy's sister! He walked up to my mother and said 'Mama...' and I jumped up and grabbed him by the arms shaking him yelling, "I'm your Mama! I'm your Mama! You call her Gran!" I shocked everyone, but I just couldn't take it anymore. My dad came into the room shouting what was wrong with me then I shouted back at him, "And you're his gramps not his daddy! He has a daddy. His name is Jericho Austin not Robert Cummings!" That day stays with me because it was the day that I found out Jericho was getting married. He had called me to see if he could come and get his son so that Duane could be in his wedding. At that time I was twenty-one and knew that I loved him. We weren't in any type of relationship, but on the inside I silently prayed that the three of us could be a family. I wanted to be his wife and give Duane the family he deserved. And

Jericho was a man in every sense of the word. Through so much adversity he stayed true. He started and still has a very successful landscaping business. And through all the mess he had to go through, he never got bitter. Only better.

My dad was so upset with him for getting his sixteen-year-old daughter pregnant that he pressed charges for statutory rape. His parents had to pay lots of money on attorneys to make sure that he didn't serve time. Even though as I understand it, he did get probation. Then after he didn't serve time, my dad made me go to court for full custody of Duane. He wanted Jericho nowhere around us. But Jericho fought for his rights to be in his son's life. How I used to pray that he'd fight for *me* to have a place in his life too, but he never did. He didn't want me.

I even tried to call his parents to apologize for everything their family had to go through because of Duane and me. But before I got the phone hung up in my face, Mr. Austin told me that they curse the day their son met me. He said that he raised his son to be an intelligent, law-abiding man and because of me his son had been dragged through the legal system like a criminal. All the things that he and his wife had worked so hard to protect their child from, I exposed him to. Then he said, "Looka here girl, I would appreciate it if you never called back here again." At that time I had no one. No one who loved me unconditionally or respected me, except my son.

I chose not to go to college because I was afraid that I would be faded right out of his little life all together. Instead, after high school I worked. I took the graveyard shift so that I could be there with and for Duane.

While he was in school I slept. When he came home we did homework, I took him to his sports practices, we ate dinner together and while he slept, I worked. When my baby woke up the next morning, I was walking through the door to get him ready for school. Duane was my life, he was so unbelievably special to me that he became the center of my world.

I never made him call me Mama. That really didn't matter. But I did take charge of his life determined to let him know just how much I loved him, and he gave me nothing but love back. After high school, I continued living with my parents so I wouldn't have to struggle financially. At the factory I made pretty good money. Some weekends I worked with my neighbor, sewing wedding dresses. After I saved up enough money, I bought my first new car for me and Duane. On the weekends we'd drive to the beach, or get his favorite: a big bag of M&M's with peanuts and we'd just drive around to no-place-in particular talking and laughing and we wouldn't head home until we had eaten all the candy leaving nothing but the empty bag. Sometimes we'd take his buddy, Tompy, who lived across the street. By the time my son went off to college, he and I had become so close that I knew no one could ever take my place in his life.

After Duane made the Mavericks squad and was able to cash that multi million dollar signing bonus the *first* thing he did was bought me the house of my dreams. A four bedroom split level home in Lawrenceville Township, New Jersey. So at age forty, I *finally* felt good about my life. Like I had proven to the world that I was running the show... instead of the show running me!

"Oh Miss Sylvia! Can I please have this picture?"

"Fancy, I done told you he already has a girlfriend in Arizona."

"Please, oh please, oh please?"

The chile was just plain nuts. "Go on and keep it, girl." I took the other twenty-three snapshots and put them back in my pocketbook. As I sat down, Fancy kissed the picture then shoved it into her drawer.

"I'ma get a frame for this tomorrow!" Taking my hand in hers she grabbed a wad of cotton and moistened it with polish remover. "So how do you want them done today?"

"Give me something really spectacular." I had changed my mind from the simple French Manicure, I wanted something jazzy, *like me!*

GREENWOOD AVENUE

My mind was swept away by the late March snow falling lightly outside of the classroom window. After erasing the blackboard and wiping it clean with a cloth I wrote the morning salutation along with the date in large cursive letters to greet my second graders bright and early tomorrow morning. When I was in elementary school I remembered a prank my teacher played on my class, that now every year I played on mine. It was the mysterious gremlin drawing. I would draw a picture of a gremlin on the board and pretend that I couldn't figure out who had put it there. The kids got such a big thrill out of trying to solve the case and I got a kick out of watching them. Smiling, I turned off the lights and closed the classroom door behind me.

It was Wednesday and that meant payday. It was also the day I did some light grocery shopping for my parents. My mother never worked outside of the home, and now since my dad was on disability, there just wasn't enough money to go around. They had me late in life and now they were both senior citizens. I don't have any siblings so I was the only immediate family they had. After fifteen years of them trying to conceive, my mom told me, I was born. I love my parents and help out as much as I could. Along with buying groceries once a week I also pay their utility bill.

After dropping the groceries off, I went home to get my own business taken care of. Sitting down at the kitchen table - turned desk - with my paycheck on one side and all of my bills lined up on the other, I agonized over which bills to pay and which one to hold off on until next pay day. I had been robbing Peter to pay Paul for so long, my finances were in shambles. Everything was marked, urgent, final notice, or cancellation. The phone rang.

Closing my eyes, I rubbed at my temples feeling the tension building in my head. *"Look, I already told you I'll send the money next week, what more do you want me to do?"*

"You have five days, Ms. Heartly. If we don't receive it, you'll be telling it to the judge."

"What?!" I grabbed the ringing phone, yelling into the receiver.

"What's up with you?" It was Crystal my sister-friend. "Oooh, girl. I thought you were one of those bill collectors. Where do they get off with those funky attitudes? I work every freakin' day. I have to pay *my* bills *and* my parents' bills, but do they *see* a sistah trying? *No!* They just see some irresponsible woman who's not paying the darn bill! Girl I'm sorry for screaming in your ear, but *oooh,* they make me so damn mad!" I took a deep breath, held it, then in a sweet little voice said, "And how was your day today, dear?"

"Uh oh, somebody needs a hug." Crystal and I started cracking up. "Wow, are you finished venting. Cause I mean, I can call you back later if you want." She teased, "Damn, I'm glad I didn't come over there. You probably would have punched me out."

"No, I'm sorry, girl. I just have so much on my mind, and if I have to talk to one more bold-ass bill collector, calling my house, for the sole purpose of telling me off, I think I'll flip." I sighed in disgust then my heart got heavy, "Crys, when I talked to my mom today, she told me that daddy hasn't been feeling well lately." That news really concerned me. Being that my parents were up in age and I worried about them a lot. "Girl, I feel like I'm losing it over here." Closing my eyes all I could do was shake my head.

Ever since we were children, Crystal and I have been there for each other. We met in elementary school. She was the new kid in class, an army brat and her father had just finished his assignment in Germany. We bonded almost immediately when the kids shunned her because of her naturally blond ponytails, pale skin and afrocentric features. My heart went out to her. I felt her pain because I was a loner myself. The kids in my class also teased me about my parents being so much older than everyone else's in my class. I chose not to be around anyone who couldn't keep their mean comments to themselves.

Crystal still has the same lanky body she had as a child, but now her five-ten frame was that of a woman and the ponytails have been replaced with dreads that hung past her behind.

"Well don't lose it, Love. You just have to be strong. I wish I could do something to help you Asia. But you know we're all in the *same old funky ass sinking boat.*"

"I know you would help if you could, but I just have to do this on my own. I've been thinking about getting a second job." My voice drifted off. To pay off my lawyer fees and to get a grip on my bills, I worked two jobs for a while right after my divorce. I hated every second of it then and just the thought of doing it again tortured me.

"A second job? Look chile don't kill yourself. For now, why don't you go on to the gym and work your frustrations off there. I know how much you like that shit."

"Canceled. I couldn't keep up the membership. But you did give me an idea though." I said licking the back of my water bill and sealing the envelope shut. They were definitely getting paid because they were crazy! They turned my service off once because I had an unpaid balance of twenty dollars. "I'm gonna throw on my sweats and hit Trenton High's track." Glancing down at my notepad where I had calculated all of my expenses and subtracted them from the amount on my paycheck, I realized that I was left with twenty-seven dollars and thirty-eight cents to make it to the next week. I was so mentally drained. "Crystal, something has to change girl. I'm so tired of living this hand-to-mouth crap."

"Me too, girl. You go and hit the track and I'm going to Seven Eleven to buy me a *lottery ticket.*" We both laughed. "I'll break you off a piece when I hit."

After I hung up the phone, I went upstairs, threw on a pair of sweats, grabbed my coat and was out the door. Life was feeling so complicated and darn unfair and the weight was *crushing me!*

Daylight was lasting longer these days, and the snow on the ground had all but melted away. Only traces of white dusted the tree limbs and evergreen bushes.

I ran around the track until the hazy blue sky faded to black. Just as I was finishing my last lap, a red Porsche pulled up to the curb. I noticed him from the distance as he stepped out in his running gear, it was Duane and he jogged over to where I was. Couldn't figure out what he was doing in this part of town.

An awkward feeling came over me and I really wasn't too thrilled to have run into him. Duane was sending mixed messages. Before we had dinner, he was ringing my phone off the hook. I admit that I was stressed during our dinner two weeks ago but he was the one talking about, how I made *him feel*. But since that night he hasn't called me once. That only led me to believe that I was right. That he was after one thing. So I really didn't have time for his kind of games.

"Small world." He said in a weak almost uncertain tone like maybe he wasn't thrilled to have run into me either.

I was breathing hard ready to collapse from exhaustion, so I threw up my hand while I caught my breath.

"How you doing, Lady?"

"Fine, just getting ready to go home. I had a long day. What are you doing around here?"

"My grandparents live around the corner off of Hamilton. So I just decided to hit the track before I went home."

As he spoke I was looking down the street at the traffic light by my house, then I looked up at him.

"Ah, sorry I haven't called you…you know, since you were over for dinner the other night. But I kinda figured that…you know." He stammered, "That maybe you wanted some space."

"Whatever Duane. You don't owe me any explanations." Again I threw up my hand only this time I started to walk away. Just didn't even want to pretend that there was anything deep or worth having some emotional exchange about. If he didn't want to call, he didn't have to explain anything to me.

"Asia," Duane said catching me by the arm. "You think you can wait up for me until I get my run in. It's been three days since I worked out and I'm really starting to feel it. It'll only take fifteen minutes. Promise."

"I really need to be getting home." All I wanted was a shower and to be left alone.

"Please Asia." Duane said soberly, "I really want to talk to you."

I inhaled deeply then said, "Fifteen minutes," to indicate not one second more.

"Cool," he nodded his head softly, "You can wait in my ride if it's too cold out here for you."

"No I'm fine."

"Yes you are." He looked down at me, then set his stopwatch then jogged over to the track.

He was fine too, but more so for the way he carried himself rather than his looks. Duane was not bad looking, but it was so apparent that his attractiveness came from the inside rather than the out. He would never be called pretty, that's for sure. But Duane had a light that shone this *all man* kind of confidence through the textured skin on his face, which was kinda rough rather than smooth. And he had this big, wide thing in the middle of his face. Like God gave him a second helping of nose, 'cause it sat real broad and prominent. His eyes really didn't make much of a statement either, just regular eyes medium in size and dark brown. But he did have these nice lips, though. Looked like they were made for blowing steam away from hot soup. But to me, his complexion was what made the biggest impression about him. Aside from the other eye-catching features like his towering height and size, he had the richest, darkest complexion. So dark it seemed like if you licked him you'd go into sugar shock. You know, 'the darker the berry, the sweeter the juice'. He should be called Sugar Cane.

I was standing by the bleachers with my hands sunk deep in my pockets to protect them from the cold. It was dark out, but the streetlights along with the lights around the track gave off a gray-blue glow to the night. Duane ran with such perfect form. His upper body slightly tilted, with arms and legs swinging in sync with each other. The thought of watching him on the football field came to my mind for the first time. Yeah, I bet he would be awesome to watch on the football field.

After the fifteen minutes were up Duane jogged back over to where I stood. One at a time he stretched his long legs out on the bleachers. "It felt good having you here waiting for me."

"Did it?"

"Yeah, I miss talking to you Asia." Duane stood up close to me and I was shivering. "Can I drive you home?"

"I'm just up the street. You can walk me there." I never gave him my address.

All the way down the tree-lined street to the front porch of my semi-detached house, we both small-talked. The traffic passing through this city street had lightened since all of the rush hour congestion had long since passed. Greenwood Avenue was a part of historic Trenton and you could tell that back in its day it was something to see.

As we stood on the front porch, once again a hopeful uncertainty registered in his eyes. "Is it alright if I come in for a few?"

I really wasn't in the mood for company, but I didn't want to come off as rude. "Sure, but you have to excuse my house." As I opened the door I felt a flush of embarrassment.

The first thing your eyes made contact with when you walked through my front door was the plaster falling from the gaping hole in the ceiling. Being that no one new had come over since the damn thing started falling, it never embarrassed me before. It was just something else on my to-do list.

I took my coat and slung it onto the chair. Perspiration had made its way to the surface of my clothes and I could smell it. "Turn on the television, make yourself comfortable. I'll be right back." The beautiful living room set that I had just bought sat on top of unpolished, paint stained, wooden floors.

Tired and not in a very good mood, I went upstairs and locked the bathroom door while I showered. As I soaped up my towel I thought to myself 'Girl, what's wrong with you?' Here I had, Duane "The Hitman" Cummings, in my house and all I could think of was that I had at least ten other things I'd rather be doing than entertaining him tonight.

After the shower, I jumped into a comfortable pair of jeans and a big cotton shirt, and when I returned downstairs there was a new smell of stale sweat hovering in the air. *Duane's manly scent.* His gym bag rested next to him and it caught my eye because it wasn't there when I went upstairs.

"If you don't mind, can I use your bathroom to change my shirt?"

"Sure, go right ahead. Upstairs to the left."

"You know I love these beam ceilings," he said to me.

His statement caught me off-guard because out of all this junk, which I thought he would be focusing on, he had found some beauty. I folded my arms, looked up at the ceiling then at him. "I think they were the reason I agreed to buy this old house. For the abundance of wood." There was sculptured wood everywhere: trimming the doorways, across the mantle of the little fireplace, up the banister, on the stairs…everywhere.

"How long you been living here?"

"About two years. I never wanted a fixer upper, but my ex-husband Bryant convinced me it was a good deal. Said he would do all of the work. At the time it was owned by the city. Although he had a good job as a sales representative for a security service, he said that he wanted to get into real estate by purchasing houses from the city and fixing them up. It wasn't exactly what I wanted to do, but at the time it really wasn't worth fighting over because Bryant was good with his hands. He could fix anything." Just the thought made me angry, "We lived here together exactly six months, which in that time he did two rooms, the bathroom and master bedroom. Now I'm stuck 'cause I really don't have the money to get anything done." My tone softened, "I guess you can tell with all the junk laying around."

"Naw, I can dig it. I always wanted to buy an old house and restore it into tip top shape, always did."

"Well I don't know about tip top shape. With the expense of everything, if I just get it to my liking I'll be happy."

"You gonna give me a tour?"

I was honestly surprised by his interest, "Sure, why not. Come on."

Duane followed me into the basement where I turned on the light. It was unfinished and water usually seeped in during heavy rains making it damp and smell of mildew. Other than that it was clean. We walked towards the back.

"I want to replace this oil tank and change to gas heat. I'm still saving up for it. That's my next big project." The tank gave off the sound of a bass drum as I slapped the side of it.

"How much is that going to set you back?" He asked also placing his hand on the tank.

"Bout a couple grand."

"Well how close are you to that goal?"

I laughed at the thought, "I said that was my next *big* project. It'll probably take me until next year when I'm ready to use it for next winter again. Until then I'll just keep calling the oil man."

We headed back upstairs as I turned out the light closing the door behind me. We then walked outside onto my back porch and I turned on the lights. The grass was chest high except for a walking path.

"See I have to put up a new fence. The kids, they keep cutting across my yard to get from the alleyway to the front street and I hate that." I pointed to the broken down, rusted fence. As I described my plans I could feel my eyes light up. I had such high hopes for my home. Since my divorce I sort of made fixing it up my positive point of focus. Right now though, the only thing I could do was dream. "I always wanted an herb garden. My mother had a friend, Miss Sarah. She had the most exquisite herb garden. Miss Sarah had mint, and basil, hibiscus and wild parsley. The aroma...Umm." My eyes closed as the pungent spicy smell filled my memory bank. "The aroma was so strong in her backyard. It was my favorite place to be. And I always said that when I bought my home I was going to plant me an herb garden." By now I was shivering from the cold and I guess Duane noticed.

"We better get in the house. I don't want you getting sick out here." He said rubbing his big hands across my chilled arms. His touch felt like he was awakening me from a dream.

Duane and I toured the rest of the house room-by-room as I shared my visions with him. I didn't know if Duane was genuinely as interested in my home as he let on, but he listened. He even gave me some good improvement ideas. "I really do need to get out of these clothes, they're starting to stick to me."

"Do you have a pair of pants to match that shirt?"

"I always carry an extra set, why?"

"You can use my shower. I mean if you want...It's no big deal." To my surprise, I was enjoying his company.

"You sure?" he asked just as surprised by the suggestion.

"I really don't mind. There are clean towels in the linen closet next to the bathroom. Help yourself."

It was seven-ten p.m. when Duane went upstairs and my stomach was growling. I went into the kitchen and took two steaks out of the fridge, a couple of potatoes, and a can of corn out of the cupboard. It was at that very moment that I noticed how lonely I actually was. I hadn't even asked him if he was hungry, if he ate red meat, or if he *wanted* to stay for dinner, for that matter. All I knew was I just wanted him to stay a little while longer. After my divorce, to lessen the hurt, I had become great at keeping myself busy. But with all the talking Duane and I had done over the past several weeks, I realized that I knew a lot about him. I didn't know much about his career, but I knew a lot about his likes and dislikes. His ambitions for the future, that he loved God and gave Him all the praise for his ability and life. Over the last several weeks I had learned so much about him but I was so busy waddling in my own self-pity that I didn't realize just how much I had learned. And how much I liked the qualities that he possessed.

As I turned on the broiler, it dawned on me that there was a man in this house for reasons *besides* being there to fix something and it was a nice thought.

The crisp clean smell of Dial soap preceded Duane's entrance into the kitchen. "I feel one hundred percent better. Now you can breathe easy." He smiled, flashing his teeth at me and for the first time he looked charming and his regular brown eyes seemed to sparkle.

"I left the wet towels on your tub. I didn't know what else to do with them."

"That's fine." I said feeling almost giddy. "I don't know about you, but I'm starving. I put on an extra steak, just in case you were hungry too. You know it's not hospitable to eat in front of your company's face and not offer them any." I laughed.

"Yeah that would be cold. I'll help you." He picked up the unopened can of corn, "One thing though, I don't eat canned foods. Do you have any lettuce, I want to make you the best salad you ever tasted."

"Whatever you need should be right in the fridge. If it ain't there, you don't need it." I cut corners on a lot of things, but food wasn't one of them.

"I like that." He was smiling.

After dinner we got so caught up into one another's conversations that we lost track of the time. The music of the eleven o'clock news blasted from the television and I could not believe that we had actually been engrossed with each other for that long.

"Duane, I hate to rush you, but I do have to go to work in the morning."

"Okay, gorgeous. I can take a hint." Duane took my hand as he stood up from the couch, "Walk me to the door."

As I grabbed the knob ready to open the door for him, he wrapped his arms around me and gently pressed his warm thick lips to mine. Bryant had been my first and only. The only one I ever gave my body to…the only one I've ever kissed with passion and often I wondered if I would feel good to another man. If I even had what it took to satisfy another man?

Slowly I opened my mouth as Duane's tongue wrapped around mine and I became so overwhelmed by the sensation. His arms squeezed tighter around my body and I felt myself melting into his chest. It was like I was saying goodbye to the old me and hello to someone new, but I didn't know who this new me was or what role this new *young* man would play. As my hands wondered freely up the back of Duane's thick neck, the palms of my hands made contact with the thousands of natural pea sized curls that made up his short crop of hair. It felt like soft fur in my hands. Our kiss was so intense that I wanted to cry because he was feeling too good and it scared me. And moans were slipping from my throat like liquid bubbles in a jar blown from a child's lips.

"I'll stay if you want me to." Duane said with his lips pressed against the side my neck. "Baby, you want me to stay? Baby?"

Yes, I wanted him to stay and put out the fire he had started inside of me. I wanted to feel his lips on my breast and his penis deep inside the river flowing between my legs. I was so curious to see how that big, black, beautiful body looked with not a stitch of clothing on it. *Yes*, I wanted him to stay! "No, not now."

"Babe, you sure?" He had this dazed look in his eyes, and his bottom lip was moist and hanging. Gripping my face in his hands, he put his tongue in my mouth once more and I had to ask God for strength. Duane took my hand and put it up against his sweats, gripping it around his erection. "Look what you done to me."

"Go home, Duane." I said pushing him out the door.

"See how you treatin' me. You gonna send me home like this?"

"Yes I am." I kissed his lips softly, "Now good night."

That night as I laid in bed, I couldn't stop thinking about Duane. He'd grown up so much. I remembered him and his little friends coming to the movies to hang out at my concession stand. Sometimes if it were a slow day, I'd let them catch a free movie. I didn't do that for everyone, but they came around so much that they grew on me.

I laughed out loud at the thought! "Who would have believed that he had a crush on *me* for all those years?" But now that little boy was a grown man…but at twenty-four years old compared to my thirty he was just a baby, and had a whole lot more living to do. "Slow down girl." I said out loud as I envisioned him in my life. But there was now a melody ringing in my heart, 'Duane and Asia sitting in a tree, k-i-s-s-i-n-g…' He was in me.

THEY DON'T KNOW WHAT I KNOW

That boy knows he loves to eat some soul food, and I love cooking for him. Ever since I was a little girl my mom cooked a feast for me, my sister and daddy every Sunday. During the weekdays we'd have small meals like franks and beans, hamburgers, or soup and sandwiches. But when Sunday rolled around mom would be mixing up in the big pots. She'd have me on one side and my younger sister, Terry, on the other. The whole neighborhood would be lit-up with the aroma coming from our kitchen.

And you name it I could cook it. From West Indies, to Italian, to deep southern soul, and I can bake my ass off too. Make a sweet potato pie so rich and creamy it would make you dream about it after it's gone. Everyone asks me, 'girl, how can you cook like that and stay as skinny as you are?' And I tell them it's because I know how to put the fork down. At five-six, I'm one-thirty-eight and the only rolls on me are curves. Dangerous curves, 'cause along with knowing when to push away from the table, I work out. My son's not the only one sporting six pack abs in this family. I have a washboard of my own.

Even though mom and dad are the only ones living in this house now, Sundays always brought us back together around the dinner table. And since Duane was home for the off-season it was just like old times. Daddy and my sister Terry's husband Lawrence went to the liquor store to pick up a case of beer, and I asked them to stop by the supermarket to get some butter and pure vanilla flavor so I can put my yams in the oven.

Mama and I danced around each other as we moved from the sink, washing up used utensils, mixing bowls and pans; to the refrigerator and pantry getting and putting away food; to the stove. Terry, who was also in the kitchen adding her helping hand, flew into the living room when Duane came and they'd been huddled on the couch ever since. He had the remote in his hands flipping through the channels when what they were talking about caught my attention.

"How did you meet her?" Terry asked him, and I was thinking...meet who?

"Actually I knew Asia from way back. She used to work at the mall when I was a kid."

"You know her from school then?"

"No, she's older than me."

"Older? How much older?" My sister had this strange look on her face.

"Asia's got me by six years."

Oh I couldn't have heard him right? "Six years?!" I yelled from the kitchen, "That means she's in her thirties." No, this was not sitting well with me. That woman probably been dragged through the mud looking for someone to pay her and her kids damn bills and here he was just volunteering his damn self to be used...and I didn't like it. "Has she been married, and how many kids she got?" I had stopped cooking and was standing in the doorway of the kitchen.

"Sylvia stop buggin'. She ain't got no kids."

"Well what about the married part?"

"She's been divorced almost a year."

"Oh great, a whole freakin' year. Have you done lost your mind, boy?! You need to drop that tramp like a bad habit. Duane she don't sound like nothing but trouble. What do you want with some old, divorced woman anyway? There ain't enough single young ones for you?"

"How you gonna put her down if you ain't never met her?"

"And I don't even want to meet her." I continued, "Besides, you already got a girlfriend. And most men would kill for a woman like Missy. She's young, beautiful and besides being a Mavericks cheerleader, *the girl's a pre-med student,* for goodness sakes." I looked at Duane like he was a fool. Missy was a beautiful young lady and I liked her right from the start. I'd met quite a few of them things my son has brought home and I tell you, I could see right through them all. I love my boy and as his mother, I look out for his best interest. Like the saying goes, 'all that glitters ain't gold,' and half the time he don't realize they're fake because he's too caught up with what's up under their skirt, thinking he all in-love.

Missy was the only one out of the whole clan who *I* liked for my son and I didn't know what his problem was? They were perfect for each other. She's young and building a career and so was he. And because of their careers it would be years before the two of them could think about getting serious. By that time at least Duane would have had the chance to make a name for himself in the PFL. "What kind of job does that woman you cooked dinner for have?"

"*Asia's* a second grade school teacher." He said kinda nasty.

Terry patted him on the arm, "That sounds nice Duane. If you like her, I'm sure she's a good person." Mom was in the kitchen fumbling around and I knew she was just as concerned as I was.

Duane must have been thinking the same thing, "Gran, I'm sure you have an opinion too, so let's hear it."

"Just be careful, honey. This girl *is* older than you and she *has* already been married before." Mom shook her head full of silvery gray hair, "You worth a lot of money, just be sure she's not after you for that."

"She's not like that." He had the nerve to sound bothered, but I really didn't care. "Once y'all get to know her, you'll see how special she is to me."

"Special! Boy you better snap out of it."

"Duane, you serious about her, aren't you?" Terry makes me so damn sick coddling Duane the way that she does.

"That's what I'm telling you. She's the one."

Mom stopped what she was doing to really get a good look at him then she jumped on the bandwagon, "You really serious about this girl, Duane?"

"Hell, he better not be!" I wasn't trying to hear it! My son had come a long way professionally, but he still had a long ways to go. I just wanted to see him accomplish great things in his life. To help him see this football career through to its fullest. Duane had only been in the PFL for two years and he was a really good running back. Damn good! But like most young folks his age, his attention span needed constant refocusing. He had a brand new career that needed to be nurtured if he wanted to amount to anything in the pros. As his manager, Duane and I had so many business opportunities that we needed to lay foundations for. And there was a lot of work to be done and he didn't need to be pulled off-track now, especially by some thirty-year-old woman.

"Sylvia, when love strikes it just strikes."

"Terry, don't be encouraging him with that nonsense." Standing at the kitchen door, I waived that mixing spoon in the air ready to slap somebody with it. "How you gonna be getting involved with someone like that?" I yelled at Duane, "Six years older than you that makes her in her thirties! What would she want with a kid like you, anyway?! Old opportunistic *tramp*!"

Mom and Terry both looked at me like *I* had lost my mind then Duane stood up out of his chair, "Sylvia, I'm a grown man and I don't need nobody to encourage or discourage me when it comes to who I choose to be with!"

"Go on and be stupid then. Don't say I didn't warn you!"

"Yeah, thanks a lot!" He said sharply.

As he headed for the door mom called out to him, "Son, where you going? Ain't you gonna stay for dinner?" She asked sounding upset by the exchange between Duane and me.

"Can't do that, Gran." Duane stopped at the front door, then came back into the kitchen and kissed her on the head, "Tell Gramps I'll catch up with him later." He eyeballed me again, then left.

After the door closed, both Terry and my mom jumped on me about Duane being a "man". Now I can respect where they're coming from and-all-that, but the fact of the matter is, he is my son, and if I would have listened to them years ago Duane wouldn't be the athlete he is today. Many times they told me that I was driving him too hard, or had him into too many after school activities. Yes, I've always demanded a lot of Duane, but that's because I only want the best for him, that's why I constantly raise the bar. My son is a strong, talented millionaire and on top of that, *still* has potential that was untapped. So if seeing to it that he became all that he could be made me the unpopular one around here...so be it.

LONG DISTANCE LOVE AFFAIR

June had come and gone faster than I would have liked. Although I was anxious to get to training camp, I knew I was going to miss Asia like crazy. We spent so much time around each other, well as much time as possible with her working two jobs. That shit kinda pissed me off 'cause I offered to pay some of her bills off for her but she wouldn't let me do it. But the good part was she did let her guard down enough to accept that my feelings for her were real. She said all she wanted was for us to be was friends because we both had issues to settle before she could think about us going any further.

I did try to *hit it* a couple of times, but she wasn't having it. Asia was a church girl and told me about her pastor's teaching on celibacy. Said he preached how intercourse was God's covenant for marriage. And that every time you lay with a person you marry them and how your souls were forever connected. If that's the case I had a Harem! But I wasn't trying to knock her flow. If that's what she believed, then that's what she believed. I could respect that. It actually made me appreciate her even more.

When I got back to Arizona I had three days to rest up before I was due to report for camp. I had Asia on my mind and I was feeling so strong about her and knew I had to get in touch with Missy and handle my business. Spent the first two days washing my clothes, packing and buying some things to take to camp, the whole while thinking how to break things off with Missy. Finally I decided to take her out to dinner so we could talk. Didn't want to go over to her place and I didn't want her coming to mine because I didn't want to send any mixed messages. At the restaurant I was having a hard time telling her it was over. Wasn't going to say I found somebody else. That wouldn't have been fair to

Missy because it actually wasn't an Asia thing. It was a me not wanting to go any further with Missy thing. But I didn't know how to say that shit without hurting her feelings. Finally, I just came out and told her that I wasn't happy being in the relationship, which she already knew, and it was time for us to call it quits.

The part that tripped me out was when her jaw dropped and eyes welled up with tears and she asked me what I was talking about. Like she didn't have a damn clue! She was sitting there crying and everybody from the people at the other tables to our waitress was looking at me like I hit her or something. I felt bad for her, but at least I stepped to her like a man and told her it was over rather than playing some fucked-up head games. As for me, I was feeling great and couldn't wait for the next day to begin training camp!

I was in my condo, in the den with a glass of Hennessey in one hand and the cordless phone in the other as I talked to Asia. I had been home from practice for awhile and already ate dinner. Already took my shower and was sitting on the floor in pair of gray boxer briefs. With my bare back leaning up against the chair as Musiq Soul Child's *Love* played in the background.

"I can't believe September's almost here and school will be back in full swing in two short weeks."

"I know. You coming to my pre-season game against the Tritons this Saturday, right?" I had already asked her, but I just wanted to make sure. "I don't want you to drive though, I want you to be with my family. I already asked my aunt to pick you up. Everybody's gonna be there. And you already know Tompy."

Asia had come over a couple of times when he was home and they liked each other. Tompy was like, "Man, she's quality. If I were you, I'd lock that down, dawg." Tompy was my boy and it felt good for someone to see what I saw in Asia 'cause she was most definitely quality! Besides, he was one of the little dudes who I used to drag to the mall to see her, back-in-the-day.

I was real concerned about how Sylvia was going to be acting, though. And I told her, don't be tripping and making Asia feel all uncomfortable but I knew how Sylvia could get sometimes.

All the time we spent together I never brought Asia over to meet my people. I felt bad when she asked me what their reactions to my dating her. I didn't lie though, I told her. But I made it clear that it was their problem and not ours. Even so I wanted Asia to meet them, but she said she wasn't ready to go there yet. Maybe it was just as well.

We've been talking ever since March and here it was August and there were certain things that she still wouldn't open up to me about. I swear, I had deep feelings for that woman but her hang-up with her ex made me wonder about her.

Sure I wanted Asia bad enough to overlook that, but knowing me, it would always be in the back of my mind. So once again I asked her what the deal had been between the two of them and why it seemed that she was having such a hard time with moving on. I needed to know! But this time like the last few times I asked I didn't expect her to answer.

Asia paused and got real quiet. I didn't say a word, just let the question hang in the air and become heavy on her head like for the last five months it had been on mine. Her stressing would have been understandable if they had kids, but it was nothing like that. So the only thing that kept running in my mind was she must still have feelings for the brother. And if that was the case then I needed to step off and let her go her own way.

Once again, frustrated by her silence, I told Asia that I had to go. Just as I was about to hang up she said, "No, wait, Duane." Then I began to feel the load that she carried.

"I knew he was cheating on me. And I can't begin to tell you why I stayed as long as I did. But laying in pain on the doctor's table not the first, or the second, but the third time getting a shot of penicillin injected into my butt I decided that I would never, *ever* go through that nonsense again! Then I thought, well at least he gives me S.T.D's that penicillin can cure." She said sarcastically.

"Damn, Baby." Just sort of slipped out. He burnt her three times! No wonder she was so cautious about herself. I couldn't even imagine Asia having to go through that mess.

"But then I thought, what if the next time I wasn't so lucky? And that's when

I divorced him. But from the time he moved out and our divorce was final he started doing all sorts of mean ass things to me. The one that he knew would hurt me the most involved something that meant everything to my dad. Daddy had a 1946 baseball signed by Satchel Paige from the Negro Baseball League. He got it the same year that Satchel helped pitch the Kansas City Monarchs to their fifth pennant." She laughed, but I also heard a sniffle. "Now Duane, you know I don't know a thing about sports, but I know all about Satchel Paige because my dad cherished that ball. He called it his good luck charm. Right after it was signed, he said he met my mom and wanted to pass it on to my first son."

"How you know your ex took the ball?"

"I thought the Negro Baseball League would be something empowering to teach my second graders. My father had memorabilia that he let me hold, the ball, a bat signed by Josh Gibson, and some old pamphlets from some of the teams. They were in my bedroom ready for my presentation at the end of the week. When Bryant left I didn't change the locks right away so while I was at work he came in my house and took all of my furniture and in the middle of the empty living room floor he left the bat. When I ran upstairs the pamphlets were still there but the ball was gone." As she spoke, I hit the stereo's remote to repeat, Musiq's "Love". "My father had told him the whole story about how he drove all around following Satchel Paige to finally get that signature and what it meant to him. Out of all the things to take, he went for the one that meant the most to my dad and he knew that kind of disrespect would kill me.

But the hard part was, knowing that my dad trusted me and I had to look him in his eyes and tell him his ball was gone. I promised him that I would get it back."

"Your ex just wanted something to tie you to him." Just the thought pissed me off 'cause it was working.

"Duane, that 1946 ball is something that I cannot make better. When my parents' house went into foreclosure because they refinanced it to pay for my college tuition, then couldn't make the payments it cost me everything but I made that right to the best of my ability. So that's why I carry this hurt because he just wasn't satisfied with ruining my life with his cheating, he had to go far and beyond to fuck me over in the process and that hurts because I trusted him. He was someone who supposedly loved me. And to think I trusted him, you know?"

Sitting there listening to her on the phone, I just wished I was there to hold her and reassure her that she was not to blame. Instead I just told Asia, thanks. Thanks for finally letting me in!

MEET THE FAMILY

It was Sunday, September twelfth, eleven o'clock in the morning and I had a nervous excitement rushing through me. I had never felt like this before. Excited because after three months since he left to return to Arizona for training camp, I was going to see Duane in the Mavericks pre-season opener against the New Jersey Tritons. Although I didn't give Duane the title of *my man*, his presence in my life sure filled the voids. And even though we talked almost every night on the phone, I missed him!

Even though Duane and I were just friends, I was also nervous because I didn't know how his family would act towards me. He mentioned that his mother wasn't thrilled with the idea of him being involved with someone older and who had already been married. On several occasions he wanted me to meet his people but I wasn't ready for the scrutiny. And that's not to say that I was ready for it today either, but it was important to him that I be there, and sit with his family during the game.

Dressed in my fuchsia-colored nylon sweat suite and white sneakers I was looking sporty. I checked myself in the mirror to make sure that everything was in place. Just in case things didn't go smoothly I also made sure I had train fare home. I was cautious like that!

When I heard the sound of a horn blowing, I stuck my head outside to let Duane's Aunt Terry know that I was coming. She was double-parked, sitting in a sharp maroon Acura.

I grabbed my purse then locked the door behind me and headed for the car. It was gorgeous outside! The sun was shining high in the deep blue sky with big white cotton candy clouds and a warm breeze blew, indicating more warmth for the rest of the day.

There was a storefront church directly across the street from my house and on this Sunday morning the doors were wide open. As I walked to the car I could hear the organ intertwined with the piano. The congregation sang out loud and clapped along. All of the sounds from the church and the cars driving by were instantly sealed out as I closed the Acura door, replaced by the low volume of the car's stereo.

"Hi, I'm Terry." She smiled warm and friendly.

"Hi, and I'm Asia." We shook hands.

She had short sassy hair, maybe an inch long that was perfectly shaped up around her face and it was colored blond. Razor-sharp arched eyebrows and a diamond chip earring sat in her nose. Terry had on this tough denim outfit. She sort of looked like Duane. I believe she had his eyes. Maybe they were family eyes.

Recalling that Duane told me his mom was sixteen when he was born and his aunt was fifteen, I thought Terry looked to be at least my age even though she was nine years older than me.

"Oh, believe me, Asia I feel like I've known you my entire life, as much as Duane talks about you."

"Really?" I blushed and was so relieved that it seemed we were getting off to a good start.

"Yes, girlfriend. Every other word that comes out of his mouth has Asia attached to it." Terry laughed as she checked her rearview mirror before she pulled off.

"Wow, now that's nice to hear." I was pleasantly surprised.

As we drove along the New Jersey Turnpike headed towards East Rutherford, the traffic had a nice flow. And so did our conversation. When we arrived at Harry Clay Stadium, I had to admit it was a little overwhelming. Terry was a nice person, but the idea of meeting all of Duane's other family made me nervous.

I followed her through the crowd of people to our seats. Duane asked us not to wear any Mavericks clothing because the Tritons fans were known to be rowdy! Duane's whole family was there and, so was Tompy. Terry introduced me to her parents - Duane's grandparents, Miss Nancy and Mister Robert Cummings. They seemed sweet. But when she introduced me to Sylvia, Duane's mother, it was a whole different story. I smiled and extended my hand ready to shake hers when she without even saying hello, turned her head from me and started talking to Tompy who was seated on the side of her. Motionless, I stared down at her feeling zapped like I had stuck my finger into a socket and even though it had happened, I couldn't fathom someone being that cold to someone they had never met.

Seeing me standing there with my hand dangling in the air, Tompy extended his hand shaking mine then gave me a warm smile and hello. We had met a couple of times before and we got along great. He was a really nice looking brother, caramel brown skin, bald head, tight physique and big hands that just swallowed mine as he welcomed me.

Terry looked at her sister shaking her head pitifully as to tell me, *don't let it bother you*, then said, "And this is my husband Lawrence."

The arctic wind that had been blown in my face still had me somewhat dazed and distracted. Duane told me to overlook her if she got ill, but I wondered if he knew Sylvia was this *ignorant*? If so, that was trouble because I had *no* intentions of putting up with her attitude.

Terry leaned over and kissed her husband on the lips. Lawrence and I shook hands then Terry and I took our seats in the packed stadium.

Lawrence was seated between us. Turning to me he said, "So you're the one who's got Duane's nose wide open." Liking the sound of that, I smiled. "Seeing you makes me understand what Duane's been telling everybody." And for good measure he threw in, "and don't pay no attention to Sylvia. There's one in every family." He circled his finger around the side of his head, and I laughed.

The game was so exciting, far beyond what I had expected. I stood, I shouted, even participated in the wave! Lawrence was a football fanatic, as he called himself, and explained everything that was going on as simply as possible.

Much to my delight, he explained that Duane was a marquee player. That meant the most valuable player on the team.

From the articles I read about Duane and his *alter ego* "The Hitman", I don't think that side of him had sunk in, until I actually saw him on the field that day. He knew what row of seats we were sitting in so every chance he got he pointed in our direction. Duane's team wore blue, red and gold and his number was twenty-nine…my new favorite number!

Rock music blasting from the speaker system charging up the stadium with energy. The Tritons' cheerleaders dressed in their black and silver danced on the sidelines, while the beer man yelled, "Cold Budweiser!" and Duane was right, the Triton fans were rowdy! But my favorite few seconds of the game was when Duane made his two touchdowns and did his endzone dance. I was loving it, and there was such an excitement in his family!

The Tritons and the Mavericks both played their hearts out that afternoon, but the Tritons beat Duane's Mavericks 31 to 27. My voice was half gone from all the yelling.

After the game ended, masses of people made their way out of the stadium. We followed until we turned off, walking down a long hallway to the reception area. It was a really big room in the basement of the stadium. Nothing impressive looking at all. Just a bunch of people standing around. It reminded me of the Motor Vehicles Agency or the Unemployment Office, only this room had tables set up with snack foods laid out on big trays. Sylvia had a pass that she showed security to let us in.

I got the chance to talk with Duane's grandparents for a few, then Tompy and I talked before Terry and Lawrence came over. I didn't approach Sylvia and she had no words for me either, which was fine. For the most part, I was comfortable around Duane's folks.

Thirty minutes into our wait, Duane came bopping into the reception hall with a black Kangol hat turned backwards on his head so that the emblem sat on his brow. He had a garment bag thrown over his shoulder, looking so fine all suited down in a beige suit and black mock neck shirt, with shinny black gators on his feet.

Duane didn't have much time before his team was scheduled to fly back to Arizona. His bus was due to pull out in another hour. He rested his bag then hugged and squeezed everyone all the while having his eyes glued to me, and I had this big *cheese* grin plastered on my face. He led me by the hand out of the reception area and I couldn't believe how happy I was to actually be touching him in the flesh.

"Where are you going?!" his family complained.

"I'll be back." He shouted over his shoulder walking me out into an empty hallway. As Duane wrapped me in his arms, I pressed my cheek snugly to his broad chest. We stood there just holding each other and it felt so good. "I miss you girl. I'm glad you could make it."

"Oh I *miss* you too," I said with more passion than I even thought existed between us.

Duane lifted my chin and kissed me real slow. His tongue tasted like he had been eating peppermint.

Just being around Duane made my spirit take wings. Inside of me there was dancing and singing and a big ole celebration. It was an internal holiday! But through all of that, I still had a nagging inside of me, "Did you take care of that situation in Arizona?" I asked referring to his ex-girlfriend Missy. As much as Duane and I have talked, we never talked about her. I wanted to know but I never asked and he didn't bring it up either. But now that he was here and I was feeling enamored, the question was very relevant.

"By you asking, does that mean that you ready for me now?" He joked.

"That means, I don't want to be standing here tonguing somebody else's man."

Duane laughed out loud, then took my hand, "Come on, I know my family's freaking. *Where's Duane? Where's Duane?*"

We walked hand-in-hand over to his mother, and I could feel my stomach churned. Not from nervousness, but this time from restraint. I didn't care whose mother she was, respect was due to everyone, and I wasn't about to let her flat out disrespect me again. This time I was going to be ready.

"Did you enjoy the game, Asia?" Sylvia asked, almost pleasantly, catching me off guard once again.

Oh no she didn't, I thought to myself! But then I looked at Duane's face smiling down at me waiting for me to respond. "Yes I did." I had her number, but I wasn't about to play her little games. Sylvia gave me a *polite* smile that irked the mess out of me, then she put her arms around Duane kissing him on the side of the face to dominate her space. By this time the rest of his family and Tompy crowded around him getting their time in before he had to leave.

It wasn't long until the coach signaled for all of the players to report to the bus. Duane took his time hugging all of the ladies in his life, first his grandmom, then Terry, then Sylvia. He shook hands with his grandpop, Lawrence and Tompy. Then Duane pulled me in his arms and gave me another deep hug whispering, "I love you, girl." Then he tenderly planted one on my lips. "You should be coming back with me."

I held him tight, "Call me as soon as you get there." As I looked up into Duane's face, there it was again. That same cumbersome, involuntary feeling of sadness that I experienced when he left for training camp in June. Standing there I wanted to ask him not to leave me. As he disappeared into the crowd, I just stood there hypnotized until I felt Terry's hand rub across my back. "Asia, you alright, hun?"

When I looked around, Duane's family was halfway down the hall and Terry and I were the only ones standing there. Watching him walk away, I couldn't deny that with him, I was *in-love!* I knew it when he went back to Arizona in June. I had such an *aching* to see him and to be with him and it was *strong!* When we talked on the phone and we did a lot of it, it only intensified the fact that he wasn't around.

My body had become used to his arms around me, and his warm body next to mine. I desperately missed the taste of his tongue in my mouth, looking into his eyes, and the way he smelled...I just missed being close to him.

MAMA'S BOY

For the past three years since I've been with the Mavericks, Sylvia would take a two-week Christmas pilgrimage to Arizona to be with me for the holidays. She loved it here. The hot climate, scenery and most definitely the *royal treatment* she received from the Mavericks establishment. Dinner at Coach's house, all-expenses-paid nights on the town, treated to the best restaurants…all compliments of the Arizona Mavericks. There were only a few guys on the team that they bent over backwards to keep pleased. I just happen to be one of them. They called us the media darlings. The ones who had the most newspaper, radio and television time. We were the guys who represented the Arizona Mavericks franchise to the world. So we were courted accordingly to make sure that gratitude and goodwill spilled from our mouth when we had a microphone or a tape recorder shoved in our faces. But as in life, everything came with a price. Some people view football only as a sport, but after you sign on that *multi-million dollar* dotted line you best recognize that this was indeed a *business*! And your ass was bought and paid for.

Love of the game was most definitely a dominant factor, but it took more than love to make an injured player in all kinds of pain go out on the field and perform. One thing that was understood from the door was if you couldn't perform you were no longer a commodity, you were a liability. And franchises don't like liabilities.

I really dug the time my mom and I spent when she came to town. It gave us a chance to talk and shoot the breeze like when I was a kid. One of Sylvia's favorite things in the world was going shopping. She already had more shit than she knew what to do with, but whatever turned her on! All my life I watched my mom work with no one there to treat her like the queen she was. No one ever made her feel special like every woman should be made to feel. That's why now *nothing* was too good for her. So she wouldn't have to work I financed her retirement, bought her a new house and a car. I made sure as far as finances was concerned that she was set for two lifetimes.

We were hanging out at the Arizona Arrowhead Mall and she must have dragged me into damn near all the stores there. And after two hours of walking around we stopped at the food court and as usual started talking business. Since she was also my business manager we did that a lot.

Because the Mavericks were a second-rate team I was feeling really frustrated and personally I was ready to fly. Despite our fucked-up season of seven wins nine losses I secured a position on the PFL's All Pros game for the second year in a row. I was feeling like a big fish in a small pond and I was ready for something to change! Over a slice of pizza, I told Sylvia that I wanted the opportunity to play in the Champion Bowl but I knew Arizona was *not* a Champion Bowl team.

Sylvia didn't share my passion to see me in the Champion Bowl. Instead she was more interested in grooming me for my post-PFL life. She told me that I already had the dollars, just go with the flow and in a few years I could get off the playing field and into a PFL office spot.

She was constantly at me to look into commentating. Said since I knew the game of football inside-and-out, and had good diction, that I would be perfect as a sports talk show host, or a game day live commentator.

Sometimes I felt more like her damn project than her son. Maybe that was the business manager inside of her, to always look for the next great opportunity. But I was a man now not a boy and I was getting tired of people telling me what to do… agents, coaches, reporter, fans, Sylvia… everyone had a damn opinion. While I was in college Sylvia told me, "You stay focused on your studies and football *only,* Duane. You don't have time to be messing around with no fraternities and leave them damn tramps alone!" She was to the point of paranoia when it came down to me getting into a relationship while I was in college.

"Those girls will trap you! And you don't have no time for that nonsense." I had to admit though, that she was right. Not all of the college women I ran into were like that. But the ones who hung around the players, most of them had that hungry look in their eyes. You knew to double up on the rubbers because they would make your life miserable if they caught your seed. So I took her advice and I didn't get into any serious relationships while I was in college.

But when Sylvia found out I pledged Omega she freaked! Not only did she freak, but she *froze me out.* Didn't speak to me for two whole months and that had me trippin' in a bad way. She couldn't beat my ass or nothing so she froze me out to make it known she was mad.

"Hey Hitman!" A passerby shouted.

"Whasup?!" I shouted back with my mouth full.

Just then out of nowhere two little boys ran over to our table, "Hey Mr. Hitman, can we have your autograph?!"

"Alright, sure. And who might you be?" I looked at Sylvia motioning my hand for a pen.

As she dug in her purse the little boy said, "I'm Curby!"

"And I'm George. We're *big* fans of yours Hitman! I mean, Mr. Hitman."

"Is that right?" I took the pen and signed the back of Curby's shirt.

"Yeah!" they both said in unison.

A woman walked over, "I hope my son and his friend aren't bothering yous?"

"No Ma'am. The kids are always nice to talk to. I was a kid once myself you know?" I joked, winking at the boys and they cracked up.

The lady, star-struck herself, blushed until her peach complexion turned red, "Hi, I'm Doris, Curby's mom."

I shook her hand, "Nice to meet you Doris. And this is my mom, Sylvia."

"I want to be just like you when I grow up Mr. Hitman!"

"How you doing in school, George?" I asked while signing his shirt.

"Okay I guess." He shrugged his shoulders.

"Well if you want to know anything about me, it's that my mom always stayed on me to get good grades. So you always study hard and whatever you do in life you'll be the best at it, alright?" I rubbed my hand across his head, ruffling his blond hair. George nodded his head.

"Well come on boys." Doris said, "Let's let these nice people get back to their lunch. Nice to meet you both."

"Nice to meet you too," we both said. The boys ran off giving each other a high-five. On any given day, I sign at least twelve autographs. Made me feel good to see how excited people got and I didn't take any of that for granted like some of the fellahs did. They would just crush people by getting ignorant on the fans by not speaking, being short-tempered or not signing. As for me...if I didn't feel like being bothered, I just wouldn't come out.

Sitting there in the food court of the mall, Sylvia and I continued to assess the end of my third season that I just completed, my fourth year coming up, and my free-agent status at the end of my fifth. I wanted to keep my options open in regards to being traded to a better team, but Sylvia *strongly* encouraged me to stay faithful to the Mavericks because she thought I had a bright future in Arizona. I was their hero she said.

As we talked, my attention was diverted by this lady walking past. She was wearing this form fitting dress that showed off her apple-shapped behind, and she was walking like she knew her shit was good.

"You got X ray vision now?" Sylvia said biting into her pizza.

"What?"

"You looking right through that woman."

I laughed not noticing that I'd been staring. "No it's not that. She just reminds me of Asia." The words just blurted out 'cause Asia was definitely packing in the back.

Sylvia sighed hard, "You keep talking about her all the damn time. I hope this is some shit that's gonna pass."

"What are you talking about?"

"That married woman, that's what."

I shook my head, "She's divorced, Sylvia. Anyway, what's your problem with Asia?"

"Her by herself, nothing. Her in your life, *everything*. Duane, you are only twenty-four years old. You don't need to be tied down to no woman who already been around the block. She's much older than you are, and besides she *thinks* she's all that and ain't even got a pot to piss in."

"Now you know that ain't right, Sylvia. So, she's been married before. And so, she ain't got no money, but neither did we before I turned pro. I dig her. She's got a lot going on for herself in spite of all the shit she's been through. Asia's got a good heart."

"Well I don't care, I still don't like her, and I know you can do a lot better than that."

"Whatever." I dismissed, drinking from my large cup of Sprite.

"Well what are you going to do about Missy? I know you still fuckin her. Y'all stayed out all last night. Got that girl on a string like some little lovesick puppy."

When I got home from training camp, Missy had written me a letter telling me how *in-love* with me she was. Said that even though we couldn't be a couple that she wanted to know if we could remain friends. That was the first of like seven letters she wrote me on flowery notepaper sprayed with just enough perfume to let me know what she must have smelled like when she wrote it. When I didn't respond, she called me to ask if she could come over…just to talk. I told her yeah, even though I knew what was on her mind. By that time I was in need of some *sexual healing* and she understood the rules. *There was no us!* We'd just hook up every once-in-a-while, and it was no more than that.

"How do I explain this to you." I looked into my mom's eyes, "We want different things out of life, and I'm sick of pretending that there is something between us when it's not. It's not like that when I'm around Asia." Just the mention of her name made me smile. Asia and I talked about everything. She'd have me cracking up with some of the stories about her second graders…she was proud of them. And even though she didn't know jack about sports, she'd listen for hours as I went on about my game. When I couldn't focus, she knew exactly what to say to have me seeing straight again. I loved that about her. "Me and that girl, we just vibe. It's like we're in total sync. I can relate to her and she can relate to me." I laughed, "Well almost relate. She still ain't tryin' to hook a brothah up none."

Sylvia looked at me strange, "Y'all ain't do it yet?"

"Naw, she be tryin' to give a brothah blue balls." I laughed.

"Well *good*. I hope when you get it, it's sour. Then maybe you can leave her ass alone."

I started rolling, "You crazy."

THE MORNING AFTER

All that fanfare for a day that absolutely sizzled out! I spent Christmas morning with my parents, which was nice then I came home to this big empty house. Still under my Christmas tree were presents for Crystal and her son, my godson, Lil Allen. Couldn't talk to her because they were in Washington to her in-law's house for the holidays and wouldn't be back until after New Year's.

And speaking of Christmas presents Duane gave me a biggie! On December first, that was the day I always put up my tree, I was listening to WMSJ fm and Luther Vandross was singing carols when there was a knock at the door. There was a big truck parked in front of my house and I thought it must have been a mistake. I opened up my door ready to send the man away but before I could say anything he said, "Major Heating and Cooling Service." Come to find out Duane had sent him over to convert my oil heat to a gas system.

So many emotions were colliding in me about Duane. Here I was working my two jobs to make my ends meet, and many times Duane offered to pay some of my bills off for me. If I said I wasn't tempted I'd be flat out lying but I just wouldn't...couldn't allow myself to let him. Now here he was putting me in that same position again and I resented it. While the service man was taking measurements in the basement, I came upstairs and gave Duane a call.

"Asia, I'm learning you. You talk about your father being stubborn and full of pride, but you've got to be worse than him. All you have to do is take the heater, babe. Why is that so hard for you to do?"

"Because,"

"Because what?"

"Because I don't want to be confused about the reason I'm with you. About the reason I care for you the way I do. But mostly, I don't want you to become confused about the reason I'm with you"

Duane told me he loved me and his gift came from the heart, and I couldn't argue with that.

As I stared at the tree glittering with its thousands of colorful blinking lights, I felt both bored and a little empty. Last night I talked with Duane and he said that he and his mother were going to be gone all Christmas day and that he'd call me once they got in, but it was already after nine. Since I didn't have any plans for the rest of the night, I figured now was a good time to read. I had stopped by the Mind and Soul Bookstore on Broad Street a few days ago and bought a juicy romance novel. It was from a lady new to the black romance circuit named, Paulette Blue. Her newest was called *Jubilant*.

Except for the Christmas tree lights blinking, and the lamp that sat next to the living room couch where I was curled up, my entire house was dark. I was snug in my cozy nighty and from the heat of my new central heating system. Sitting in front of me was a large bowl of popcorn that I had popped and an oversized mug of hot chocolate.

Two hours later all of the chocolate and half the popcorn was gone and I was *totally* engrossed in the lives of Colin and Elizabeth, the two main characters of *Jubilant*. Reaching out, I had the phone to my ear, saying hello before I even remembered the phone rang. I was more concerned with finishing the next sentence than with who was on the line.

Bryant was on the other end, "Merry Christmas, baby." Although I was deeply hurt by the way he'd done me and our divorce, I found it hard to hate the man whom I once loved. If anything, I felt sorry for him, because I knew, until he changed his ways he would never be able to have anything real in his life. Bryant was the type of person who would continue that cycle of hurting anyone who tried to be close to him.

"Hey,"

"I know how much you love the holidays. I took a chance on calling, but I really didn't expect you to be there."

"No, I'm just sitting here."

"Alone?"

"Me and this beautiful tree."

"Asia, I need to talk to you. I'm going through some things and I could really use a shoulder right now."

Listening to him talk, my mind wandered on Monique, the woman he left me for, and where was she tonight? As I sat there with the phone to my ear I wondered if she ever thought about me when she and Bryant were fooling around behind my back. How *ironic* that her man would need to talk to me. Bryant and Crystal's husband were first cousins. Bryant and I were the ones who set Crystal and Allen up on their first date, so Crystal had already told me that my ex was starting to reap what he sowed. Apparently, Monique was *the wrong sistah to mess with!*

I still had a lot of issues with Bryant. Only two years ago I was to the point where I'd get migraine headaches and just couldn't function from agonizing over what he did to me…the broken trust, the life he robbed me of. The only thing that helped was when I asked God to *help me* forgive him! So many nights I prayed to be released of the bitterness and hatred that just gripped me. It was like he had this wicked power over me that I couldn't control. Since we've been talking, Duane had done so much to help me move on with my life, and I know he's an answer to my prayer.

"Asia, I could really use a friend."

I don't know what I was trying to prove, but I told him that he could come over. I often dreamed of the day when someone would pay him back for how he treated me. Give him some of his own medicine. When Crystal told me what Monique did to Bryant, I can't lie we both had a good laugh and part of me screamed, 'Yeah! Now how does it feel? Not so good, does it?!' I guess I just needed to look him in his pathetic eyes to see if it would give me any satisfaction or back any of the dignity that he robbed me of. I gave him my heart, my life, my virginity. What he gave me in return were several trips to the clinic, a rotten house, divorce papers, then left me alone to pick up the pieces. His roosters were coming home to roost and *I wanted to see it!*

Moments later he was knocking on the door. When I let him in, Bryant kissed me on the side of the cheek, "Merry Christmas." He handed me a flat wrapped box.

There was a beautiful sheer scarf inside, "Thank you, Bryant." I smiled, "Why don't you rest your coat?"

He was always soft on the eyes. Not much taller than me at five nine and a half, compared to my five-eight. To me he looked like Mr. Corporate America. Clean shaven, caramel complected skin, navy blue suit, starched white shirt, spit-shined shoes. He put his coat on the back of couch.

About an hour into our conversation I really couldn't stand anymore. Here he was almost to the point of tears over this woman leaving him and taking everything that he had and he was actually looking for me to console him. And all this after he took my father's collector baseball and stole my furniture out of my house while I was at work. So he called Monique every name in the book. I kept quiet then when he had run out of words and quieted down, I looked at him and said "Bryant you have a long history of hurting people. And until you can recognize that and start doing the right things, Monique just gave you a taste of what's in store for you." I wasn't as strong as I thought I was because I felt my anger growing inside of me. "This ain't happening. I'm sorry, but you have to go." I said standing to my feet.

"I'm sorry, Asia. You didn't deserve to be treated the way I treated you." He looked at me with more sincerity in his eyes than I had ever seen before. Hopefully he was starting his transformation into a better man.

"Nobody deserves to be treated like that, Bryant."

When he left I turned the ringers off on my phones. All I wanted was some quiet time to myself 'cause I felt heavy on the inside. Pain was pain and I got no satisfaction out of seeing him like that. Nor did being in his presence contribute anything to my dignity, which was a stupid thought anyway because I knew that dignity was internal and no one could give you that. After I unplugged the Christmas tree lights, I left the popcorn bowl, my empty mug and book on the coffee table, went upstairs and slid under my covers.

The next morning as I sat at the kitchen table eating a bowl of Honey Nut Cheerios I wondered why it was so quiet until I remembered I had turned the ringers off. Reaching under the phone I restored the sound and before I removed my hand from the dial, it rang. "I called you seven times last night. All last night!" Duane's bass rumbled through the phone without so-much as a hello, "Where were you?!" He demanded.

His tone took my breath away and the spoon dropped into my cereal bowl. As the milk splashed onto the table I said, "I was home."

"Asia, I called you all last night. Way up until three o'clock this morning."

"Duane, what's with the third degree? I am over twenty-one and I'm not wearing anyone's ring on my finger!" How was he going to call me shouting over the phone like he had rights?

"Oh, so it's like that? Just answer me one little question. Was it Bryant?"

"Who even said that I was with anyone?" The sudden onset of the highly charged, negative, discussion had my heart racing. Who in the world did Duane think he was talking to?

"Come on, don't even take me there. Was you with Bryant last night?" He pressed. "Asia, ain't no need to hide it…just tell me the truth."

"He stopped by. But…"

"But ain't nothing happen. But he just a friend…what? Which one, Asia? Damn!" The sound of his breath blew hard through the phone. "So what, y'all getting back together now?"

"No we're not getting back together," I stated matter of factly. "I don't understand your reaction, Duane. When I asked you if you had broken things off with your girl, Missy, you two-stepped around that question so well your name could have been Mr. Bo Jangles."

"You don't understand my reaction?!" He blasted. "So the reason you fucking your ex-husband is because I ain't never gave you a straight answer?!"

"Don't you dare disrespect me like that!" I yelled into the phone. "I have too much respect for myself to be using my body as some get back tool!" I felt like Duane had just blindsided me. But I knew what was going on 'cause Bryant used to do the same thing when he was messing around...become accusatory. Duane sounded guilty! He called me last night and since I didn't answer the phone he assumed that I was doing what he must be doing. I started to hang up, but I wanted to say my peace first. "Duane, I'm not stupid! I know you're still involved with your situation and I..."

"Is that what you're waiting for Asia?" He cut me off mid-sentence. "You know how I feel about you. I want you in my world and this shit is tearing me apart. Is that what you're waiting for?"

My heart was beating so fast and I believe I had started perspiring, "Duane you won't be leaving her for me. You have to decide where you want to be. Because whether or not you want Missy you have to make that decision based on the two of you. But I'll tell you one thing for sure, I do not share my man with any other woman. And if you do leave her, that still doesn't mean a thing between you and me."

"I don't want you with no other man, Asia." He talked over me.

"Duane, you need to handle your business and not worry about me and what I'm doing."

"Asia, I don't want you with no other man." He stressed once again.

We argued back and forth over the phone for twenty-three solid minutes and all that was going through my mind was, 'I could not see myself having to explain my every move to this man. Here he was going off because he couldn't reach me on the phone and he was so blinded by his own apparent guilt and jealousy that he was acting like this! At this point in my life I was not willing to go back through this again.

His yelling faded into the background of my mind and I felt so hurt and let down by his actions. I guess what we had was too good to be true. That I could find someone who loved me and wanted to make a life with me. Guess the angels in heaven must have had a good laugh at my expense. Why do all the men that I let into my life have to have these kind of issues? Duane had gone from some guy to my friend, to someone I had fallen in love with. I loved him so it really hurt me when I told him, "Duane, I think we should just call it off. Maybe we should go our own separate ways for now. Give us both some time to think. Cause I really don't like what's happening right now."

Duane got real quiet like all of the air was let out of his system, then he said, "Don't do this. Asia don't do this."

"Duane I'm going to hang up now." Bryant's visit had affected me even more than I thought. When I looked at him I couldn't help but to see what should have been between us. I had put so much of myself into making our marriage work, just to be spit on. I wasn't willing to give that much of myself to anyone again. And Duane sure wasn't acting worthy of my effort.

"Asia!" He called out to me right before I hung up the phone.

I sat in front of the soggy bowl of cereal with my hands over my face. My head was spinning trying to digest what had just taken place. The phone began to ring, and ring, and ring, but I wouldn't answer it.

HOME IS WHERE THE HEART IS

I felt like shit when she told me we should go our own separate ways. Like every drop of arrogance had dried up like a prune and I heard Teddy Pendergrass singing in my ear calling me a silly fool, asking me how'd I lose such a good thing.

I loved Asia and I couldn't stand the thought of her ex anywhere near her! The shit made me insane. How she be tripping like he was still inside of her head somewhere. But he'll always be her number one, right? The first to hit it, the first to marry her... and you know what they say about a woman and her first. What it came down to was I was afraid to lose her.

All that day I called her, but Asia wouldn't pick up the phone. When she finally did pick up that night her guard was up like she didn't want to be bothered, which wasn't right. She was freezing me out of her life, but she gave that muthah fuckah a hundred chances... she couldn't give me one more? My head was messed up.

Asia had become the one. No matter what the news, I wanted to share it with her first. She was the one whose voice, laughter and smile lifted me up from the inside out. And her tears could break my heart. Over the phone that night she told me the same thing that we should just cool things down for awhile. I told her that I wanted to see her face to face, and the next time I'll call would be to tell her that I was on my way. She told me not to come.

I was scheduled to start toning up for the All Pros game next week, but I couldn't concentrate on anything except what was going on with Asia. Even though it was going to break my training regimen, when Sylvia caught her flight back to Trenton, I was on the plane with her. And before she even got started about me missing the first week of the All Pros training, I told her I didn't want to hear it. But first I went to Missy and finally put an end to our charade. She turned it into a shouting match, trying to pretend that we had something to fight for. We didn't!

By the time I got to Asia's porch ringing her bell it was almost nine o'clock at night. After the few days of us not speaking I was hoping that she would have thought things over and changed her mind. When she opened the door, she didn't say anything. Didn't look surprised to see me, didn't smile, didn't frown. She just walked into the living room and sat on the couch tucking her leg underneath her. Dressed in a beige cotton pajamas pants set, she stared at the television ignoring me.

Closing the front door I just stood there and watched her. Okay, okay, I had to admit that I was wrong for the way I came off on her about not picking up the phone on Christmas night. And jumping to conclusions about her sleeping with her ex, while I was the one doing the sleeping around. I knew she was hurt, and I was hurt too. But most of all, I was scared.

I walked in front of the television and turned it off then her emotionless eyes looked up at me. It was dead quiet in the room as I stood there looking down at her. I felt myself choking up and my heart was pounding because she didn't seem anymore forgiving now that I was here, than when we were on the phone. Ever since our argument and all the way during the plane ride here, I was rehearsing what I was going to say. That I apologized for coming out my face on her like I did. That I knew I was wrong and to give me another chance cause I wouldn't cheat on her no more. But I know that was exactly what she expected me to do because she had heard it all before. And I knew she was going to let me say my peace then send my ass right back out the door. It was written all over her face, so instead of going there, I just poured out my soul.

"When I saw you at Maxine's Restaurant on your birthday last year. Asia that was one of the best nights of my life, because…" I stopped because I wasn't sure if I really wanted to tell her this: to reveal my innermost weakness so that if she wanted she could later throw that shit in my face. What I was about to tell her, I didn't like to deal with so I kept it to myself, even though the thoughts were always there. "…because I never really felt like anyone ever accepted me for who I am on the inside. Oh sure, I have lots of so-called friends. And I can't walk down the street without people yelling, 'Hey Hitman!' But they don't know me," I banged on my chest. "Asia, they don't give two shits about Duane Cummings! I was nothing but some little black ass ugly boy who just happened to be good at sports. And that's all they ever saw. Now all they see are the dollar signs, and I'm sick of this shit! Well what about me, Asia? Huh? What about me?"

It was easier to just play the role like everything was cool. But to be a little kid and have people laugh at me and call me black, not as in black as a people, but in a derogatory sense because of my skin tone. They'd make fucked-up jokes at my expense. It just tore me down on the inside, made me self-conscious about who I was. But almost simultaneously when I hit junior high and I became recognized for sports, then all of a sudden the jokes stopped…well in front of my face anyway. From that point on, I became the one everyone wanted to hang around and I always resented that. All I've ever wanted was to be accepted for who I was, but that just never seemed good enough. The shit still gets cloudy sometimes, but I knew Asia connected to the real me and yeah, I played myself. But I wanted this woman by my side and I was afraid, "I messed things up, but I'm asking you for another chance." I would rather have lost my pride than lose her and I would have even gotten on my knees if I had to 'cause she meant just that much to me. "Don't close the door on us, Asia."

"Don't do this, Duane! Don't come in here playing with my emotions. I cannot handle this right now and I want you to leave…just leave."

"I need you!"

"Why are you doing this to me, Duane? Why can't you just let me be?"

I walked over to where she sat feeling all exposed and known-about. Still not sure if those were the right things to reveal. Even though I loved her, my weaknesses were confidential. Now I felt like maybe I should have just kept that shit to myself. "Because I love you and I don't know what to say. I need you in my life. I need you."

"Well I don't need you or these games that you're playing!"

Her rejecting my plea made me wonder if she ever cared for me at all and I got angry, "Well, I guess I had you all wrong then!" I can't even remember the last time I cried. And for sure, I have *never* cried over a woman. But even though no tears were coming down my eyes, I was crying!

Maybe I was wrong about her being the one. Maybe I just fooled myself into believing that Asia was feeling *the real me. Maybe* she was just like the rest but hadn't blown her cover, *yet*. Just the thought of it hurt like hell, so I told her, "Oh I get it...too ugly for you too, huh?"

Asia chewed on the side of her lip and now her eyes were glassy, "You're wrong. You are beautiful, Duane," she said in a whisper. "And it has nothing to do with your profession or your money." She closed her eyes as tears continued to roll down her cheeks. "You are so loving, and strong. And when your fans come to you screaming, 'Hey Hitman', the reason they *stay* your fans and love you even more is because you give yourself to everyone of them. You make them feel special and what you share with them is real." Asia's sad ebony eyes penetrated my soul, "But I need you to be real with *me*. Just like you said you wanted someone to be all the woman you needed her to be, that's what I want from my man. And I don't want to hurt anymore, Duane."

All I heard was she thought I was beautiful! Asia had to be the one because just a word from her gave me strength. She built me up from the inside. I reached my hand out hoping that she would reach for me, but instead she looked at my hand as if wondering about the impact of doing so. Then she looked into my eyes.

Come on baby, take it, I said in my heart. If I had to walk out of here tonight without her in my life, I didn't know what I would do. "I love you," I whispered to her with my arm still extended, still reaching for her. Tears continued to drip down her cheeks as Asia pressed her soft palm to mine.

Pulling her to me, I buried my face in her neck and in her arms I felt understood, I felt black, I felt strong!

"I'm so scared." She whispered. "Duane?"

"Yeah?" I said looking down at her.

"It doesn't bother you that I've been married before, or that I'm *six years* older than you?"

"Should it?"

"I don't know, does it?" She searched my eyes for the answer.

"All I care about is you. That's all that matters to me." My body, my mind, my soul ached to make love to this woman that I loved! One by one, I unbuttoned her pajama top, kissing her gently under her neck all the way down to her small full breasts, "Marry me, Asia."

Bending down I caressed her erect nipples with my tongue.

"Duane," she said breathlessly, "We can't."

I understood where she was coming from with the whole celibacy thing and what intercourse meant to her. But she needed to understand, *I meant* I wanted her in my life forever! "I want to marry you."

"Duane, I..."

"Shhh, Asia, it's been ten months and I love you, and I want to *make love to you*. I want to marry you. Tonight. Right now." I pulled Asia's pajama bottoms down over her round hips and she wasn't wearing any panties.

With my eyes glued to her precious body, I pulled off my jacket and removed my shirt. Someone once told me that my biceps and pectorals looked like chiseled rock and I worked hard to maintain it like that. From my back pocket I got my wallet, took the three condoms that were inside and put them in the palm of her hand. I wanted her to know that I would *never* hurt her, that with me she would always be protected. Asia's mouth opened slightly and she looked down in her hand as if I had given her gold coins.

Lifting her chin, I put my lips to hers and I wanted her so damn bad! Unzipping my pants, I finished undressing and stood bare in front of her. Asia's eyes roamed all over my body but when she saw the nine inches I was *working* with, her stare just sort of lingered a while. I pulled her body close to mine and the heat from our flesh seemed to set the room on fire. Her skin was so soft as I gripped her behind, rubbed her back and stroked her sides. We sucked deep on each other's tongue and my erection throbbed as I grind it into her belly.

I led Asia up the stairs to her room. "Tonight, I marry you." But first I explored her with my finger then sampled her with my tongue and it was umm, umm good! Ripping open the condom, I gave it to Asia and let her do the honors. After she rolled it on I penetrated her, sinking deep inside the wet warmth of her walls. I was literally overcome by the fact that I was here, in Asia's bed making love to her.

"Ah, Duane," she cried in my ear. And as I stroked, she did a slow wind with her hips baring her soul for me just like I did for her a little while ago. And I don't mean bare, as in naked with no clothes but bare because as I made love to her, I knew she was taking a chance on me. Her body smelled so good, and around my nine she was that right kind of tight and I was *drowning* in her sensation.

"Thank you Lord, Ahh." She prayed.

And I was thanking Him too, "I claim you. You my wife now." I whispered in her ear, and was going to be a good man...shit...*husband*. "I'ma be a good husband, Asia. Your husband." She must have been feeling me, because when I started talking all soft in her ear she started calling my name, and in each other's arms we jumped the broom.

GUESS WHO'S COMING TO DINNER

Seeing how distraught my parents became during my troubled marriage and divorce to Bryant, I promised myself that I would not involve them into my love life unless it was serious. Well how serious was marriage? My mind was stuck in the night when Duane and I made love. He was so gentle, and so sweet, and he calls me his wife now. I got so filled when I thought about it, then it got scary because I was so *high*! I looked at him and not only did his eyes glow, but his whole darn body glowed and it was like I was caught up in his aura... wide open. And I couldn't help myself, I was crazy *in love* with Duane!

Up until now I wasn't ready to introduce him to my parents because I didn't want to build any false hope. Duane went to church with me and we were on our way back to my place when he brought the subject up of meeting them again, and this time I gave in.

It was around two o'clock on a bone-chilling January afternoon when Duane and I pulled up to my parents' house. I could see daddy through the window, sitting in his Lazy-boy watching television. I opened up the door with my key and Duane stood behind me.

"Hey Daddy."

"Hey Shugga," he said not taking his eyes away from the television. He was watching the PFL playoffs. "Go on in the kitchen, your mama's in there."

I looked at Duane and we smiled at each other.

"Well, hello to you too," I slung my hands on my hips.

"Oh, oh, I'm sorry buttercup. You know how I am about these games." My dad finally looked up.

"Daddy I have someone I want you to meet."

He sat on the edge of his chair with his eyes narrowed. Duane's face must have looked familiar but he just couldn't place it.

"Daddy, this is Duane Cummings. Duane, this is my father, Walter Heartly."

Daddy looked tickled, "Duane Cummings? The..the "Hitman" Cummings?!" He got this wild-eyed I can't believe it grin.

Duane smiled and replied, "Yes, Sir."

Daddy jumped out of his chair and did sort of a shuffle, "Well hot damn!" he yelled, came over and shook Duane's hand vigorously. "Come on in and have a seat. What you doing in these parts, boy?!"

Mama hurried out of the kitchen, "Walter, what's all the commotion going on in here?"

"Baby, you ain't gonna believe who your daughter done brought home this time! Duane Cummings!" Daddy looked so excited we thought he was about to have a conniption.

"Who?" Mama asked looking confused. I stood in the background with my arms folded leaning up against the door amused by my parents. And poor Duane, but he wanted to meet them. Standing up from the couch that my dad nearly shoved him into, Duane extended his hand to shake my mother's hand. Mama still couldn't figure out why Daddy was acting the way he was.

"Janie get the boy a beer." My dad ordered zealously. "Would you like a beer, son?" He asked after-the-fact.

"Yes, Sir, that would be nice."

My mother walked out of the room, flabbergasted. I followed behind her laughing.

"I think the last time I seen Daddy that happy was when I told him I was moving out."

"What's wrong with him? Who is that man?" Mama whispered.

"He's a football player. Ma, do you remember me telling you that I ran into an old friend of mine who plays professional football?"

"Yeah," she said with one arm folded across her chest and the other up under her chin.

"Well that's him. He plays for the Arizona Mavericks."

"So that explains why Walter's actin' the fool out there." Mama laughed clapping her hands together. "Thought the man done seen a ghost or something, the way he's carrying on." Mama had a short afro that had gone almost completely gray. She had more gray hair than daddy even though he was three years older than she was, but at seventy-two her mahogany skin was wrinkle-free.

She grabbed Duane an ice-cold beer out of the fridge, and another one for Daddy.

As my mother prepared dinner, I sat in the kitchen watching Duane and my dad talking exuberantly and refereeing the game. To see them together, one would've never known that they just met not even an hour ago.

Mama and I stayed in the kitchen while the men effortlessly bonded in the living room. My mother fixed my father's plate and served him on the TV tray that sat on the side of his Lazy-Boy recliner.

"Have some supper Duane?" Mama offered.

"No thanks Mrs. Heartly, I..."

"Nonsense." Daddy interrupted, "Janie, fix the boy a plate. What's your rush? It's only halftime. I know you wanna know which team's out for the season."

"Daddy?!" I shouted from the kitchen. Mama just shook her head. We were used to Daddy blatantly dismissing our voice, but even though we knew he meant well, we weren't sure how others would interpret it.

"What?" Daddy put his hands up in the air unaware of what we were so upset about.

Duane was laughing. He thought it was funny, "Asia, it's up to you. Do you want to stay?"

Affectionately, I looked at my father through the corner of my eyes then cut them sharply, "Back off Dad, he's my man."

Duane started cracking up and Mama laughed shaking her head. Once again she went back into the kitchen to fix Duane a plate.

"What?" Daddy questioned once again, as he loaded up the hot sauce over his fried fish.

EMPTY NEST SYNDROME

Hawaii was just as beautiful as I thought it would be, and for the second straight year Duane's division won the All Pros game. When we got back into Trenton, he announced that he would be staying at Asia's house instead of Tompy's like I *thought* he was. That next weekend for Sunday dinner Duane brought Asia over to mom's house. Given his new living arrangements I was hoping that his nose wasn't so open by that woman that he'd stop joining us for dinner, but I hadn't counted on him bringing her along. After all, Sunday dinner was for the *family*.

When they got to the house they both were dressed up. Duane had on a suit and said that they had just come from church. Church? As much as we go around here, he never showed much of an interest in going to church.

Terry and Asia had become pretty close ever since Duane started going out with her. Terry had been over to her house on a few occasions and Asia had gone over to hers. Duane also brought her around to my house once, I guess he was trying to get me to cozy up to her, but I wasn't feeling it.

As I was on the stair steps going up to the bathroom my eyes made contact with this huge diamond ring that was sitting on the ring finger of her left hand. I slowed to a stop until my eyes made a photographic copy of it in my mind, then I looked at her as she burst into laughter at something Terry had said. I continued upstairs and went into the bathroom. As I closed the door, I leaned against it feeling shaken, threatened and *jealous!* I was losing my son to her. Duane had never put anyone ahead of me before, especially those females he got involved with, but now everything was different and I was no longer number one in his life. I felt this coming about for a while now, like he'd been slowly pushing me to the side for her.

Pulling my clothes down, I sat on the toilet wringing the blue tissue paper around my hand when images of Ralow Ferguson conjured up in my mind. Duane was thirteen when I was dating him. We had been seeing each other for six months and it was so hard for Duane to accept the fact that I was dating. Up until that time I was never into anyone enough to bring them by the house and go through the whole scrutiny of my parents, so I kept my relationships casual. But when I met Ralow. We got close. And at twenty-nine I was ready for the intimacy that I had missed out on for so many years. Ralow was so good to me, and he tried to be good to Duane too, but Duane was at that age where he was very protective of me. He didn't understand that I *needed* Ralow in my life because there was a part of me that was starving. Duane didn't see it and he gave Ralow such a hard time. I tried everything I could for the two of them to bond but Duane just wouldn't open up. He got so rebellious. Then one afternoon when the three of us were having a cookout in my parents' backyard, I went into the kitchen to get some ice out of the freezer. By the time I came back outside, Ralow had the neck of Duane's shirt balled up in his fist yelling at him. That was my baby, and I don't care how much of a smart mouth Duane had, I wasn't going to let no man that wasn't his father or my daddy, put their hands on my son. Ralow apologized to me for losing his cool the way he did, but I had to be a mother first. Duane was my first priority…over love, over companionship. I was irresponsible once by getting pregnant, but all I could do from that point on was be responsible and raise him right.

The entire evening I kept my mouth shut, because if I said anything it would have been the wrong thing. I couldn't keep my eyes off of that ring, though. It was a band that couldn't have been silver, so I imagine it had to be platinum and it had three rows of diamond. There were like forty! It had to have cost a fortune. I also thought that would be an event that he would want his *mother's* advice on…picking out a ring for his special someone. Even though I damn sure didn't want it to be her. I looked at Terry and wondered if they had told her they were engaged. I bet they did.

As we all sat down to dinner, Duane announced to the whole family that he had asked Asia to marry him and she said yes. On the inside I cried, I swear I did but no tears came out. My daddy once told me, "girl, you just too ornery to cry." But that wasn't it, I was just always afraid that if I started to cry, I wouldn't be able to stop.

I didn't make a scene either. After dinner was over I politely excused myself from the dinner table as the family all continued to sit around congratulating them.

Into the frosty backyard...the same backyard where twelve years ago I told Ralow that he could no longer be apart of my life...I went to have a smoke and half way through my cigarette Duane came out and stood in front of me. I sucked hard on the filter taking in a lung full of smoke, "Don't you think you could have *warned* me about this shit first?"

"I want you to be happy for me, Sylvia." He looked at me like a part of him needed me to be okay with this. But I wasn't.

"Boy, I ain't gonna lie to you." Holding the cigarette between my two fingers, I picked at my natural nail that had grown out on the side of the acrylic nail then I took another puff. I wanted to tell him exactly how I felt: that *that woman* who had him all starry-eyed was taking my place in his life, and I hated her for it. I wanted to tell my son that when it was just him and me, that I knew my place in this world. I had made him my life, my reason for being for so long that without him to guide and direct...I didn't know who I was.

I continued to puff on that cigarette like the whole world was coming to an end. The other girls who were in his life were so young and dumb, that I never felt threatened, but this one was a whole different story. Duane sheltered her like she was gold. I didn't know how to ask for some time...to adjust. Was an eternity too much to ask for? Nor did I know how to ask for his understanding because I didn't know what was going on myself...*within* myself. All I knew was that the game had changed from me and my baby boy against the world, to all this uncertainty. And of course he didn't understand that. But oh well, I was used to being misunderstood.

"Well then at least you know, right?" He spat, irked by my reaction, then he said, "I guess you just gonna freeze me out like when you found out I pledged Omega, right? You ain't gonna speak to me for another two freakin months?" He looked down at me with his eyebrows in a knot, "You know what, I'm sick of not having *my* decisions respected by you. So fuck it. At least you know."

Placing the cigarette to my mouth I said, "I guess I do." Turning my back to him, I inhaled then blew the smoke up into the deep blue sky.

BABY TALK

It was July and Duane had gone back to Arizona a month ago. During the three months that he stayed with me during his off-season we had such a good time together. But being in love was the easy part; learning to live together was going to take some time. Although my house structurally was falling apart, I was the neat freak. Everything of mine was clean and in its rightful place. Duane on the other hand was a mess. Wherever he stepped out of his clothes that's where they stayed until, *I* picked them up. Duane would kick off his shoes at the front door and keep on walking. Would eat and leave his plate on the table, but what *really* got on my nerves was that after he finished taking a shower he wouldn't wipe the shower walls dry. He was a full-time job in addition to the one I already had.

But on the other hand Duane couldn't understand for the life of him, *why I couldn't cook!* One night when I was seasoning yet *another* steak to put in the oven, Duane stood over my shoulder looking less than satisfied and asked me what was the deal with my cooking skills. I had to confess that my cooking was pretty much limited to cooking breakfast, broiling steaks and making hamburgers.

"What did you do when you were married before?" He asked me.

"Baby, we were a two-career household. Never had enough time to sit and eat together, let alone cook. So it didn't matter."

"That don't make sense. How could a woman be married and not know how to cook? Somebody wasn't on their job!" Duane walked out of the kitchen then came back with a pencil and pad handing it to me, "Call your mom up and get her recipes." He then took the pencil from me again and scribbled a number on the paper, "And when you're finished with her call Gran, 'cause you gonna learn. I eat out of pots not bags."

I had to give it to him as far as my finances were concerned because he *put it down*! One afternoon Duane sat me down at my kitchen table and had me pull out everything that I owed and he was writing checks. Duane paid off everything, my student loan, credit cards, bank loans…everything! Plus he gave me money to spend! That was the first time since…ever…that I felt financially free! Now I could actually hold on to my money rather than put a stamp on it and mail it away. At thirty-one, I found it so hard to believe that at twenty-five Duane was so grounded. I mean most men *my* age were still trying to find themselves.

Now that money wasn't my issue, my dad's health was. He hadn't been feeling well at all. Mama had called me over because his ulcers had been acting up again and he was in real pain. After some effort, I convinced him that he needed to go to the hospital and I'm glad I did because they kept him for three days.

After another hectic day of running around my body was totally out of sync. All week I had been driving Mama back and forth to the hospital, then when daddy was released I had to take him for his follow-up visits and I was worn out!

The phone began to ring just as I finished putting away my food for the night and cleaned up the kitchen. At thirty-one years old I was no spring chicken, but I was taking those stairs two at a time to get the phone. I knew it was Duane and I wanted to get in the bed so I could relax while I talked to him. The first thing he did was asked about my dad and it made my mind wonder. It was hard to see what old age had done to him. All his life my father provided and supported, and now that he was in poor health it was hard for him to accept being taken care of. It was in his eyes every time Mama or me had to make him take his vast assortment of medications for everything from acid reflux, to high blood pressure, to his insulin shot for his diabetes. I didn't know exactly, but I could imagine what he had to deal with.

"You come on your period yet?"

"No."

"See, I told you you're pregnant. You carrying my seed." Duane said and I bet he was smiling.

"No I'm not Lovah, I'm just under a lot of strain right now. My periods are crazy like that. The smallest thing will knock my chemistry off-track." I told him last week that I was late, but I just knew I'd be on in a couple days. Stress did that to my body. The first time it happened, I was in college studying for mid-term exams. After they were all over and the stress was gone, my period poured like red rain.

"Why don't you go to the drug store, get a pregnancy test and put me out of my misery, since *you* ain't worried about it then." Duane said sarcastically.

"It's ten o'clock at night here. You can't be serious?"

"Yes I am too. Go to the store and call me back as soon as you get home. I want to go through this with you."

All of a sudden the idea started to register that it *was* a possibility. "What if I am, Duane?"

"Let's find out first, then we can talk about the what ifs."

I got out of my pj's, dressed, went to the drugstore then called Duane when I got back home. With the cordless headset pressed between my ear and shoulder, I narrated my every move. After I peed on the stick I got so nervous. It was the longest ten minutes I had ever experienced. "Talk to me, Duane."

He was laughing at me as I stressed, "What do you want me to talk about?"

"I don't care, just talk." I said going into the bedroom and flopping down on the bed. Duane with his crazy self started messing with me about buying himself a full-length fur coat. I once told him that I couldn't stand to see men in fur because it made them look like a bear, or worst a pimp. He was rolling and had me cracking up, then he said, "Time's up, baby. Go on in there and tell me if I was right."

"Oooh Duane," I whined as I reluctantly got off the bed. When I went into the bathroom I was shaking, thinking about how much my life would change if I were pregnant. A part of me hoped that I was. It was that part of me whose biological clock had begun to tick, that part of me who wanted something little and precious of my own to nurture. That part of me who had fallen so deeply *in-love* with Duane that I wanted to have his child and him in my life forever!

Then there was the other side of me that had heard and understood what Duane said he wanted from a wife and the mother of his kids…and that was for me to give up my career. The only reason I even entertained the thought was because *in theory* it sounded so good when he talked about it. After working most of my life, to be home taking care of the children I always wanted and a man that I loved didn't sound half-bad. It all just sounded so romantic and it was *not* hard to get swept up in the dream.

I never told Duane that I'd give up my career, though. Whenever he'd start talking about it I'd tell him the truth- that I worked hard to get through college and I was a darn good teacher. My second grade classes have consistently, year after year, scored higher on their standardized test than the other two second grade classes in my school and that was no fluke or coincidence. That was the result of the skill, time, love and dedication that I put into those kids and my career. Teaching was my passion. I loved what I did for a living and it just didn't seem logical for me to have to give that up.

When I asked Duane why he felt so strongly about his wife staying home he told me as a kid he knew how it felt to be on both ends. He had watched his mother work hard, but he saw how his grandfather took care of his grandmother. "Asia", he told me, "I had to be about six years old when I realized that my mom had a job. I got sick in the middle of the night and I went into her room and she wasn't there. Her bed was all made up and it was like midnight, pitch black outside. I was crying and going off, when Gran came into the room and explained that Sylvia was working. I still remember the feeling." Duane got quiet then continued, "felt like she had abandoned me, but on top of that I was scared as shit for her. Here I was looking outside and all I could see was darkness and she was out there somewhere and I could never shake that feeling. Even as a teenager, I remember one night it was around ten o'clock and it was raining rough. I was laying across my bed listening to my stereo headphones when Sylvia stuck her head into the room to let me know that she was leaving. I tell you Asia the shit was killing me inside. All those years of watching her working her ass off for me. All those years came to a head that night. That was the night that I *knew* I *had* to make it to the pros. If not for me, I had to make it for my moms. Gran always had Gramps and to me that was the right order of things."

When Duane spoke about how he wanted his household set up and the roles everyone would play, I realized his ideas were planted when he was real young so the roots of his beliefs ran deep. I admired that about him. He was a man with direction who knew what he wanted not only from a career standpoint, but from his family as well. Wasn't that what I always wanted from a man?

As I looked in the tiny window of the white stick and there was a double pink line, "Oh-my-God," I said slow and low, then it picked up speed all the way until my voice was a piercing squeal. "Oh my God, oh my God, oh my God! Duane we're having a baby!" I heard him on the other end laughing.

"So when are you coming to Arizona with me?"

"Huh?"

***

Crystal took the day off to accompany me to my doctor's visit then we met up with Terry for lunch at Maxine's Restaurant. I had just gotten my very first ultrasound. I was so excited as I showed off the black and white strip of paper with my baby's image on it. Terry ate from the buffet since she had to return back to work, but we had time so we ordered off of the menu. As we waited for our food my mouth watered for a Long Island Iced Tea, but for the next eight months nothing alcoholic would be going into this body. The lunch crowd was on the medium side on this July day. Our table was right in front of the picture window overlooking Warren Street in downtown Trenton.

Maxine's was always one of my favorite spots in the city because the atmosphere was so upscale. From its beautiful décor that ran from the bar lounge and into the split-level dining area where the second floor overlooked the first. All the way to the black baby grand piano that sat in the corner of the room. But what made it my all time favorite place now was that every time I came here I remember when I ran into Duane again and he asked for my phone number.

It didn't take long for our food to be served. I had the stuffed mushrooms and Crystal ordered fish. The three of us had somehow gotten on the subject of me teaching once I made my inevitable move to Arizona. It was kind of strange because neither of them understood when I told them I was going to give up my teaching career, and our casual discussion got quite emotionally charged.

Once the idea of me having a life inside my womb sunk in, my priorities began to shift. In the short fourteen days that I've known about this miracle Duane and I made, all I could think about was how much I loved it and wanted the best for this baby! So at least with my mouth anyway I made the commitment to resign from my job. But even I couldn't help but to wonder if I would lose myself by giving up my career and I was getting *no support* from my girls.

"Asia, I don't see how you can just totally submit everything to him like that, especially…" Crystal said then caught herself.

"Especially what Crys?" I already knew what she was going to say.

"Especially since you been through a fucked-up marriage already. Asia, you have to keep a little something for yourself, girl. I just don't understand what's the big deal about you keeping your job if you want to. Don't let him control you like that!"

"Yeah Asia. I love my nephew to death, but I totally disagree with his views that a man has to be the breadwinner and a woman's place is in the kitchen fixing his ass a plate. We have come such a long way as women from the 'bare foot and pregnant' mentality. Girl, you have a college degree in Early Childhood Education, plus you have eight years of teaching to your credit. How can you just give all of that up because he asked you to?" Terry asked, cutting a small piece of lamb smothered in gravy. "Lawrence and I have been married for thirteen years and we both built our real estate company from scratch. We are *equal* partners."

Terry and I had talked a lot. And she was a stone cold women's libber. She *loved* Lawrence, but there was this hard edge to her almost like she kept score so he wouldn't have one up on her. Like she was always proving that she was capable. Whenever they went out with Duane and me, if Lawrence drove there, she *was going* to drive back. I noticed that same take-charge, *I am woman* attitude with Sylvia, but I always thought that was because she had to stand on her own for so long.

The whole tone of our discussion was not sitting well with me. We were supposed to be there to celebrate my baby, but instead they were making me sound weak because I was going to abide by Duane's wishes. Yes I had some misgivings of my own because I wasn't totally sure that I was ready to stop teaching. And heck yeah, as Crystal so bluntly put it, I already had one fucked-up marriage and the thought of trusting again was most definitely scary. They thought I was crazy for giving up my career, but I think that it would have been crazy if I didn't give it up. If I didn't give Duane and me that chance at love the way he envisioned… and I had been too *afraid* to envision, I will never know if it actually can be something wonderful. So in my defense I said, "I think that the women's liberation movement is about many things… but mostly choice. It's the *choice* to stay home and raise the kids if circumstances permit. Or the *choice* to pursue a career." I emphasized to Terry.

"Exactly… the *woman's* choice." Terry smiled changing the subject as she dug in her purse and pulled out a pack of birth control pills, "I also have a baby announcement to make." Crystal and I looked at each other quizzically. "Lawrence and I have finally decided that we are ready to start our family so I won't be needing these any more! Crystal and I both spread our arms out and Terry leaned from one side of the table to the next so we each could get a hug. At forty years old, both Terry and Lawrence had accomplished all of their financial goals she said. Now that the hard work of creating a business and building a home was behind them, they looked forward to putting their attention on becoming parents. I was happy for them!

UNCHARTED WATERS

As I stood inside of Arizona's Sky Harbor International Airport, I saw Asia's flight taxi down the runway. I politely handed back the pen and magazine that bore my script to the seventh fan that had excitedly asked for my autograph.

I felt myself physically, mentally and emotionally exhale at the thought of Asia *finally* being in Arizona. I knew she had serious issues about leaving Trenton, giving up her career, leaving her family, *trusting* that I would be a good man. I also knew what my Aunt Terry and Crystal were trying to fill Asia's head with. With all those odds against me, I swore I wouldn't breathe until I saw her with my own eyes and held her in my arms.

I waited by gate number 9 until I saw Asia walking through the tunnel and into my world, my life. Glancing at her stomach from afar, I thought she'd be showing by now, but at three months she still wasn't. Asia had on a pretty light peach sleeveless top and a short matching skirt showing them beautiful brown thighs that I loved so much. Watching her I couldn't get enough of her fineness. I waited in my stance as she walked over to me. Smiling ear-to-ear, Asia's eyes were cut into their half-moon shape.

I was sporting my designer sports gear, with matching Kangol cap, and my proud papa smile! Wrapped my outstretched arm around her waist and held her, kissing them luscious lips like we were the only ones around. "Hey mommy." I gave her another slow delicious kiss. Then, from behind my back, I pulled a little blue stuffed elephant I bought at the airport's gift shop. I put my hand on her stomach, "I got this for my boy."

"And you're going to be so crushed when your daughter comes out instead," she said sounding all sweet in my ears.

"It's all good. Girl, boy, don't matter to me, long as I have you." I wrapped myself around Asia and she kissed me on my Adam's apple. The sensation felt so good, I had to laugh. "Lets go get your bags and get out of here."

Loaded down with her five large suitcases we walked out into the scorching 110 degree August sun and up to a spankin' brand new black BMW 525i.

"Um! This is nice Duane, whose is it?"

"It's mine." I said pressing down the remote as the auto alarm deactivated and the locks popped up.

"Yours, where's the Porsche?"

"It's home in the garage. I got this last week after I knew you were definitely coming. You gonna need something to drive, and I sure can't fit no baby seat in my ride." We talked about so much over the phone, but I wanted to surprise her with this.

Asia squealed, then started bouncing up and down, "So I'm gonna be driving this car?!"

"Yeah, if it was for me I would have gotten a stick-shift instead of this automatic."

Asia dropped the overnight bag and grabbed me by the side of my face kissing me on my jaw. I was hoping she would like it and it looked like I made a good choice. I opened the passenger side door to let Asia in then loaded up the trunk with her luggage before I got in.

"It has that new car smell in here!" Asia said stroking the beige leather seats. Then she looked up through the tinted moon roof and grazed her fingers across the CD stereo system. "Oh Duane," she sounded so excited as she pointed to the back of the car. "That's where our baby's car seat is going to go. Can you see it?"

I was looking at how beautiful Asia was in Arizona with me, "Yeah, I can see it baby." As I drove, I had one hand draped on the wheel, leaning towards Asia. And she couldn't keep her eyes off me. "I can't believe you're here." Reaching over I ran my finger across the side of her face.

"Me neither," Asia smiled taking in the scenery.

"I want to show you off before we go back to the crib." Truth was, I had to pick up my check. In order to get to the Airport on time, I had to leave practice early and didn't get a chance to swing by the front office.

"I can't wait to see your place."

"If you would have come up here to visit like I tried to get you to do, then you would know how it looks." I gave her the eye.

"But I'm here, ain't I?"

"Yes you are lady, and I ain't letting you go nowhere now." Intertwining my fingers in Asia's I brought her soft hand up to my lips.

Our first stop was the Arizona Venturis Dome, the home of the Arizona Mavericks. I pulled up to the security bunker and was waved into the personnel parking lot. We got out of the car as Asia took in the view of the enormous dome. Holding hands we walked inside to the business office.

"Hello, Duane."

"Helen."

"I believe I have something for you." She reached in her file cabinet and handed me my paycheck. The bulk of my money was wired directly into an account that was managed by my financial advisor, but I kept a couple grand out as my spending change.

"Helen, I would like you to meet my lady, Asia Heartly. Asia this is Helen Gratty, one of the nicest people I've met since coming to Arizona."

Asia and Helen shook hands as Helen blushed deeply. She was a portly woman with graying hair and rosy pink cheeks. She looked like if she weren't there working, she'd be in the kitchen baking cookies and pies like the grannies on TV. "Oh, you have yourself quite a charmer there, Asia," Helen said batting her eyes.

"Is Coach around?"

"Yes, as a matter of fact, Bill just left here not even ten minutes ago. You can catch him in his office."

"Thanks Helen."

"Nice to meet you," Asia smiled.

"You too darlin', and you have a nice day ya' hear."

We walked around the dome until we came to the Coach's plush office. I knocked on the door. "Coach Barnes?"

"Duane, come on in," he said, upbeat as usual. Coach was a heavyset sixty-year-old man who never played football past his college years, but he had been coaching in the PFL for over thirty-five years. I let Asia walk in first, and she looked around the room excited as her eyes peered through the huge window behind Coach Barnes' desk. It had a full view of the football field and stadium seats.

As we talked, I couldn't help but feel a sense of rightness as I watched Asia and the man I held so much respect for getting along. For the four years that I had been with the Mavericks, Coach Barnes has taken me under his wing. He become coach, friend, advisor... almost father-like, and to see him welcome Asia meant a lot to me. She was my heart and she deserved respect from my world. I didn't want her hurt, or made to feel bad because she was with me, like most of my family made her feel.

Even Gran was acting ill. After we found out that Asia was pregnant, I asked her to reach out and at least *try* to get to know Gran. Asia wasn't really feeling the idea at first. She told me she wasn't comfortable with pushing herself on anyone. I understood what she was saying, but I really wanted Asia and my family to get to know each other. When she saw how important it was, she did it just for me. But when Asia told me how Gran was acting towards her on the phone... answering questions, but not really saying anything to keep the conversation going or trying to learn anything about her. All I could do was tell Asia thanks for her effort. If they didn't want to be bothered, then later for them.

After a quick tour into the weight room and the sauna, I introduced Asia to some of my teammates who were just finishing up for the day, then we went out on the field.

"Want to race me?" I played squatting to a starting position.

"Boy, if I didn't have this skirt on, I would tear your butt up out here." Asia laughed.

"I'm sure you would, with your fine self."

We strolled from one end zone to the other holding hands. Asia was so impressed, and she asked me a zillion questions. She knew next to nothing about football. The girl cracked me up by bending down pretending that she was hiking the ball to me. Squatting behind her, I squeezed her butt.

"So that's what y'all *really* be doing out here, huh?" Asia teased.

"Naw, girl go head." We both laughed out loud then I picked Asia up off her feet.

As we walked back to the car, Asia wrapped her arms around my neck and once again we went into our own little world kissing each other down. "Thank you for that tour."

"You're welcome." I smiled looking down at her.

"I want to drive."

"Girl, you don't even know where you're going."

"So, you'll tell me."

Looking at her from the corner of my eye I sighed then dropped the keys in her outstretched hands.

"Thank you baby."

"Yeah, just don't kill me."

"Oh Duane, you don't trust my driving?"

"I trust you girl, come on." Actually I only lived two miles away from the stadium so Asia didn't have that far to drive. My condominium was in a high-rise on the fourteenth floor and everything in the condo was on one floor.

Once we got there, I opened up the door and the expression on Asia's face told all. After living in her run down house for all those years she deserved a place like this.

We walked into the oversized living room and Asia went over to the huge floor-to-ceiling window that overlooked the highway. Stretched alongside the highway was a river and far off in the background was nothing but mountains. And the shit was beautiful, especially when you come from the city like us. There were no mountains in Trenton. Asia fell in love with the kitchen. It had brown marble floors with matching counter top, and stainless steel appliances. It was almost like new because I didn't really cook in it. Just my luck, there was a restaurant in the lobby of this building.

I…I mean we…I have to get used to saying that…we had a huge master bedroom with a full bath: Jacuzzi and Bidet. And down the hallway was another full bathroom that was just as nice. Lastly, my cool out place…the den. I had all of my music, trophies, football mementos, and my weight bench in there.

"Do you ever get used to this?" We walked back into the living room and Asia stood at the window staring out.

"It's the best of everything, girl. And, naw, I ain't get use to this shit yet."

She commented on how nicely everything was decorated, and I had to confess that I didn't know the first thing about decorating. "Sylvia picked out mostly everything in here." When I moved to Arizona Sylvia also moved down for the first five months to help me get situated. I gave her a blank check and she had a ball shopping for the furniture, putting color schemes together buying pictures and artwork. I really don't care for all that stuff. Long as it was comfortable and looked right, I was good-to-go. Sylvia had that expensive, good taste, so I knew I'd like whatever she put together.

Asia was hungry, and even though there was plenty of food in the fridge, nothing was prepared.

"There's a nice restaurant on the first floor. Let's go and eat down there." That restaurant was my saving grace. I'm not a junk food eater and I don't do fast foods. The restaurant cooked home-style food, and I was a rice and potato man. I went down there so much I even gave Frances, the owner and chef, the recipes to Sylvia's potato salad and collard green. Frances liked it so much she put it on her menu. And yeah, she had Sylvia's blessings to do so.

"That sounds good baby. But let me call my mom and tell her that I'm here and see how daddy's doing." Before Asia hung up the phone, she passed it over to me. I spoke to her mom and pop and assured them both that I was going to take good care of Asia and their grandbaby.

Before we went to the elevator, I knocked on my neighbor's door. They were the Chows, Siani and Po. They were real cool people, both of them in their early thirties. Po was a cardiac surgeon, and Siani was some kind of abstract artist. She worked from her house. When I moved here they were the ones who pretty much showed me the town. I give them free tickets to the games and every now and then we'd get together and go out to a nightclub or to eat. When I told Siani that Asia was moving here with me she was excited. I knew where she was coming from 'cause there weren't many young people that lived in this building. We kicked it with them for a few minutes then we were on our way.

We got back from dinner around six. I turned up the central air and then went in the den and put on some music. Asia joined me in the room as I sat on the floor.

"Get comfortable, make yourself at home."

"At home...with you, hum? I like the sound of that." She bent down and kissed my lips then kicked off her shoes and sat on the floor besides her man. We stayed close together talking, laughing, and caressing for hours.

We took our party into the bedroom where I pulled off my clothes down to draws. My things went on the chair and I lied across the bed. Asia undressed down to her red matching bra and panties and neatly hung her skirt and top in the closet. With no clothes on I could see that her belly was a little round.

Picking up my things, she rolled her eyes at me, "I didn't know what shape your place was going to be in when I got here. I'm impressed that it's clean."

I rolled onto my back, pushing the pillow up under my head watching her...glad that it *was her* here with me instead of some woman that I really didn't want to be with. "Took me all week to clean it too. I do it once a year so you were in luck. You got good timing," I kind of laughed at my own story.

I had a cleaning lady come in and clean during the week. I hated that shit too. The first company I hired to clean, their workers had sticky fingers. After they left I'd notice my shit missing. Nothing big, just dumb shit. They beat me for two Kangol hats and this African wooden giraffe Sylvia bought me turned up missing. But the lady I have now seemed pretty good.

Asia smirked, "I'm just in time, huh?"

"Yup." Watching Asia walk around in her panties gave me a hard on.

"Where do you keep your towels? I really need to take a shower."

"In a minute, come here first." I stretched my hand out to her, "Just let me hold you." Lying down in front of me, Asia pressed her soft behind into my bulge. Her head rested on my biceps. "You smell so good," I had my nose all up in her neck. "You already smell like roses." I kissed her neck and wrapped her tighter in my arms, "I'm really glad you came to be with me, baby. Thank you."

"I'm glad I'm here too. This really feels right." She snuggled in even closer to me. Closing my eyes, I drifted off to sleep.

The next morning I woke up at five, then propped myself up on my elbows as I watched Asia asleep next to me in *my* bed. I kissed her lightly on the cheek then got up, jumped in my jogging gear and was out the door to begin my routine. Go for my run, jump in the shower, eat my breakfast usually a big bowl of oatmeal, then be out the door. Our team meetings start at eight but I am always there by seven-thirty. Shit, some of the guys come in looking like they just rolled out of bed, complete with mucous in the eyes and all. Then be complaining all practice long. By the time I got to work, my wind was up, stomach full, head was clear and I was in my zone ready for whatever came my way.

Forty-five minutes later I got back from my four-mile run feeling strong and completely awake. After my shower, I went into the bedroom to get dressed. I had little over an hour before I was due at the stadium. Asia was still knocked out lying on top of the covers, on her stomach. Her arms were wrapped around the pillow with one leg arched and the other straight. Them red bikinis was looking good as candy and I wanted me some. Reaching down I ran my hand across my full-grown erection knowing that from now on, I was going to have to allot myself some extra time in the mornings.

Crawling in the bed behind her, I moved the crotch of her panties with my finger, penetrating her from behind and she felt so damn good. Asia began working that body like she wasn't really sleep, but just laying there waiting for me. Cupping her chin with my hand, I turned her face sideways so I could get some lips. She stuck her tongue out the side of her mouth and I caught it with mine…morning breath and all. Since I was pressed for time I allowed myself to cum quick, but man, I could have stayed in her all day!

After I got cleaned up and dressed, I ran into the kitchen to put the kettle of water on the stove for my oatmeal. Just as I sat down to eat, Asia walked into the kitchen. We both looked at each other and simultaneous these big grins came on our faces. Asia walked over to me, put her arms around my neck and kissed the side of my face. Her breath was now minty fresh. She was looking good in my sleeveless T-shirt with no bra, showing off those tangerine-shaped breasts as her thick nipples poked against the shirt. Made me wish I had at least *another* hour to give it to her nice and slow.

"What time are you going to be home tonight?" She was sitting next to me on the kitchen's barstool. The sun was just waking up in the sky.

"I'm not really sure. I'll call you later and let you know." I dug in my wallet and placed my bankcard in front of Asia on the table.

"What's this for?" She asked picking it up.

"Just in case you want to go some place or buy yourself something pretty. Maybe you and Siani can go to the mall or something." I smiled at her, "The pin number is eleven fifty."

"What's my limit?"

"You don't have one."

Asia smiled as she leaned over for a kiss. Then she got up and poured me a glass of juice before I left to begin my day.

SUNRISE

I wanted my child to come into this world right, with my name. Asia and I talked about getting married quickly by a local preacher, but something in me wasn't sitting right with that. My mind went back to our first date over Tompy's house a year-and-a-half-ago. Just like then I knew Asia was a queen and deserved the best that my money could buy. This time I was going to do it right. We had already set the date for the Mavericks bye-week, which was coming up in October. That was our only vacation week during the season. Asia had no idea what I had planned for her.

Helen, who also served as the Mavericks travel administrator, booked Asia and me on a flight to St. Thomas so we could get *legally* married. I explained my plans to Helen and she outdid herself. Once again, it paid to be a marquee player, because accommodating my personal travel business was not a part of her job description. But just like with Coach, Helen and I had become friends.

Sylvia didn't quite know what was going on, 'cause we hadn't told anyone our plans, but she must have smelled it in the air. She wasn't excited about the news of my baby, so why even go through the letdown of her trashing my spirits about my wedding…but anyway. When I told Sylvia that Asia was moving to Arizona with me, the first thing she started talking about was that I should get a lawyer to draw up a prenuptial agreement. Just to cover myself, she said. I told her I'd think about it, which I did and from a business standpoint it made sense. Asia and I had even talked about it and she was like, "Duane, you're asking me to give up my career and if we do separate after a long time that would mean I could be out in the cold. I won't be equipped to return to school and teach without going back to college first. With how fast technology is moving I would be too far behind. And not to mention that my pension stops growing when I stop working."

Our conversation brought to light that we both had valid concerns about our finances. So not only did she sign the Prenuptial Agreement that my lawyer drew up. Asia hired her own lawyer who drew up an Entitlement document stating that she and all children born into this marriage would be taken care of in the manner that they had become accustomed if we decided to get divorced for "just-cause". And I signed it. Seemed strange to be making provisions for the end of our marriage before it had actually began, but Asia put it best. She said after we locked those papers away in the safe, they'd never see the light of day again because we were going to make our life together last forever.

Once we got to St. Thomas, we stayed in a honeymoon mansion. The front yard was landscaped with all these exotic flowers and trees and in the back there was this huge patio with a built-in pool. Beyond the patio was nothing but beach and ocean.

We had the whole place to ourselves along with a full staff of servants. It was dinnertime when we got there. Our luggage was taken care of so we went right for the food. Asia didn't eat much, but I threw down. I had some kind of shrimp and cabbage dish and it was delicious. Asia and I sat out on the patio sipping tropical drinks, non-alcoholic for her. Then bout an hour later we jumped in the pool. That night we had to sleep in our own separate rooms. As I laid there trying to get to sleep, I didn't have too much on my mind. Wasn't real excited or nervous. I was just hoping that Asia was alright because she got a little queasy after dinner, and at four months she still got sick some mornings.

I drifted off to sleep and at 4:15 in the morning my butler woke me up. A hot bath was waiting along with toast and tea breakfast. From the brochure, the real breakfast was after the wedding. He had laid out a white linen ceremonial outfit across the bed. They were simple looking clothes, looked almost like what someone would wear to get baptized. After I got dressed, I was escorted, bare feet to the beach. In all of my twenty-five years I had never seen anything like this…I mean the shit was sweet! It looked like something from the movies.

It was 5:20 in the morning and dark, lit only by the moon, a million stars and three, six-foot bamboo torches. There was this nice breeze blowing off of the ocean and the sounds of the water swishing in and out of tide echoed in the air. By now I was moved inside! Standing there feeling the sand under my feet waiting for Asia...to be my wife...in every sense of the word. I stood there thinking about God and paradise, and Him making a woman from man's rib, and God saying that, *it was not good for man to be alone* then I thought...I have her. Duane, man, for the rest of your life, you won't ever be alone. My mind went to the little boy inside me that took so much grief, was laughed at, called black and ugly, and I wanted to reach back in time and tell him that everything was cool. That it was alright. That we had found someone who loved us completely. Just the thought put this heavy sensation in my chest and I had to catch myself.

A guitarist, a keyboardist, and a barrel drum player played a soft Caribbean melody as I waited for my bride. Just as the black sky began to crack with blue, Asia was escorted by her maid onto the beach. Apparently they had the choreography of the sunrise wedding down to the tee. Asia was also barefooted. She had on a white Kimono style dress draped over her round belly, white flowers in her naturally crimped hair and I couldn't take my eyes off of her. The light from the video recorder came on, but it in no way distracted me from her simple beauty. Holding an armful of white tulips, Asia's big brown eyes melted my heart as I reached out my hand to hold hers. Her maid took the flowers then Asia put her other hand in mine and I pulled her to me kissing them lips before we turned to the officiator.

As he read from his book, I repeated my vows to Asia as the sky went from gray to light blue. As Asia repeated her vows to me the tip of the burnt orange sun reflected off of the rippled waters. I wasn't nervous about none of this. I was only sorry that our people couldn't be here to see us.

My butler brought over a chair and a short bench. Asia's maid carried over a foot basin filled with water and two large white towels draped over her arm. Asia sat in the chair and I sat on the bench so I could wash and dry her slender feet. Her maid handed me a pair of silk slippers to put on my wife's feet. When I was finished, I sat in the chair and Asia sat on the bench. She washed, dried and put slippers on my feet. The officiator announced that by our washing each other's feet it was symbolic of us being partners in life. Servants to and for each other.

As the sun came up high in the sky, Asia and I exchanged rings, then I kissed my bride! I took Asia in my arms and held her to my heart. And after I tasted my wife's lips, I bent down and kissed her stomach, our child inside. Then the music started playing and Asia and I had our first dance as Mr. and Mrs. Duane Jericho Cummings.

That night we stayed in the honeymoon suite *together*. The next day we went sightseeing around the island, which was a lot of fun. On that third night me and the wife were headed back to Arizona.

Whoever said that staying at home wasn't a job needed to call me for a second opinion! Sitting on the couch in front of the huge living room window as the morning sun flooded inside, I had the cordless phone pressed to my ear. Mama was on the other end and I was just *venting!* The entire dynamics of our household did a one-eighty in a matter of months. When I first came to Arizona up until after the baby was born was a serious honeymoon period…but now, the marriage *had begun!*

I flipped through the channels and stopped at the game show, *The Price Is Right.*

"Duane fired the maid 'cause *he said* we didn't need her anymore. And instead of me cooking every now and then, like when I was pregnant, he wanted me to cook dinner *every night!* Duane even had the nerve to complain that the bath towel he used was scratchy, then had the nerve to ask me why didn't I use the Downy fabric softener in the wash like *he* liked!" The way he was going I really could have knocked him out. Thinking I was going to get some sympathy from my mother she laughed at me. "No really Ma, this is bothering me. Duane is starting to remind me so much of daddy."

"And that's a bad thing?"

"Ma, what I'm trying to say is, you know how daddy always has to be right about everything? Well that's how Duane is coming at me, and I don't like it."

"Well what happened?"

"For instance, last week Duane came home from work around seven and I wasn't finished cooking dinner yet. The way he went on, you would have thought that I slapped his mother or something. We've eaten late before. Now that we're married, I'm supposed to jump when he snaps his fingers?! I don't think so!"

"You young girls have so much to learn."

"Mama, now come on."

"Chile, Duane's just getting comfortable in his new *husband* skin. Marriage is hard work, now. I should know, married to your father for forty some odd years. And he ain't the sweetest man in the world either."

"Ma, no offense, but I have watched you and daddy for so long. He can be so stubborn and chauvinistic at times. That really burns me up, but you always remained so calm. How do you do it?"

"Still waters run deep, honey. Just 'cause there ain't no movement on top don't mean there ain't a mighty current raging below!" I heard mama laugh out loud, clapping her hands. "God-almighty-knows!"

I sat up straight charged by her excitement.

"You just never seen it, but me and your father had our share of times. You can believe that. But honey, I comes from the old school where a man *is head* of *his* household. Like it or not. Yes, Walter's a stubborn man, but he's a good man," she said with conviction. "Always took good care of his family, always very supportive, and God knows honey, he loves us. See Asia, the whole key is to know *when* to fight. You can't open your mouth and fight about everything, 'cause then you turn them off. And then when something worth fighting come about, you done fussed so much about nothin' they done learned to tune you out."

"Desensitized!" I was hyped because I really understood what she was trying to say.

"That's right. You young girls have to stop wanting to be the woman and the man. It's all about compromise. *The way* you compromise." I sat straight up, hanging on to mama's every word.

"God made you a *woman*. You need to learn how to be a woman to your man. You young women these days get all mad at your men, don't cook for 'em, don't clean for 'em and don't give 'em no lovin'. And you wonder why they be down the street messin' around."

"Oh, no!" I was cracking up. To be seventy-four, my mother was one of the coolest people I knew. She didn't mind telling it like it was.

"But am I right?"

"Yes you are."

"What you need to do Asia is close your mouth and win your battles with the arsenal that you born with. You had it since day one, and most of you poor things don't even know about it. Your womanly nature. How many times I done opened my bible and read about women using their nature to persuade *the most powerful men*. And Miss Teacher," Mama stressed, "How many mythological..." she mispronounced the word, but I knew what she meant, "... stories were written about the same thing?"

"So in other words, I've been going at this all wrong then?"

"If you're coming at your man, like a man, he'll beat you at your own game every time. A man is hard, so hard and hard...there's no balance. Put your two clenched fists together," she instructed. "But if you come at your man like a *woman*...now open one fist and wrap it comfortably around the closed one, then you have hard and soft. The perfect balance. He knows how to be hard, that's in *his* nature. It is *your* nature to be soft. When you get mad at him, go and take yourself a nice hot shower, put on some nice, smell-me-good, fix your hair. *Give him somethin' to look at*." She stressed. "Fix his food, clean his house and by all means, *keep a fussin' mouth closed*. You will learn, your nature will win you more fights than a big mouth any day."

I talked to my mother for three hours straight. She helped me to adjust to my new *wife* skin. And by talking to her she helped me to realize that Duane and I *were* on the same page. I wanted that old-fashioned love and environment to nurture and raise our family in as well. And we felt so much like a real family since the baby was here.

Her name is Epiphany Zion Cummings and she had perfect timing. Epiphany was laying on top of her blanket, on the couch next to my leg. As I talked on the phone, I admired how beautiful she was as she slept. As soon as I told my mother bye, Epiphany started to squirm. No bigger than eighteen inches from head to toe, I picked her up with my two hands and her little body was curled up into a crawling position. Then her little arms lifted up in the air and her lips pressed tight together as she made a whinny sound from the back of her throat. I kissed all over her little face as it turned red from making a little poop.

Duane couldn't get enough of his little Piff Piff. That was the nickname he gave her. When I was pregnant I had that glow, but now whenever he saw her... held her, he glowed!

All morning long I thought about what my mother and I talked about... Duane and I getting used to our new spousal skins. Our contrived social roles as Terry called it. After I changed and breastfed the baby, I bundled her up, jumped in the Beamer, and we went grocery shopping to stock up on food. While there, I made sure I got the *large* bottle of Downy fabric softener.

As I stood at the checkout line with the baby harnessed to my chest and slid my bankcard through the slot, Lord what a wonderful feeling! What a change from the sweaty palms I used to have as I wondered if I had gone over my limit. If my credit card was going to be rejected. Shopping used to be this necessary evil that always reminded me of the debt and seemingly hopeless situation I was in, but now I actually liked shopping! And I still get tickled at the thought, because that was something that I never thought would be possible. As I took the receipt from the cashier I looked around the entire grocery store, looked at the top of my new born daughter's curly black hair leaning up against my chest asleep and my cart filled with groceries... and for the first time I felt like one of them... a stay-at-home mom. The thought just sort of hit me at that moment. Looking at my watch it was one-forty in the afternoon and somehow the time made it official. I had no clock to punch, no lunch hour to rush through. At this time of the day, if I hadn't been with Duane, I would have been standing at my desk right in the middle of a teaching a lesson at school. Well, a summer school lesson since it was July.

When I got back home the afternoon sun was overshadowed by thick rain clouds and I was glad that me and the baby got back home before it started to pour. I laid Epiphany in her bassinet, then turned on the stereo as I unloaded the fold-up shopping cart that I used to lug my bags from the trunk of my car inside the condo. It saved me from making trips up and down to the garage.

After I was finished putting away the groceries, Siani stopped by to show me her latest canvas creation. She was very talented, but what surprised me was she didn't have any one area of concentration. She painted everything! My favorites were her landscape drawings. The depth she put into her pictures…and I mean down to the smallest detail…made her pictures just seem to come to life. For our wedding present, Siani gave us a picture of lovers in silhouette. You couldn't actually see them just the outlines of their bodies behind a waterfall and it is *gorgeous*!

Today, though, I had to rush her out the door so I could get busy. When she left, I rewashed and softened all the towels in the condo, even the ones that weren't dirty. Then I cooked Duane a really nice dinner. Baked fish with lemon juice, steamed fresh vegetables, brown rice and cinnamon apple sauce. I must say that my cooking skills have definitely improved. I recently started collecting recipes. And since I actually had the time to cook now, I was surprised at how much I enjoy it. But my favorite part was watching Duane throw down and when he was finished to hear him say, "girl you put your foot in that pot." He had me grinning all over the place.

Around seven in the evening I was in the living room holding Epiphany. Had the television on, but I wasn't really watching it. I was too busy looking at my precious little angel that Duane and I created as she nursed from my breast. The aroma from the dinner circulated throughout the condo and I was tired from all the work, but I felt so good inside.

Just as I took Epiphany off of my breast, I heard Duane's keys rattling in the door. Even though it was July and the PFL preseason began one week earlier, Duane had been going strong since the first week of June. He was working out with his trainer. This was his fifth year with the Mavericks and the year that he would become an unrestricted free-agent and he was *stressing*. Kept emphasizing how important it was for him to be at his best this season and I knew this was going to be a long...*long* six months!

As he walked through the door, Duane had on his purple and gold Mavericks shorts and shirt that he cut the arms out of and his muscles were bulging from everywhere. That man had the most beautiful body that I had ever seen.

"Hey," he said looking drained then dropped his gym bag on the floor. Duane flopped down on the couch next to me leaning his head back on the couch. He closed eyes and sighed heavily.

"Hey baby. You hungry?" I asked rubbing one of his big hands.

"Starving." He replied reaching for Epiphany. "Hey Piff Piff." He held her up then started kissing her all over her tiny little cocoa brown face.

Taking Mama's advice, I had given her a bath not even thirty minutes ago, so she smelled fresh and clean from the *Baby Magic* products and she had on her pink one-piece sleeper. Epiphany's head full of black hair had just started to curl, and she had the most precious, almond-shaped glassy dark brown eyes. Only six pounds at birth, and at three months old she was still a lightweight.

As Duane cuddled his baby, I got up and went in the kitchen to get his dinner. Moments later I came out with a medium amount of food on his plate. Duane was very particular about the amount of food he ate before he went to bed. Now he would eat a big breakfast, and a big lunch with a lot of fruits, juices and water in between, but dinner was actually his smallest meal of the day.

"Yeah baby, this looks good." He said as I put the plate on the coffee table in front of him. I went back into the kitchen to get him a big glass of water and a fork. When I came back out I sat next to Duane and took Epiphany so he could eat. The rain had started to pour down outside and it quickly became dark inside the room. Reaching over to the end table, I turned on the lamp.

"Asia, you wouldn't believe this stupid ass rookie they got. Boy don't know the plays, don't know who he supposed to be guarding." Duane vented with his jaws full of food then he pointed his fork at me. "I told that boy, if he thought he was going to make it through the month-long, away training camp, next week and actually make it into the PFL that he better get his head out the fucking clouds and into a playbook. Learn what the fuck he supposed to do." Duane shoveled more food into his mouth and continued, "This the year I turn free-agent and all eyes gonna be on me, baby. I have to shine this year so I need everybody to pull their weight. I don't have no time for bullshit."

When Duane said that, I had a feeling that he was talking about me also. One thing I learned from last year was that Duane had *two* speeds…off-season and season. During the off-season, Duane and I cuddled and laughed all the time. It was just heaven to be around him, but during the season… He was just so intense and the house just took on a whole different vibe. Sometimes I felt like I had to walk on eggshells around him.

After Duane ate, he showered then came back and we relaxed together just the three of us, watching television. At nine o'clock, I put the baby down for the night. Lately she had been sleeping straight through 'til six the next morning. It was such a relief because that waking up every two hours was starting to make me cross-eyed.

Duane also headed to the bedroom but before I turned in I washed up the remaining dishes from dinner. Twenty minutes later, I headed to the bedroom. The room was dark and the only sound was from the humming of the central air unit. Duane was laying underneath the sheets and I crawled next to his warm bare body. I thought he was sleep, but he began kissing me slow and I was feeling my husband in every cell of my body…I *loved* that man! If I had any doubt about if I had made the right decision in giving up my career for him and our child, he erased them all that night.

As I laid there he undressed me, taking off my night gown, nursing bra and panties then he started kissing me between my thighs. Duane made love to me so strong that night that I knew he was thanking for me going the extra mile for him in my wife skin. So oh yeah, Downy fresh towels, sheets…dinner, breakfast or whatever else he wanted! That old-fashioned kinda love. I was…to use my man's words…diggin' it!

CYNICISM

The end of the season was always kind of a low point for me because of the team's personnel changes, players being trades, others retiring and as for me, my shit was up-in-the-air. It was January seventh and I was officially a free agent. This past season I worked my ass off because I wanted to give myself leverage. I wanted to start off a bidding war throughout the PFL on who would have a chance to obtain the greatest running back going. And just like I had anticipated, teams were ringing my agent, Zigna Rodregues' phone asking her to name her price. The New Jersey Tritons organization was one of those teams. The Tritons were an old team with a lot of veteran players, which made them a solid organization. They were a Champion Bowl team and were going strong to win it again this year, but with all of that going for them they were still in need of a quality running back.

I got a really good offer from Miami. Dallas was second on my list, and Chicago put a pretty good package together as well. But as far as making the transition worth my while, none of them were actually as strong of a Champion Bowl team as the Tritons. And that was my objective…the ring!

I took a couple of days and thought about it. Played all of the probabilities over in my head. No matter which scenario I put to the test I continued to come up with Jersey being the best decision. I wasn't particularly interested in living back in Jersey. I loved my family, but it was no secret how they felt about my wife so I figured a little distance would be best for everyone. Then my mind went to Sylvia. She was so convinced that I should stay in Arizona even though I kept telling her how miserable I was being on a second rate team. She told me some bullshit line like, "short-term discomfort for long-term gain." I knew she was going to flip if I left Arizona. I also started thinking about her and Asia together both living in the same town again and wondered how that shit would play itself out.

Epiphany was born last April and we flew to Trenton a month later in May. When I told Sylvia that we were coming she invited us to stay with her, which to me made sense because she had a big four-bedroom house. Asia wasn't trying to hear it, but I let her know that's where we were going. Big mistake! They started *warring* over the baby. It was so fucking unbelievable!

The first instance was when I overheard them arguing over whether to give Epiphany water or not. Asia was trying to explain to Sylvia, that she didn't want to give Piff Piff water yet because she was a light eater. Which she was. Asia was breast-feeding Epiphany like a full-time job. Piff would suck just enough milk to put herself back to sleep. Then she would wake up within the next fifteen-to-twenty minutes and do the same thing…drink just enough to put herself back to sleep again. So Asia wanted to make sure that she was getting enough milk for the vitamins and minerals that she needed in her system. Well Asia was trying to tell Sylvia this, when Sylvia said something slick to her and they went at it. I had to come in the kitchen, grab my wife by the hand and bring her in the room with me so the two of them could calm down.

The second argument, I was downstairs waiting for Asia to get the baby dressed 'cause we were going to her parents' house and spend some time with them. I was chillin' watching television when Sylvia came charging in talking about, "Duane, would you tell her that she should not have washed that child's head if y'all were getting ready to go outside!"

With Epiphany dressed and in her arms, Asia was right on Sylvia's heels, yelling, "Duane, tell your mother that this is *my* child that *I* carried around in *my* womb for the last nine and-a-half months, and not *her baby*!" And there they were—both standing in front of me arguing their cases, *expecting* me to take *their* side. They were fucking *killing me*. I was too glad when it was time to leave!

All the contract negotiating had my head messed up, and I had some making up to do with my wife. I know I wasn't the easiest person to be around. I'd catch myself biting her head off about petty shit and a few times it led into shouting matches so I just wanted to let her know that I was sorry and I appreciated her tolerating my ill side.

We left Epiphany with our neighbors, Siani and Po for the night and I took Asia to the Regency Hotel. It felt good just us two escaping into a whole new scenery. It was the first evening we spent alone since Piff Piff was born nine months ago. Asia and I ate at the hotel's restaurant, did some dancing in their jazz room, then headed back to our room drinking Champagne until we were both damn near drunk. The next morning we checked out early and caught a matinee at the movies before we went home. It felt so good just to be hangin out. Walking into our building, we were even holding hands again, something that we hadn't done in months. Asia had that spark back in her eyes when she looked at me, and I was sparkling my damn self. We picked up the baby and headed back to our place.

When we got in there were three calls from Sylvia. All sounding urgent.

"Duane, you better call your mom. She sounds upset about something." Asia said putting Epiphany into her playpen.

Shaking my head, I picked up the phone and started dialing.

"Bout time you returned my call," Sylvia snapped.

"What's up?" I ignored her tone.

"You tell me. What's this about you asking to be signed with the Tritons. Duane, have you lost your mind?"

"Sylvia, I really don't feel like arguing right now."

"No, I want you to talk to me, and if you hang up this damn phone, I'll be on the next flight to your front door, so start talking."

Not wanting Asia to hear the conversation, I took the cordless phone and went into the den for privacy. Asia didn't know that I had made up my mind and already spoke with Zigna to start negotiations with the New Jersey Tritons. In addition to the Tritons being a Champion Bowl team, Asia's dad's health was getting worse and it just seemed like Jersey is where we needed to be. "Look, before you even get started, I'm doing what's in the best interest of my family."

"How about doing what's in the best interest of your overall career, Duane. You have worked so hard. All your life you wanted to play professional football. And I made sure that happened for you. I am the one who have managed you from the time you were in peewee football, and now that you're in the PFL, thanks to my devotion, you don't need me anymore? My input is irrelevant? You're making a big mistake, boy, and you're about to blow it."

"How am I about to blow it, Sylvia?" I was sick and tired of the—*what I did for you*—speech.

"How?!"

"Yeah, how Sylvia. How am I blowing it?" I was pissed. Sylvia went on about how Barnes appreciated what I brought to the team, but that wouldn't be the case with the Tritons' coach, Maxon. I wasn't trying to hear it, but it didn't stop her from telling me what she thought just the same.

"Duane, please think about what you're getting ready to do. What does Asia think about this?"

"I haven't told her yet."

"Why not?"

"I wanted to surprise her."

"*Surprise her?* Well isn't that *special?*" Sylvia mocked

"Come on Sylvia!" I said sharply.

"No you come on. What if she doesn't even want to come home? What if she's fine in Arizona?" Sylvia sucked her teeth, "Put her on the phone."

"What? Naw Sylvia, I'm not even going to go there."

"What are you afraid of, that I might be right? Put her on the phone, maybe she can talk some sense into you."

I felt like hanging up the damn phone, but instead I covered the receiver and opened the door, "Baby, pick up the phone!"

Asia peeked her head into the hallway from the kitchen, and I raised the phone indicating for her to pick up the other line.

"Hello?" Asia said.

"Hi Asia, it's Sylvia. Duane, you still there?"

"Yeah, I'm here." I replied dryly.

"Asia, as sweet as my son is, he wanted to surprise you, but he's making some major decisions that I think you should be in on." I couldn't believe Sylvia. She didn't give a damn about me keeping my news from Asia. All she cared about was changing my mind.

"Oh really? Decisions like what?"

"I asked to be signed with New Jersey." I sighed.

"Really?" Asia sounded confused, "So what's the problem?"

"The problem is, yes you are a good football player, Duane, but the Mavericks organization and Coach Barnes are interested in making sure that my son is utilizing his full potential. Coach Barnes was the one who suggested that Duane take the communications instruction, and got him the gig on their cable program. They see Duane as the person he is—an excellent player, but also the person he has the potential to be off the field as well." Sylvia pleaded her point passionately.

"Well couldn't he take a similar training through the Tritons organization?" Asia interjected.

"It doesn't..." I started before Sylvia cut me off.

"No, absolutely not! In fact, the only thing that Maxon cares about is his next Champion Bowl ring. If his player's don't cut it, they're history."

Now after listening to Sylvia, Asia was upset that she had to find out like this. "Baby, how come you didn't tell me about this?"

"There're a lot of reasons. Look Asia, bottom line, with your father being sick and everything, I know you would rather be there."

"Oh Duane," Asia purred.

"Duane, I know your heart is in the right place, but if Asia wants to be near her father, I'm sure you two can work it out. Maybe she can come back home and you can join her and Piff Piff after the season's over."

Flinching at the thought, I lost it. "Sylvia, how you sound?" I stood, ready to sail the phone across the room. "You just gonna split my family up on two different coasts and think that's suppose to be alright with me?!"

"See these are the distractions I warned you about!" Sylvia's words spewed out of her mouth.

"This conversation is over," I clicked my phone off with my thumb and dropped it on the chair. If she wasn't my mother I would have fired her ass right on the spot for saying some shit like that. Asia and my daughter meant everything to me. Us as a family meant everything. I was working it out with Zigna to make sure that all ends were taken care of, my family and my career and here was Sylvia making it seem like my wife and kid were in my damn way. The game had changed. I was a man now! *I* was in charge! But she was still treating me like I was a kid.

Sylvia and I didn't have the typical mother-son relationship. It was more like older sister-younger brother. Sometimes it was a plus, sometimes not. The plus side was we kept it real with each other. Growing up it used to trip some of my friends out that I called my mother by her first name, was allowed to swear in front of her and as I've gotten older, we've even gone to clubs together. Yeah, even though what we shared wasn't typical, I don't know anyone who was as cool with their mother as I was with mine. But on the flip side, being that she *was* my mother it was hard dealing with her as my business manager. A true manager would have an objective view about how to manage my career. They wouldn't come at me thinking about what *they* wanted for me, feeling that I was *obligated* to see things their way…because they raised me. That was Sylvia's approach to managing my career and it was starting to cause some serious conflicts between us…mother to son as well as manager to client.

By the time I made my way back up into the living room, I heard Asia tell Sylvia, "I'll talk to him and see what's on his mind, but Duane'll have the last word." Then she hung up the phone and joined me in the living room.

I took Epiphany out of her playpen and put her on the floor where I was sitting. At nine months old she was crawling around, and loved playing with her daddy. My hands were stretched out and Epiphany had a big grin on her face as she tried to stand and wobble to me. "Da da, da da." I picked her up holding her over my head then gave her a big, big kiss. Epiphany grabbed my ears and put her little mouth on my eye. Drool ran down the side of my face.

"Hey Piff Piff, you slimed me girl. You slimed daddy." I tickled her tummy as she laughed hard, showing all four of her teeth. She looked just like Asia. I didn't see me in her at all.

Asia sat quietly on the couch looking at Epiphany and me wrestling on the floor. "Duane, you think Sylvia has a point?"

"Maybe babe, but I already made up my mind." I said in one quick breath, "I had a long talk with Zigna and she backs me up with this." We just got back from having a nice twenty-four hours together and in fifteen minutes Sylvia's phone call took me from feeling good to completely pissed off. I really didn't want to get into some heavy conversation with Asia right now.

"Well what happened to the talk with me, Duane?" She snapped.

From the corner of my eyes I looked at her, "Asia, I had to decide what I wanted. I know that we're in this together baby, but I'm thinking career choices as well as family choices. What would have happened if I got your hopes up all high about moving and then changed my mind? With Pop sick and everything that wouldn't have been fair to you. I had to make up my mind first." Feeling my anger rising, I looked up at the ceiling and took a few deep breaths. I was tired of the strife between us. It went on for the last couple weeks, and I didn't want us to go back there. But mostly, I was tired as hell of everyone second-guessing me. Like I couldn't make a damn decision without checking with them first.

"Sweetheart," she diplomatically added between closed teeth. "I would like to be informed about decisions that affect our family." In spite of Asia trying to get my full attention I continued to play with Epiphany. "Well what did you decide?"

"If Zigna can get me signed, we're going to Jersey." I gave her the *just drop it* look!

"Why Duane?" Asia insisted, "I hope that you're not doing this just for me. I don't want you blaming me if things don't go like you expect them to. And besides, what about the issues Sylvia mentioned." I could hear it in her voice, Asia was getting frustrated 'cause I wouldn't focus on her conversation. "Duane, what about your communications training? This is important, Duane." She tapped me on the shoulder, "Duane?"

"Don't worry about it."

"Don't worry about it?!"

"Just drop it!" I yelled and Epiphany who was steady crawling around, froze and looked up at me, alarmed. Asia glared hard in my direction.

I stretched out my arms reaching for Epiphany, "It's alright, come on." I smiled softly, focusing my attention solely on my daughter and ignoring Asia. Asia was so upset with me that she got up off the couch pushed me in the side of my head with her hand, grabbed her keys, and walked out of the condo, slamming the door behind her.

I looked at my baby, "I think mommy's mad at me, Piff Piff. What do you think I should do?"

"Da, da da da." Epiphany squealed, slapping her little hands against my face. "You think we should go after her?" Epiphany started laughing. With the baby in arm, I went out into the hallway only to see Asia get on the elevator and the doors closed behind her. I wasn't really trying to catch her, I was actually kinda glad she was gone. I went back inside and finished playing with my daughter.

Three hours later, Asia walked through the door. I was sitting in the living room, deep in thought gazing at the setting sun, listening to the mellow sound of my favorite old George Howard jazz tune *Love Will Follow*.

"Where's Piff Piff?" Asia asked quietly.

"I wore her out," a smile crept up one side of my lips. "She's in the room sleeping."

"Baby, I want to talk about this." Asia started right in again, "I still can't understand why you would make such an important decision without even talking with me. I can't tell you how much this hurts, Duane."

"Come here." I said softly. Reaching out, I sat Asia on my lap. My head was in a much better place now than it was when she left earlier. Plus, I realized that I did owe her at least the consideration of answering her questions. "Baby, like I said before, I had to make sure it was in the best interest of my career, then I had to see if Zigna could even manage to get me signed to the Tritons roster."

"What made you want the Tritons? I know you're concerned about daddy, but..."

"I know you need to be near your family and I want to make that happen for you. And that shit Sylvia was talking about is out. There's no way I could be separated from you for half a year. That shit is *out*."

"Well, I feel the same way you do about that. I'd go crazy without my man." Asia gripped my head and pressed her lips on my jaw. Wrapping my arms around her, I squeezed Asia around the waist.

"And your man would go crazy without you too. Don't let nobody tell you any different."

The evening sky had burning streaks of deep orange and reddish pink. From outside the window the cars' headlights going west and the taillights going east on the highway across the water made the beautiful red and white moving picture show.

"Well baby, what about the other points Sylvia brought up?"

Gripping Asia's chin, I looked into her eyes for the truth, "Do you have confidence in me?"

"Of course I do, Duane. Why would you ask that?"

"I'm asking because I have confidence in me too. The most important things in my life are you and our baby. I know I'm one of the best running backs in the entire league, and with that I can go to any organization and make it work. Another reason why I feel it's time for me to leave Arizona is because I'm getting too relaxed. I don't want to become someone's pet and lose my competitive edge. If I do go to another team and have to work my ass off, then so be it. I'm not gonna lose baby. You with me?"

"Always."

"You forgive me?" I asked stroking her chin with my thumb.

"Only if you promise not to do this again. I'm serious Duane. I want to know what's going on in our lives. I need to be a part of it."

"Deal." I kissed her cheek.

"Now what?"

"Now we just wait and pray for the best."

Three weeks later Zigna called and told me it was a done deal. I was officially a New Jersey Triton.

THE ART OF SEDUCTION

When we spoke last night Asia said everything was going well with the house. In the short month-and-a-half that she and the baby had returned to Trenton, the developers had broken ground, framed out the entire three-car-garage, five-bedroom house, and started bricking in the exterior. Asia was having a ball going out to the site, taking pictures, and driving everyone by our soon-to-be new home in Hamilton-Mercerville.

I stayed in Arizona to get the last minute things done like finalizing my business with the Mavericks organization, calling the Mayflower movers who were coming at the end of the week, and squaring away our condo lease 'cause we still had half a year before we were released from it.

I was excited to leave but for the last five years these people had been like family to me. For three days straight my teammates from the Mavericks were taking me from party to party. It was a lot of them, so there were a lot of goodbyes to share.

Two nights before I was due to leave I was sitting in my condo with three of my Mavericks partners. All four of us were tore down drunk.

"You our brother now, but when we encounter your ass this spring, we ain't gonna take no pity on you then," Vince the Italian said.

"Natural born enemies, man," Raymond said gesturing a clothes line strangle at me.

"Man, please. Y'all know I was carrying all y'all sorry asses. It ain't gonna be no team after I leave." I laughed chugging from the bottle of Budweiser. "So y'all just might as well get used to the idea of finishing last in the division."

"Ahh fuck you." Clyde yelled. He was tore up, "We gonna kick the Tritons ass in the spring and I'm comin' straight for you." Clyde pointed at me, then fell off the chair right on his behind.

We started cracking up.

"Somebody pick that drunk muthah fuckah up off my floor," I waved Clyde on and laughed. Just then the doorbell rang. We were so engrossed in our rhetoric we ignored it. The doorbell rang again, this time I got up. Standing there wet from the heavy rain pouring down outside was no other than Missy.

Blocking the entrance way with my arm, I wondered what the hell was her problem, "What are you doin' here?" I asked pissed, feeling a little lightheaded.

Apparently she didn't catch my negative vibe, "I came to see you before you left. You don't think I was gonna just let you leave without saying goodbye, do you?" Missy smiled that naughty kind of smile, "And besides your mom called and told me your wife and baby are in New Jersey." When she said that something on the inside of me didn't feel right and I knew she was up to no good. Besides, I told Sylvia to stop telling that girl all my damn business.

"I got company." Looking down at her, I was put off by the fact that she even thought it was alright for her to show up at my door.

Swaying her body slowly, Missy poked out her bottom lip and gave me puppy dog eyes, "I came all this way to see you and you're not even gonna let me in. You're starting to hurt my feelings, Pookie," she said in this low penetrating whine. The tone in her voice just sort of broke down all that frustration I was feeling and my logic started clouding up.

Standing there staring her down, I couldn't help but to think how Missy's ass was my kinda fine. Deep chocolate skin, them lucious lips, dimples that dug in her cheeks and the most beautiful white teeth I've ever seen. She was a tall glass of water, five feet eleven, and with her heels on she was almost staring me in the eye.

My first time seeing her, she was cheering at our home game and all that body was packed tight into the short shorts and tiny top, that they called a uniform. Even tough I knew the cheerleaders were off-limits to us players, I just *had* to have some of whatever she was willing to give.

Pookie, huh? I could never deny that girl her way when she called me Pookie in that baby voice. Against my better judgment, I stepped to the side so she could enter, but I gave her the *you better behave yourself* look. As she walked in Missy brushed her body close to mine, even though she had enough room to pass. When I felt my nine starting to rise, I knew it was a bad sign.

All the fellahs ooowed and ahhed knowing my former history with her. Clyde spoke up belligerently. "Girl, what you doin' here?"

"Same thing y'all are, saying goodbye to a friend," Missy snapped at Clyde then she said politely to the others, "Hey Ray Ray, hey Vince."

"Hey there Missy," they replied with their eyes wide like she was their secret desire.

"Why you so mean to me, huh, huh?" Clyde said drunk as a skunk. "I ain't never done nothin' to ya." He went over and stood in front of her, "I think she likes me that's what it is. I'ma get that when you leave Hitman. I got too much respect for you to try that now though." He slurred, acting like she was my woman or something.

"Get on away from me you drunken fool." Missy pushed him out of her face.

"See, see what I'm talkin' bout. That's alright though, I'ma getcha and make you forget all about that brothah right there." Clyde pointed at me.

"Yo Clyde, man. Chill out and have a seat." I stood up ready to get with him if I had to because I didn't like the direction his conversation was going.

"No, no man. I'm cool. But I was just saying though." Clyde retreated back to his seat.

Missy rolled her eyes at him. Then sat on the end of the couch with her wet coat still on and crossed her legs. She was wearing black high heel shoes with no stockings.

"Let me get your coat," I offered.

Like she was savoring me, she slowly said, "No."

"Come on girl, you're messin' up my couch."

"I said no," she teased.

I waved her off, "Suit yourself."

The fellahs and I continued our wild style conversation, laughing, hooping and hollering for the next twenty minutes or so. I looked at Missy and she looked both bored and disgusted. She gave me the *why don't you tell them the hit the road* look.

"Yo fellahs," I said standing up, "It's been real, but ahh..." and I motioned my head towards her.

"Oh, oh, yeah right." Vince said laughing rubbing his hands together.

Raymond stood up and looked down at Missy nodding his head in agreement, "You the man, D. Go on and handle your business."

"See ya Missy." Clyde snapped.

Missy looked at him with much attitude, then waved goodbye by dangling her fingers. For the last time as their teammate, I saw them to the door, embracing each one. I knew the next time we saw each other we'd be trying to take each other's heads off on the field. I waited until they got on the elevator to close the door.

"Bout time you asked them to leave, all that male bonding was starting to bore me," Missy said rolling her neck.

"Oh yeah. Well if I knew you were coming I would've baked a cake. You the one who invited *yourself* over here. Remember that." Tipsy, I nearly missed when I sat on the arm of the chair my damn self. I was on the opposite side of the room from her.

She patted the sofa seat next to her, "You not gonna come and sit next to me?"

I looked at her feeling the blood rushing to my lower extremities, "No. You *want* me, you *come* to me." Slowly, Missy walked over standing between my open legs and put her tongue in my mouth.

"Why don't you take your coat off?" I asked sucking on her neck.

Untying the belt of her cream trench coat, Missy took her time unbuttoning each button letting it drop to the floor. She stood there in a sheer blue, thigh high robe and black high heel pumps. Digging her sexiness, I stared totally turned on.

"Surprise." She laughed playfully, looking at me for a reaction but I didn't give her one. Even though I was feeling her, I kept my poker face. Taking my hands Missy placed them on her behind and she was naked under her robe. I ran my hands down the back of her smooth legs then slowly up until my fingers felt the curl under her well-endowed behind. Once again we started kissing hard.

"You so bad, girl," I said slapping that butt just hard enough to make it sting a little bit.

She flinched then said, "Make love to me, Duane." As I sat on the arm of the chair, Missy rubbed her nipples against my lips.

My mind flashed to Asia and I pushed her back. "*Make love to you?* Girl, It ain't even that kinda party." My damn conscience started kicking in and I wondered where was it when she was standing at the door before I let her in?! Well I guess, better late than never. Missy was all about the bullshit. Here she was sitting up in my wife's house talking 'bout, *make love to her.*

"Yo girl, I can't do this." I got up and went into the kitchen to pour myself another drink. This shit was foul…I'm a married man! I should have never even let her in the door, I said kicking myself. When I came back Missy was sitting on the single chair with her robe neatly retied and her legs crossed looking dejected with her head hung low. I don't know why she couldn't understand that I had moved on.

"It's getting late." I said sarcastically as I sat on the sofa in front of her dreading the drama I knew she was capable of. The crying spells, the shouting matches.

"You know what Duane, I don't understand you. I thought we were suppose to be together." Acting like she wanted to cry, Missy said, "*I* still love you, Duane. How could you do me like this? We had something good! If you don't care for me, tell me you don't care. That's the one thing you never said and I just need to hear you say it, then I'll leave you alone."

I didn't say a word. I didn't owe her any more explanations. Everything I needed to say to her was already said. Nursing a glass of Hennessey, I just sat there.

"You can't say it can you?" She said a little louder, " 'cause I know you want me. You may be married, but I know she can't satisfy you like I can. Can she?" Frustrated, Missy demanded, "Say something, Duane!" When I didn't respond Missy reopened her robe once again exposing that beautiful body. "I *know* you want me." Then she started doing things to herself.

"Why…why you doing this, huh?! You know it's over between us!" From my raspy voice she had me, and she *knew it*.

"It ain't never gonna be over between us. Now come here and kiss it."

I started to move, but hesitated. Leaning her head back on the chair, erotically she moved and gestured, licking her lips, and ummp the way the girl moaned my name, and had me losing the battle! I turned the glass up to my mouth and gulped down the last drop hoping that it would give me the strength to tell her to get up and *get the fuck out my house!*

"I just wanna *make you feel good, baby*. Is that so wrong?" She crooned.

I got on my knees, 'cause yeah, I wanted to *feel good* and the more she came the more I wanted her. All thoughts of Asia, and of being a good and *trustworthy* man were bound, gagged and held captive to my lust and that urgent need to have it satisfied. We were going at it hard on the living room floor when the phone rang. After the greeting of the answering machine, I heard Mama Janie's voice.

"Asia, this is your mother. I'm just calling to see if you got in okay."

Missy and I both froze and I sobered up *quick!* "Shhh!" I said to her, panicked!

"You said you would be callin' at eight and it's almost ten. You know how I worry."

I practically stomped on Missy to get to the phone, "Hello. Mom?"

"Hey baby. What, you just gettin in? You sound all out of breath." Mama Janie questioned.

"Yeah, that's it. I'm just coming in so I ran to catch the phone. What's this about Asia being here by eight?" I tried to compose myself.

"I'm sorry if I ruined your surprise, but it's past my bed time, but I can't rest until I know she's okay. Walter Lee says I worries too much, but I just can't help it."

I eyeballed Missy who was pissed off and gathering her things, "This shit is fu…" she yelled.

With my hand I quickly covered the phone; and if looks could kill. "Don't you even try that shit." I said between clinched teeth. Missy closed her mouth.

"Who was that?" Mom asked.

"That was *nobody* Ma. I just turned the television on." I lied, staring Missy down. And I swear-to-god I would have beat the shit out of her if she said another word!

She was fired up and she mouthed the word *nobody* rolling her neck because I overemphasized the word to let Missy know just who she was to me. I watched as she went into my bedroom then stormed back out. Missy threw on her coat, flipped me the bird, then left slamming the door behind her.

"Yeah, alright Ma. I'll make sure she calls as soon as she gets in. Bye." In a panic, I hung up the phone.

First of all I threw on my draws now wishing they had stayed on my ass in the first place, then I grabbed all of the empty beer cans and liquor bottles, threw them in a garbage bag, and hid the bag in the cabinet under the sink. Opening all of the windows, I wanted to get rid of any love making smells that might have been circling the air.

I called downstairs to the doorman, "Theodore, this is Duane Cummings. Look man, I need a really big favor. My wife is expected home at any time. When you see her try to stall her, but if she gets onto the elevator, ring my phone twice then hang up. You think you can do that for me, man?"

"What do you want me to do?" Theodore asked.

"I don't know, I just need twenty minutes."

After hanging up the phone, I dove in the shower. From the thought of being inside of Missy and not being able to get a nut, from all that damn alcohol, and from the thought of almost being busted if Mom Janie hadn't called, my system was accelerated like crazy! The hot water beat down over my swirling head until I was able to somewhat collect myself.

By the time I got out and was dressed the apartment was icy cold and thoroughly aired out. After closing all the windows, I threw the garbage outside into the hallway and down the chute. Still rattled by my close encounter, I turned on the television, knowing that Missy and I would have still been on the floor tearing it up *right now!* I felt bad. *Really bad* 'cause Asia could have opened the door and walked in on that shit! Just then the phone rang twice and stopped. Feeling sick to my stomach I closed my eyes with the remote gripped tight in my hand. Minutes later I heard the key opening the door and there was Asia and Terry talking and laughing away.

Standing up I went over to them kissing Asia on the lips, "Hey y'all." I said casually, and grabbed their overnight bags.

"See," Asia laughed looking at Terry, "I told you he already knew. Mama called you didn't she?"

"Yeah, she was worried about you."

"The plane was in the air when the pilot announced that he had to delay the landing because of the rain. We were delayed two whole hours." Terry said giving me a kiss on the cheek.

"Ain't that something?" I said, "Oh babe, call your mother. She's worried sick about you."

"Okay Lovah," Asia cupped my face and gave me another juicy kiss on the lips, "How come it's so cold in here? I'm gonna turn up the heat." Asia walked towards the kitchen to use the phone.

"I already did. It should be warming up soon." I replied then looked sourly at Terry, "What's up with the surprise?"

She looked at me strangely, "Why? Were we interrupting something?"

"Whose idea was this?" I whispered.

Terry mocked Asia, "Your wife's. She just couldn't *stay away from her man* one second longer. Even though you would've been home in two days anyway." Terry threw up her hands, "I still don't get what's up with the attitude?"

"Call next time." I snapped.

Asia came back in the room all smiles, "They are something else. I'm over thirty and they still think of me as a little kid. I *still* have to call home and tell them I'm alright." Asia snuggled up to me, "So how you doing? I wanted to surprise you."

"Believe me, I'm surprised."

"A good one I hope." My wife's eyes sparkled when they looked at me.

"It's always good when you're around." Squeezing Asia, I kissed her tenderly on the lips feeling convicted thinking about the places on Missy where my lips were not even an hour ago.

"So what did you do today?" She inquired.

"Clyde, Vince and Raymond came by. We were just sitting around drinking a little bit."

"I know 'cause I can taste the liquor mixed in with that minty mouth wash." Asia said walking away from me.

In spite of everything, Asia, Terry and I had a nice night. I ordered a pizza, we watched some HBO then stayed up real late talking. Around one in the morning Asia said she was tired and was going to turn in. She walked into the bedroom and Terry and I were still bugging, 'cause my aunt was the craziest! She had me laughing from the belly, and not too many people could do that. Our fun was interrupted by Asia's irate call, "Duane! Come here!" At that moment I remembered that Missy had gone into the bedroom before she left. And by Asia's tone I knew she had found whatever it was that Missy had planted.

STAND

If it weren't for my belief in God, I probably would have gone crazy by now. It was June and we had been living back in Trenton since February. During the four months that we have been home daddy's condition had taken a turn for the worse. As usual he hadn't been feeling well, but this time during his doctor's visits they discovered that he had stomach cancer. Dealing with daddy's illness and trying to appear strong for mama was difficult. But on top of that I was six months pregnant and going through my own headache and heartache with Duane.

We stayed up at the hospital all day until Daddy got out of surgery. They had to remove half of his stomach. It was a long day of drinking coffee and sitting around the waiting room, watching soap operas and trying to keep our spirits up. The operation itself took about two hours, but there was the pre-op, then there was recovery time afterwards before they moved him into his room.

Hours later the doctor came out and told us that they were able to get all of the cancer and right now things looked promising. His diet was now restricted totally to liquids: soup, vitamin enriched milk shakes, ginger ale and the like. I knew he was going to hate living like that. Especially as much as my daddy loved to taste his food.

Duane and I went through our emotional cycles of getting close and pulling away. His cheating was so hard to deal with at times that I just felt like packing up taking my child and running out of his life. When Duane and I found out that we were expecting Epiphany, I didn't get the chance to look in his eyes and that bothered me. When I found out that I was pregnant again, I wanted to tell him while we were face to face. I was so excited and I thought it would be fun surprising him with a visit. Thought it would be something romantic to tell him that I was pregnant in the place where our child was conceived.

But the surprise was most definitely on me. When I went to turn in for the night I went to get in the bed and there was an earring under my sheets and it sure didn't belong to me. What was supposed to be a beautiful surprise turned out to be an ugly fight and my whole purpose for being there never happened, well not the way I planned it anyway. Duane found out that I was pregnant but Terry was the one to tell him.

When we got back to Trenton in February, our home was still under construction, so we stayed at Duane's grandparents' house. My parents only had two bedrooms and with my dad being sick, my aunt, his sister, came up from Beaufort, South Carolina to help Mama take care of him. Even though there was no room at my parents' house for me, I packed my and Epiphany's things. We were going to sleep on my mother's pullout couch until I found us some place else to stay 'cause I had no intentions on staying with Duane. As I headed for the door, Gran was the one who convinced me to stay.

I walked out of the room with my suitcase packed. "Gran, Piff Piff and I are going to stay at my parents' house." I told her reaching to take my daughter out of her arms.

She looked troubled because Duane was in the bedroom with me and had been trying to talk me out of packing my things and leaving. When he saw that my mind was set, he stormed out of the house and Gramps went after him. "What's going on between you and Duane, Asia?"

"I really don't feel like talking about this again." I didn't want to cry. I laid ten-month old Epiphany on the couch to put her inside of her snowsuit.

Gran was sitting at the dining room table listening to her gospel songs playing on the black portable radio that was sitting by an arrangement of artificial flowers. She had on a blue, pink and white flowery housecoat with slippers, and a scarf tied around her mostly gray hair. "Is it that bad?" she asked as she stood up and walked over to me. She insisted, "Chile, please put that coat down and tell me what's going on."

I sat on the edge of the couch and started to ball. I explained to her what happened when Terry and I went to Arizona, "And with the baby coming this is just the wrong time for this to be happening."

Gran touched my arm, "Asia, you pregnant?"

I nodded my head to confirm. She held me by the arm guiding me to stand and put her arms lovingly and comfortingly around me. We just stood there embracing and she told me that it was all going to be alright, and I so desperately needed it. I just kind of laid my head on her shoulder and breathed for the first time in two days since I found out Duane had cheated on me.

"First thing you need to do is calm yourself down," she said softly. "Now Robert and Duane gone out together and if I know my Robert, he's gonna give Duane a strong-talkin'-to." She dried my eyes with her handkerchief. "And Honey, it's too cold out there to be draggin' that baby outside. Besides where y'all gonna stay, it's no room at your mother's with your aunt still there."

"Gran, I just can't stay here with him." All I wanted to do was run! Bryant told me over and over again after he got busted that it was going to be the last time. I wasn't trying to wait for three more venereal diseases before I decided to get a clue and leave... I wasn't trying to go through any of that again!

"Just you wait chile." She said with a bit more authority, "Talk to your husband. Cheating is a terrible thing, I know. Duane done an awful thing, and there's no excuse for it! But that's your husband for better or worse and you's got kids to raise. You young folks has got to stop your running from your problems and learn to just stand! Believe me Asia, this is not the end of the world, honey. And us black women ain't no quitters." Her words came out like she felt my pain. "Leave the baby here with me and you go on and take yourself a nice hot bath and try to relax your mind. You don't let no other woman cause you to throw your family away. You need to stand granddaughter." She put her arms around me once more, "We'll all get through this together, but you have to learn to just stand!"

It wasn't even so much what she said that made the difference that night for me not to walk out of Duane's life…it was the fact that she showed me she cared. About me, about the welfare of the kids, about the survival of my marriage. When Bryant and I had come to the end of our marriage and were going through our divorce, his family could have cared less. And it was a hard thing going through all of that emotional stress with no understanding and no support from anyone on his side.

One good thing that came out of this whole mess was over the four months that we lived with Duane's grandparents I finally got the chance to bond with them. The four of us had many heart-to-hearts at dinnertime. To my surprise, they openly shared with Duane and me, the trials and truths of forty plus years of marriage. And many times when Gran and I were alone at home during the day, she'd have me laughing so hard about Duane's adventures when he was growing up. It was nice because his grandparents got a chance to know me and judge me on their own terms without being influenced by Sylvia's dislike of me…I still couldn't figure out what I ever did to her.

But there was something about the way Duane looked one day when he walked in the house. Gran, Epiphany and I were all in the kitchen. Piff Piff was in her highchair and I was peeling potatoes while Gran prepared the meat for dinner. He came in and just stood there in the kitchen doorway taking in the whole scene. And I knew how much it meant to him to see his grandmother and me finally bonding. It meant a lot to me too. Through this difficult time in our young marriage, Terry, Gran and Gramps really rallied around us and gave me so much support. They told me that the children and I were their family, and that family doesn't run, but stands and conquers trouble together as a unit. Right in front of me, Gran and Gramps told Duane that he was better than a cheating man, and that his actions not only hurt me, but them as well. For the very first time I felt like I was really a part of Duane's family and it meant the world to me.

One bad thing that came out of the whole mess was that I also hurt Duane just as bad by bringing Bryant's name up, as an example while we were arguing that night. I had asked him one simple question: 'While he was in Arizona messing around on me, how would he have felt if I were in Trenton sneaking around with Bryant?' But Duane did not internalize the question like I intended. Instead he turned the argument around on me and asked if I was confessing my own ill secrets in the heat of the moment. Reminding me that he was never convinced that Bryant didn't sleep with me that Christmas night when he called. Looking back, I wish I could have taken all of that back because now Duane had trust issues with me. It was tough, but so far we were sticking it out, committed to making ours a marriage of quality.

In April, for Piff Piff's first birthday, we drove down to Disney World in Florida. The long drive really helped to focus Duane and me, and got us back on track to what was really important. We stayed there a week taking lots of pictures, and really enjoying ourselves. We had a lot of time to talk and listen to each other. It was good for a change, 'cause we weren't bitter, sarcastic, or coming down on each other like we had been. We were just being positive and determined to get our relationship back on track.

Then two months later we went to the Bahamas, and left Piff Piff home so we could have some much-needed intimacy between us. We both knew things were about to really get hectic and time alone was going to be hard to come by. It was June. We were about to move into our new home, Duane was due to report to training camp, and the baby was due in another three months.

LAP OF LUXURY

It was June fifteenth and Duane had asked me not to go to the house for the past three days. He told me he wanted to surprise me. He guided me to the backyard as my eyes were blindfolded with a bandanna.

"Don't let me fall, Duane!" I laughed grabbing on tight to his arm. The heat from the sun beamed down on my face.

After we stepped off of the patio he led me twenty paces. "Okay, stop," Duane directed. Excited, I put my hand up to my eyes ready to remove the blindfold. "No, not yet. Just be patient."

"Come on Duane." I whined impatiently as I felt my baby thumping around in my belly.

He put something up to my nose and I flinched not knowing what he was doing until the smell of fresh mint overtook my senses then I breathed in deeply, "Oh babe." Lifting the bandanna from my eyes, I gasped at the sight of the beautifully sculptured backyard. Earlier in the week it was all dirt. Now we had this plush green lawn with trees, shrubs and all these colorful flowers. But what was totally touching was the lush green herb garden and that Duane remembered our conversation when we stood in my backyard on Greenwood Avenue three years ago. My lips pressed tightly together and I became overwhelmed by emotion. Looking up at Duane, tears welled in the rims of my eyes.

Smiling confidently he asked, "You like it?"

"It's beautiful." I grabbed him around the neck and held tight. "What's that?" I pointed to a three foot high something, covered with a white sheet.

"Why don't you look and see." Duane folded his arms, amused, looking down at me. Grinning back at him with anticipation I went over and removed the sheet. Covering my mouth, I laughed. It was a cute wooden scarecrow wearing a straw hat, with a black crow on his shoulder. The scarecrow was holding a green and gold sign that read, *Asia's Herb Garden*.

I was seven months pregnant by the time we moved into our new home. We had a finished basement that stretched from one end of the house to the other. One small area was blocked off for the heating unit and storage area but the rest belonged exclusively to Duane. He called it his domain and wanted complete say over it, which was totally fine with me, because the rest of the house was mine to decorate. Duane had a weight room complete with all this new equipment. It even had mirrors on the wall so he could check himself out as he lifted. He had an office where he could study his playbook and study film of his own game or film of his upcoming opponents… he was his own biggest critique. And of course Duane's toy was this big new red pool table. He said he just had to have one, and I didn't even know he could play.

Upstairs was my area! I had never even heard of a Conservatory, but we had one! It was a sitting room that was of-but-not actually a part of the main house. It was almost like a closed-in, four-season porch, but it's more like a living room that was outside and it was beautiful! Then we had this huge country style eat-in kitchen with a solarium. The solarium was a little room on the side of the kitchen that flooded in sunlight! All three walls of the solarium were huge windows, plus there was a sky roof. The view in the morning was pure heaven.

The master bedroom suite was my favorite. The room had two walk-in closets, one for Duane and one for me. On the side of our bed were French doors that led outside to a balcony overlooking our backyard. The right side of the room was the lounge, which was another sitting room. I loved to read and it was the perfect space to tune everything out and curl up with a good book. To the left side of the bedroom was the master bath. It was decorated with french vanilla marble and gold fixtures. We had the his-and-her, double sinks, temperature controlled Jacuzzi, which meant that we could sit in the water as long as we wanted without it getting cold, and a separate glass enclosed shower.

***

It was three o'clock in the afternoon when the kitchen door that leads to the garage opened up and Duane came walking into the house. I had already cooked up a big pot of spaghetti and meat sauce, and I had my garlic bread all buttered up and waiting in the refrigerator, along with a big pitcher of fresh-squeezed lemonade. Duane, with his Kangol sitting backwards on his head, came over and kissed me on the lips. He rubbed my belly then tapped me on the behind as he passed through the kitchen to go into the family room.

"Baby, you ready to go?" I asked. He had been promising me for a week that we were going to go furniture shopping.

Epiphany was now stretched out on the couch. I had her in the backyard, in the kiddy pool playing for about two hours. When I brought her inside, she ate lunch and was knocked out ever since. Duane flopped on the couch next to her and was stroking her little leg with his fingers.

"Asia, I been out there in that hot ass sun all day and the only thing I feel like doing right now is chilling under this air conditioner." Duane tossed his hat to the side and ran his fingers across his head. "Can I get something to drink?"

"Duane, you know your dad and stepmother are coming on Saturday and we still don't have any furniture for them to sleep on. You been saying that we were going to go and get it since Monday, and it's Thursday already." I fussed all the way into the kitchen, poured him a big glass lemonade...took a sip, poured him some more, then brought the glass to him.

"Baby, I'm tired," he stressed. "Call your mom, Crystal or somebody and see if they feel up to going with you 'cause baby..." Duane shook his head then drank half of the lemonade in one chug, "...I ain't up to it right now."

I had my gospel music playing on the stereo. Tramaine Hawkins singing ,"A Change"...my 1980's music! Ump...seems like only yesterday.

Epiphany opened her sleepy little eyes, and when she saw her daddy she used his arm as a brace to pull herself up. Once on her knees she put her fifteen-month old fingers in the rim of the glass pulling it to her little open mouth with her tongue sticking out. Duane tilted the glass so she could get a sip…then another one, and when she had her fill, she laid her head on his shoulder.

"Give daddy kiss." At the sound of Duane's voice, Epiphany puckered up and gave him some shugga.

Duane's stepmother, Marie and Jericho have been married for twenty-two years. Ever since Duane was five. They were such beautiful people. Even though I spoke with them often on the phone this was going to be my second time actually seeing them. When we came to Trenton after Epiphany was born, we drove to Maryland and spent the day with them. Now for our house warming they were going to come up for the week.

I was having a ball with the house! Even though our home had five bedrooms. Duane and I just bought bedroom furniture for our master suite and Epiphany's room. We wanted to start from scratch and decorate the house with things that we got together. So when we found out that Duane's dad and wife were coming we had to go out and buy bedroom furniture, curtains and sheets for their room.

I called Crystal and asked her if she wanted to go to the mall with me. At first, she gave me the run-around but then I let her know that I really wanted her to come and for us to hang out just like old times. We both have been so busy since I came back home.

She finally agreed.

I hung up the phone and went into the family room, "I'm taking your Navigator."

"Be careful with my ride, Asia. I don't want to see no scratches when you bring it back to me, either."

Duane made me so sick treating that truck like a baby. There was a Lincoln Mercury dealership around the corner from our house and when Duane saw all those Navigators on the lot the first words that came out of his mouth was, "I'm getting me one of those." Next thing I know, he was pulling up to the house in a customized, champagne-colored Navigator with these huge, gaudy chrome wheels, yet the car was so pretty! Then he came in the house all excited, and pulled me by the hand talking about, "check this out!" And on the inside it had his initials DJC embroidered into the headrests of the leather seats. The truck had two TV screens one for the back of the truck and a mini screen on the passenger side visor. And the DVD player was one with the CD stereo system. The way he carries on about that truck…I think he loved the thing more than me.

As I drove across town, it was the typical beautiful June day outside, sunny and hot without a single rain cloud in the sky. When I picked Crystal up she was looking cool in a pair of blue jean shorts, a striped blue and white tube top and she had her dreads pulled up into a ponytail.

"Where's my baby? I thought you were going to bring Lil Allen with you." I was kind of disappointed because I was looking forward to spending some time with my godson.

"He's at my mom's for a few days. I can use the break, you know what I'm saying." Her tone was on the dry side and she was looking out the window the whole time she was talking. Then she looked at me. "Where's Piff Piff?"

"Home with Duane." As we drove, Crystal was on the quiet side, but I had been running my mouth enough for the both of us anyway.

Our first stop was to Windsor's Fine Furniture where I picked out this beautiful cherry wood bedroom set…full-size…Duane said make them comfortable, but not so comfortable they don't want to go home. To pay for it I whipped out my platinum Visa card. And I paid a little extra to have them put a rush on the delivery. Then we jumped back in the ride and headed across town to J. C. Penney at the mall. As usual Quaker Bridge Mall was crowded with people.

"You hungry Crystal, 'cause this baby has got me starving!" With this pregnancy, I didn't get a little hungry. I went from feeling okay, straight to famished! I was in search of the pizza parlor. I guess to keep the old new and exciting, they kept switching the darn stores around.

"No, I'm not hungry." Crystal had her arms folded and she cut her eyes away from me, which caught me off guard but I shrugged it off. I mean, maybe she was just having a bad day or something.

"Well let me grab a pretzel and some juice." I loved Auntie Anne's Pretzels!

And I think my baby did too! After I finished stuffing my face, we went into J. C. Penney. The entire time I was talking about the house warming and how I went to the stationery store and had them run off one hundred flyers to distribute. We had them made for our new neighbors on Honey Dew Lane, Duane took some to work with him passing them out to his new teammates and we also mailed some out to our family and friends. Then I went on about how Duane and I had so much fun with Epiphany in her stroller as we passed them out to the people on our street inviting everyone to drop by. Being that the whole development was new, we thought it would be nice to have sort of like a neighborhood meet-and-greet, slash family reunion, slash house warming all at one time. But of course only family was welcomed up inside the house. Everything else was going to be outside and in the backyard where Duane and his dad were going to be on the grill. Dad... as they want me to call him gave Duane a list to take to the meat market and it looked like enough chicken, beef and seafood to feed a small army. I was so excited and couldn't wait for them to get here.

Once we entered J. C. Penney I bought the sheet and comforter set, along with the matching curtains. Then I was in search of the finishing touches like the dresser and chest scarves, two lamps, three nice size pictures to hang on the walls, and a few little knickknacks to add that special touch. Once again I swiped my Visa platinum and everything was paid for.

The entire time Crystal was quiet. I thought maybe she wasn't feeling well, "Crystal girl, cat got your tongue or something? I have been running my mouth and you haven't said a word almost the whole time we've been together."

"Why don't you stop making such a big deal out of nothing?" Crystal grabbed a few of the bags off of the checkout counter and we walked off. By the time we got back to the truck the sun was starting to go down for the night. Looking at her it was so obvious that her attitude was about more than nothing. I knew her too well. She was like my sister. After all of the packages were loaded and we were inside, I put the keys on top of the dashboard and looked at her, "Okay Crystal, now either you tell me what's wrong or we'll just sit here in this heat until you do." I pulled the elastic waistband of my maternity shorts down under my belly. My fingers scratched across the impressions on my skin where the band once was.

I just knew she was going to tell me that Allen had been up to his old tricks again, and I was ready to tell her that I was here for her like I always did when she found a strange number in his pocket or his butt stayed out until the wee hours of the morning.

She hesitated then said, "Asia, you and I have been tight ever since the third grade and we have been through so much together…"

I sat there listening as Crystal started a sentence only to stop midway through. Then took deep breaths as she struggled to express herself, and believe me, this was a first from somebody who has never had a problem expressing what was on her mind.

"Asia I've gone with you to your house as it was being built and just to see everything coming together for you." She stopped again, but this time she had this irked look on her face and her words just started flowing. "And just like today, to see you buy all that shit right on the spot! I mean, my God Asia, you got a Visa platinum card! And I'm thinking to myself, I wonder how much money is on that thing?" Crystal looked like she had a real problem with me and I was taken aback because I wasn't expecting any of that. My mind wasn't sure what emotion to grab hold of… anger at her nerve or sympathy for her situation? I just sat there, stunned and speechless. "I just don't feel like we're on the same level anymore, Asia." Her elbow was propped up against the window and her chin rested in the palm of her hand as she stared out into the parking lot full of cars.

"Crystal, I'm still the same person and we're still girls."

"You are not the same person anymore, Asia. You're not and you can't say that you are. And our relationship has changed too. You have money now. You don't have to worry about bill collectors, or getting up and going to a job because you have to. I do! And that changes everything between us Asia, it does." She gestured as her words came from her heart, and her words hurt!

Sitting there, I thought about when we were at Maxine's having lunch before I moved to Arizona and how Crystal was so against me leaving my job to be a housewife for Duane. It didn't make sense then but it did now. She never seemed put off by the idea of a woman staying home before. Matter-of-fact, we used to laugh saying, *what we would give to have a good man holding it down for us. And if we ever found him how crazy good we would be to that man!* But I guess the idea was cool long as the situation stayed hypothetical. She wasn't fooling me, though. If her husband made it possible for her to be home, she would be there and I knew it. Bottom line she was jealous!

"Well what do you want me to do Crystal, huh? You want to stop being my friend? You want me to break you off a piece of Duane's money? What?!"

"I don't know, Asia! I don't know! All I know is I can't stand you rubbing this shit in my fucking face!" Her hand slapped across the dashboard. Once again she stared out of the passenger side window.

Before I left for Arizona I noticed Crystal pulling away from me. I guess I was trying to rationalize the distance between us away, but I knew something wasn't right. Even when I was in Arizona I even invited her and Allen to come and spend a few days with Duane and me, but she gave me these excuses as to why she couldn't make it. I thought we were too tight for anything to come between us. Looks like I was wrong.

Tears welled in my eyes. Sometimes I'd think about how we were always there for each other and all the times she bailed my butt out of a jam if I needed a few dollars to hold me over until payday. I also thought about how I would have felt if she was the one who had a lot of money and I was still struggling like I was when I lived on Greenwood Avenue. I pulled out a piece of tissue from the small tissue box strapped to Duane's visor and wiped my face with it, "Crystal, I didn't mean to rub anything in your face. I just thought I was sharing my joy with you, girl." All of a sudden, the loudness of the new leather smell in the Navigator just seemed to heighten the tension between us.

Crystal wouldn't even look at me. "Yeah, I'm happy for you, Asia. Can you just take me home now?"

Duane once told me that out of his four closest childhood friends, Tompy was the only one who could weather the fact that he was rich. One friend stopped speaking to him after he made the pros and Duane said he had to cut the other two loose because they started to act like he owed them something. So I *really did* understand where Crystal was coming from. But never would I have thought that she would stop speaking to me.

We drove in silence back home to her apartment complex. The same complex she'd been trying to get Allen to move them out of for the past four years. My insides had sunk and I felt like I just wanted to cry. Instead, I waited for her to at least say goodbye, but without a single word she got out and closed the door behind her.

NEW IMAGE CAMPAIGN

We arrived at Zigna's office by ten minutes to eight. As we rode the elevator up to the eighth floor, my son held Asia's hand. I really didn't understand why Duane felt the need for her to come today, after all this was a business meeting and not some social get together. I told him that I would try to keep my personal feelings about his wife to myself. Then he turns around and starts involving her in the business.

Even though I *love* my granddaughter, I *still* say that he didn't need to go and get married. Now they had *another* baby on the way. How could he possibly be focused on his career with a whole family to think about?

I'll tell you who wasn't upset about it…Jericho. He and Marie thought that Duane and Asia could do no wrong. When Duane called and told me that they were in town, I dropped by. When Asia saw me standing at the door I could tell that she didn't know what to expect. But Jericho, Marie and I made our peace a long time ago. Now Marie and I were nowhere near friends, as in buddy-buddy, but shortly after she and Jericho were married I called her and put it all out in the open. Everything from me lying to Jericho to my parents making me take him to court…everything.

It was not easy for me to talk to her because I didn't know if she would hang up in my face like Jericho's father did. But for Duane's sake, I told her that I was sorry for all the pain that Jericho and his family went through because of me. And I told her that I had *no* intentions on causing her any trouble. So since she was Jericho's wife, I asked Marie if the three of us could get along for Duane's sake. At that time I was so broken that *I* needed things to go right for my own sake as well. I am so grateful to her for not hanging up that phone. And for *really* listening to me. She told me that Jericho was being pressured by his parents not to have anything to do with me or Duane. But with her help, Jericho became more involved in Duane's life. From that point on the three of us decided that we were going to raise Duane in love and without the stress. Marie already had a daughter, Kimmy, from a previous relationship but she also treated Duane like he was her own son. So from that point we've always kept the lines of communications open.

The first night Jericho and Marie came into town, we all had dinner at Duane and Asia's together. Afterwards we played cards, drank spirits and smoked in the conservatory, laughed, talked and caught up on old times. There was no strife between us.

When we stepped into Zigna's office, she had fresh pastries, muffins, coffee and juice all set up in the center of the long oval conference table. Zigna greeted us all with a smile. She was in her mid forties, short of five feet even and stocky. She had this naturally curly hair that was bleached blond and cut short to her neck. She had big eyes, chubby cheeks and heavily pored skin.

Her office was a reflection of her successful career. It was large with two enormous windows that connected in the corner, which gave a view of both the western and northern landscape of the Plainsboro Executive Campus. I remember when Duane and I first walked up in here during his senior year of college. That was when I knew we were in the big leagues.

"Glad everyone could make it," Zigna smiled standing at her office door. Asia put her hand out for a shake, but Zigna pulled her forward giving Asia a hug. "Finally. You're just as pretty as I pictured you."

"Thank you Zigna. And it's nice to finally put a face to your voice too." Asia smiled.

Zigna chuckled, "Why don't we all take our seats and get started. I took the liberty of ordering up some breakfast from downstairs." Zigna sat at the head of the table as Duane pulled out Asia's chair for her to sit.

While we were getting settled, Asia wasted no time in helping herself to a blueberry muffin and a glass of orange juice. Likewise, I followed her lead by reaching over and selecting a banana nut muffin with a cup of black coffee.

As Zigna poured herself a cup of regular coffee she asked, "Duane, you want anything?"

"You don't have any fruit? I'm not big on coffee or pastries."

"No, but I can call and have them bring you up some."

"That sounds good to me."

Zigna picked up the black AT&T phone in front of her and called downstairs to the cafeteria and ordered a fruit salad. "Now, to get down to business, I did some market research on the public's perception of a successful athlete and it fell into these categories here," Zigna referred to the information on the presentation pamphlets she passed out. "I have been in this line of work for twenty-five years and the rules are always changing. The best approach is to change with the times. Back in the day, professional athletes were viewed as untouchable icons, but today fans want an animal on the field, but someone they can identify with off the field. Our job is to personalize this criteria where you'll be fulfilling the fan's needs, as well as your own objectives."

As Zigna spoke I thumbed through the booklet, "This looks thorough, but what about the endorsements that we talked about over the phone last night? I don't see them in here."

"Right, these pamphlets were already completed when you brought the new leads to my attention. I have my secretary running off copies of the additions."

Asia looked at me and she seemed impressed. It was a side of me she had never seen in action before. The cafeteria worker brought Duane's fruit salad up right before Zigna's secretary came in with the copies of the proposal I found for her.

We broke for lunch at quarter to twelve, and by one o'clock we all took our seats and continued with business. "Okay, in the morning session we talked about satisfying the public's needs. Now Duane, I want to talk about the personal side. I need to know what you want. How do you want the public to perceive,

Duane "The Hitman" Cummings?"

He thought a bit then told her he wanted to bring more attention to his performance on the field. We talked about some different strategies to make that happen. Then he said he also wanted to be known as a family man. That he wanted to use his status to show the young brothahs out there to be responsible for the lives that they brought into the world and I agreed with him one hundred percent, there. But we darn sure didn't agree on too much more.

"Good. I think I have a solid vision of how you want your image to be perceived." Zigna said scribbling on a note pad. Although it was gorgeous hot day outside of Zigna's window, it was a little too cold on the inside. Sitting there in my sleeveless dress, I felt like an icicle.

"Our next area of business is to get you connected with the right endorsements. I've been calling around and receiving very nice responses. Everyone that I spoke with sees you as a positive, untapped commodity." Zigna said smiling at Duane. "I know you're going to love this. This is the endorsement that your mother brought to my attention. Power shoe line sent me an entire spiel on how they would like to give you your own, top of the line, athletic shoe deal. The endorsements off of Power alone could run in the millions. Let's look at page twenty-two of the spec that my secretary brought in."

Everyone flipped through the pages. As the afternoon sun beamed in, Asia eyes opened wide, "Now that's some serious money!"

I nodded, to remind her who made this possible. When they found out that Duane was going to be signed by the Tritons organization, a representative from Power contacted me. Power Athletics was an international corporation. I saw that as a perfect opportunity to take Duane out of the local marketing arena and launch him into worldwide recognition as their spokesperson. He had already told me how he felt about endorsing high-end merchandise, but I was hoping that seeing the figures in black-and-white would change his mind. So I pushed for Zigna to include it in today's meeting.

"Do people really make that much money?" Asia asked in disbelief.

"If Duane agrees to the terms of the contract, it could be yours."

We focused our attention on Duane, and it was plain to see that he wasn't feeling it.

"Well Duane, you're mighty quiet." Zigna coaxed, "So what do you think? Unbelievable, huh?"

"Maybe for somebody, but not for me."

"What do you mean, not for you?" I couldn't believe him! "This contract could set you up for the rest of your life."

"I ain't no pimp, and I ain't gonna be mackin' kids to be down with a sneaker that there's no way in hell they can afford. I don't want my name associated with anything that's gonna get kids jacked, or entice 'em to commit a crime to get it. Sorry, Zig, but ain't no amount of money in the world worth that." Duane waved off the idea with his hand, "As for Power, I pass."

"Stupid!" I was fed up with my son. Here I was supposed to be his manager, but he was not taking any of my suggestions into consideration. I was just wasting my time.

"Stupid? Like you ain't never hear about people getting jacked for their expensive gear?" He glared at me.

"Well, I'm proud of you, baby. It's not all about the money." Asia said to Duane and I really lost it.

"Somebody please tell me why you are even here. How are you going to sit there and tell him that it's not all about the money when you are the main one benefiting from *his* money or have you forgotten?"

"Whoa Sylvia, hold up!" Duane jumped to the edge of his chair. "Don't be taking this shit out on my wife when we already discussed high-end endorsements. You know how I feel about that shit. Zigna, I done told you the same."

"Yes, you have Duane, so maybe we should move on." Zigna said somewhat flustered by our hostile exchange, but remained in her business composure.

"Yeah let's do that." Duane looked at me sharply.

Once again I was hurt by his defiance, "You know what, I'm finished with this. It's apparent that I'm just wasting your time, and mine so I don't want any parts of this. You need to find yourself a new manager." I slid my chair from under the table, grabbed my purse and walked out of the office. I mean who was I kidding, Duane had moved on. It was then that I realized that the question wasn't what was Asia doing there, but what was I doing there.

I stood in the elevator full of people, looking straight ahead. I dared not blink because I refused to release one single tear that had formed in the rims of my eyes. When the doors opened into the lobby, people got off and onto the elevator. I walked outside of the lobby into the hot sun. As the rays soaked into my face and thawed my chilled skin, I breathed in deeply to compose myself. Pulling the pack of cigarettes from my purse, my body screamed for nicotine. Right before I lit it, Duane called my name. When I looked up he was making his way over to where I was.

"You alright?"

"I will be." With the cigarette to my mouth, I shielded the flame of my Bic lighter from the wind and puffed, blowing the white smoke from between my lips.

As Duane and I began to stroll the manicured complex, out of nowhere I said, "I'm thinking about starting a catering business." The idea of starting my own business had been rolling around in my mind for a while now. I mean, I loved to cook and I loved a good party, so why not turn my passions into cash, right?

"Stop Sylvia."

"Stop what?"

"For once in your life, stop fronting like you got it all together. This is me. Duane. You don't have to do that with me. I've watched you putting on all my life. Fooling all of the people most of the time. But you ain't fooling me...never did." Staring down at me, Duane vented like he'd wanted to get that off of his chest for awhile. And damn, I fronted so much that sometimes I didn't even know who I was. It's rough when all you want to be is yourself, but you don't know who that self is. For the world, I am whatever I need to be at that particular time.

I took a deep pull on my cigarette as I felt the big drops of tears sliding down my cheeks, because yes...I was *tired*! Emotionally, physically and spiritually drained from always being on protection mode. Protecting myself because there was no loving man to protect me; protecting Duane from everyone who was trying to take him from me; protecting his career. Now here I found myself fighting my own son's rebellion from my protection. And I was standing there feeling like the party was over and someone forgot to tell me!

"Sylvia, if you want to start a catering business that's fine and you know I'll support you. But make sure you're doing it for the right reasons and not just to run and hide from the world." That's exactly what I wanted to do run and hide in a quiet dark place and lick my wounds.

"I'm happy," my son said to me. "Asia and my kid they make me happy. I want you to be happy too...go on out there and meet a man or something."

"Meet a man huh, so you can chase him away?" Pulling my stare away from Duane I thought about Ralow.

"I'm a grown man now, Sylvia and you can stop protecting me. You did a good job raising me and you were a good mom...the best. I know you wanted me to make football my only love and since I didn't you're hurt and disappointed in me. But Sylvia, I'm done feeling guilty about that."

Duane wiped my face, wrapped me in his arms and kissed my forehead. "I need you in my life, Sylvia. You let me worry about my football career, and you just concentrate on being a mom and grandmom, alright? But more importantly, it's time for you to start concentrating on you."

We walked back into Zigna's office together and the meeting resumed. Duane agreed to endorse a sports drink, and to do a series of commercial spots for men's deodorant. Zigna also suggested that he attend local activities to rally hometown support, such as appearances at his old schools - starting with elementary all the way up through high school for question-and-answer assemblies.

"Finally for today Duane, I've got you booked for a football signing. Three thousand to be sold on the Cable Shopping Network. Your schedule is going to be booked to the teeth. But that's the price you have to pay to be *The Hitman*. You up for the challenge?" Zigna looked at him.

"I was born up for the challenge."

"Oh, one more thing," Zigna said distantly, "I thought this was a really insignificant proposal, but with you turning down a monster like Power, I'm not so sure. On page seventy-two is a line of sports clothing from a new designer named Gary Johnson. Very nice looking stuff, but since he's an unfamiliar name I'm not sure how much he's actually worth."

Turning the page, Duane took a look and was most definitely interested. The clothes were priced affordable to moderate, and the designer was an up-and-coming entrepreneur. Duane said that he liked it because he would have the chance to help someone trying to make a name for himself, plus from his address the designer was a Trentonian. "Can you get me some more information? Maybe set up a meeting here or at his shop?"

"If that's what you want." Zigna said writing herself a note, "Well that's it for today. We covered everything and I'm very pleased. If anyone has any questions or thinks of anything else, don't hesitate to call." Zigna stood.

I did have a suggestion, I wanted Zigna to schedule a follow-up meeting for three months from today so we could monitor how effective the campaigns are. But I looked at my son and knew that it was time for me to cut the umbilical cord. Him from me, and me from him.

"Oh and Zigna..." Duane said, "...maybe we should set up a meeting to find out how all these campaigns are going over with the public."

I taught him well.

DADDY'S LITTLE BABY

It was Sunday, September twelfth and we had an early home game today. When I got home from the stadium, I was chillin' on the couch in our family room underneath the glass Cathedral ceiling watching the rain as it cascaded in sheets over the roof. I was thinking about Sylvia. I knew she had what she *thought* was my best intentions in mind when she did what she did. Even though she was hurt it was best for us to separate our professional lives from our personal. I decided not to hire anyone in her place, I'd just keep in closer contact with Zigna and manage my own career. But Sylvia was right about the Tritons organizations...they were no joke and her words of warning in the beginning of the season came back to haunt me.

My first practice as a Triton was rough. It was intense from the moment Coach Maxon stepped on the field. Drill after drill after drill in the hot July sun with temperatures in the mid nineties and we were in full pads.

The established Tritons were especially tough on the new members of the team...the trade-ins and the rookies. And in this stage of my career I wasn't about all that hazing bullshit. I just wanted to come in and do my job. But they were ranting and raving about how they didn't like the Mavericks and how theirs wasn't a soft-ass second-rate team. *We eat Mavericks for dinner. You're a Triton now boy. Let's see what you got. Is that the fastest you can run? When I catch up to you I'm gonna grab you and ram you a new ass hole. I'm the big bad Cheese. You better be scared of me boy. I'm your worse nightmare*

I beat my chest back and yelled, "Well I'm dropping the soap muthah fuckah. Come and get it!"

QB dropped back and passed me the ball. Pal LaLakie a.k.a. Big Cheese was from Hawaii. He was this three hundred fifty pound lineman, and the rest of his defensive crew was headed straight for me. Running, I stopped on a dime maneuvering myself then blasted through them for a first down.

That first day I had to come through the door letting them know I was someone to be reckoned with! Getting up from the ground, I turned around in Big Cheese's face, hyped, "I'm The Hitman, muthah fuckah, believe that!"

All practice long I was earning my respect as a Triton, and it wasn't easy. Face to face, word for word, hand to hand, scuffling in the trenches. Down and dirty, intense football was nothing new to me but I had never practiced at that magnitude. Those players were flat out ignorant. And forget all that superstar shit, 'cause they didn't give a fuck who I was.

And the pressure was on! I had been watching the local news stations and reading the sports columns and everyone had their eyes on me to produce big this season. *Cummings to have his best year yet!* It was scary because everyone was saying since I was signed to one of the best teams in the PFL that the Tritons were *expected* to get back to the Champion Bowl.

For the first couple weeks I was mad disappointed in my performance. My mind started fucking with me as I wondered if I was only good because the Mavericks *were* a second rate team and I was the coach's pet, or if I *actually* had what it took? Then I started thinking about all that *have confidence in me* stuff I was telling Asia, and just hoped that I could get myself together and start to produce.

But after the culture shock of the rugged Tritons routine wore off, and seeing a fuller picture of the *true* dedication of Coach Maxon, the team and the offensive training staff, I started to feel more loose, relaxed and like myself on the field. When I got a feel for everyone's timing and playing style, and after I learned the plays, my game started to jell. The hardest part was weathering the adjustment period. While I was going through, it was hell 'cause I couldn't get the pieces to come together. It messed with my mind, my confidence, my *manhood!* But when I mastered all that shit that had me down, I came out strong. And once again I was in my zone!

***

Dressed only in my black boxer brief underwear, I was seated in my usual position on the couch with one leg propped up against the back and my other foot on the floor. Asia was sitting between my legs wearing a silk nightshirt that was unbuttoned to her navel as she breastfed our two-week old son, Duane Cummings, Junior or DJ as we call him.

I was sore and tired from the game earlier that day, but Asia wanted us to go to church for the seven o'clock service. It was important to her, so I was with it. Between practices, games and all of the promotional gigs Zigna had me assigned to I was on the go seven days a week. Some days I'd pull a sixteen-hour workday, leaving the house at six in the morning not getting home until nine – ten o'clock at night. As hard as that shit was for me, I knew it was hard on Asia too.

Her minister was cool, though. I actually enjoyed going to church with her. He was one of those new school preachers, who was more about teaching than preaching and I dug that. Asia wanted me to join the church, but I let her know that she had to ease up on all that. Told her that issue was between God and me. For now, I was satisfied just going with her and the kids. "We make some pretty babies," I boasted stroking DJ's head, full of thick black hair. Now this kid looked like me, definitely had my nose and he was a long baby so I knew he'd be tall like me.

"We sure do," Asia agreed. As she switched the baby to her right breast, milk continued to drain from her left. "Hand me one of those pads from off of the table, Baby. Please."

I ran my finger across her nipple and put the watery milk on the tip of my tongue, "I can see why babies don't want to go to the bottle. This stuff is sweet."

"You want a glass full?" She looked at me with a teasing smile.

"And you'd be surprised if I said yeah, wouldn't you?" I squeezed her breast and the milk squirted across the room, "Daymn!" I laughed and she slapped my hand.

"I'm not cleaning that up...Come on Duane, give me the pad. It's getting messy over here."

We all wondered how Epiphany would adjust to the baby. After all, at seventeen months old she was spoiled rotten. But I had to give it to her, Asia warned everyone not to give DJ more attention than they gave Epiphany. To get Piff Piff involved, Asia would let her help out by getting DJ's diapers or the powder and Asia would praise her for doing a good job.

Epiphany loved to kiss the baby and feel his hands and legs. We had to watch her though, because we didn't want her to touch DJ's soft spot on the top of his head. Piff Piff was amazed by his small, wide eyes. When they were open, she would say "babee eyes" and try to poke them. She really loved her little brother, but love wasn't enough to make her give up her spot with me, though.

It was almost like Epiphany understood that DJ needed Asia, but she got touchy when it came to me, and hey...I wasn't mad at her.

When I gave Asia the Wet Wipe and a nursing pad, she cleaned herself up as DJ continued to nurse. He was just *like* a man...ate then fell right to sleep. Asia handed the baby to me and I put him on top of my bare chest and I stretched out on the couch watching the news. DJ was curled up on his knees with his little diapered butt sticking up. He reminded me of a snail. Asia had him smelling all good.

Couple minutes later I overheard her in the kitchen talking with Epiphany who was sitting at the kitchen table eating. I wasn't really paying them that much attention because I was watching TV but when Asia asked her for the second time what was wrong, that made me tune in.

"Nuffing," Epiphany answered in her little squeaky voice.

"You don't feel well, you sick?" Asia left the sink where she had been washing dishes and went over to feel Piff Piff's little forehead.

"Nuffing," she said again.

"What's wrong with you, girl?" I asked but this time she wouldn't say anything.

Asia continued to pry, "You mad at mommy?" Epiphany shook her head no. Then Asia asked, "You mad at daddy?" And Epiphany dropped her head and wouldn't speak. "Ooh Duane, this child is upset with you."

"Piff Piff, come here, girl."

She slowly climbed down off of the chair and walked over to me, leaving a trail of tears along the way.

"Why you mad at Daddy? Look at me." I had one hand around DJ and the other lifting Epiphany's little chin. Her eyes were big and glassy.

"Nuffing," she repeated.

Then it must have dawned on Asia. She walked over to me, and I was still without a clue, "I bet I know what it is." Asia stooped and picked DJ up then she looked at Epiphany. "Daddy got DJ in your spot?"

I had to laugh cause it was the sweetest thing. Ever since Epiphany was an infant I'd let her sleep on my chest. Made me feel close to her, but I never knew that she thought it was anything special. But now I do, "This your chest Piff Piff?" Reaching over, I lifted her, laying her on top of my chest. Epiphany snuggled in place rubbing her hands across my pecks. She was sniffling trying to stop crying. "This is daddy's baby girl. You don't have to cry. Daddy love you, okay?" I cooed Epiphany, rubbing her little back. Asia sat in the opposite chair holding DJ patting him back to sleep as she watched me and Epiphany together. As I comforted my daughter, I winked my eye at Asia, loving my place as husband and father. *This* was that old-fashioned love I had been looking for.

STACY T

I hadn't seen my boy, Tompy, in a while. Ever since I moved back to Trenton, life's been hectic. Trying to get my marriage back on track, getting adjusted to being on my new team, finding time for my kids, and fulfilling the obligations of the New Image Campaign had left me with absolutely no free time. I made a special effort to spend some time with my boy today though, which required effort on both our parts because he had to take a day-off from work to hook-up with me.

About a month ago I was driving down the New Jersey Turnpike to practice with the radio blasting. The music was sounding good when the disc jockey came on, "WMSJ! Stacy T on your radio dial. Good morning Jersey. Today's topic for the ladies. Who's got the hottest bod!? Did y'all see that game last night? Ooo we! Did Duane Cummings have his backfield in motion or what? Give me a call and tell me if you saw what I saw. That brothah is tight!"

My eyebrows sprang up in the air, as I listened in.

"Go ahead caller, you're on the air with Stacy T, talk to me."

A woman got on the phone screaming, "Hey Stacy. And yes, I saw that game last night and "The Hitman" definitely got it goin' on, you know what I'm sayin'? He can hit this any time!"

I had to laugh.

Stacy started cracking up, "Alright, let's keep this clean. This is a family show...but just for the record, he has to hit this first." She cracked up, "Next caller, who's on the line with Stacy T?"

"What's up Stacy? This is Branda from T town. What's up Trenton! I saw that game too, and I don't even like football, right. My brothers were watching the game last night and when I saw "The Hitman" make that touchdown and do his end zone dance. He ran right into my heart. He is so fine!" The caller screamed.

Then Stacey T called me out, "If you're listening out there Hitman, I want you anytime, anywhere, anyplace. But since we all know you're *happily married,* I'll settle for you being on my show. Ring me up!"

Stacy T was *wild.* I can't lie though. I did wonder how she looked. When I got to practice that morning, everyone was talking about Stacy T's morning show. Then I got a call from Zigna saying the PR person from WMSJ called to see if she could arrange an on-air interview. With all of the promotional gig's Zigna already had me booked for, I was lucky if I had time to sleep, let alone accept an unplanned interview. But after weeks of hype, everyone within radio frequency knew Stacy T was in love with Duane "The Hitman" Cummings. She was relentless and would not take no for an answer! Stacy T started this campaign involving the callers to get me on the show and by popular demand Tompy and I were on the Jersey Turnpike driving to the station.

It was a gray October morning and the rain was coming down like mist. Tompy had his big cup of Dunkachino up to his mouth. "Duane, man, you remember me telling you a couple of months ago that I put in for a promotion at Millennium."

"Yeah?" I bit into my breakfast sandwich then flipped on my intermittent wipers with the same hand.

"Out of seven candidates for the position they chose me. Damn, man, I feel so high!" He stretched his arms like if he were flying.

I stuck my fist out for a pound. "Hey, what can I say. I'm proud of you man."

"Damn straight, boy. I'm proud of myself." Tompy was just as tall as me and damn near as big. He was a Morehouse man and a damn workaholic. We both strive for perfection, but I took the path of athletics and Tompy took to the corporate life.

"Didn't you mention that if you got the job you would have to move to

Atlanta?"

"Hot Lanta GA!" Tompy yelped in a deep voice. "Check it out, I'm gonna be heading up my own unit down there. Me, man, Tompy Seagrams, Manager, large and in-charge." With this self-satisfied glare he dug his sandwich out of the Dunkin Donuts bag.

Tompy was like my brother, and I looked forward to reconnecting the bond that got put on ice, when I moved to Arizona. "Dag Tompy, it took me five years to come home, now that I'm home, you're moving away. I don't know how I feel about that."

"You'll feel like I felt when you moved to Arizona, like a part of you is missing, then you'll adjust."

Checking my review and passenger side mirror, I had to jump two lanes because I almost missed my exit. Tompy was cool, and didn't say anything. If that had been Asia, she would have been going off 'bout now. Rolling down the off ramp, I redirected my attention back to our conversation, "Well maybe while you're out there one of those fine ass southern gals'll lock you down."

"Not me man, I'm a bachelor for life. I needs my freedom."

"You sick man," I looked at Tompy laughing, "You don't know what you're missing."

From his breast pocket, Tompy pulled out his little black book and held it up for me to see, "Naw, my brothah, you don't know what you're missin'."

"So how long you got before you move?"

"It's October now and they were going to give me until after the Christmas holidays. But I told them all I need is a couple of weeks to fly down, and find a place and I'm out. So I should be out of here maybe in the next three weeks, four max."

Sticking my fist out, I offered up another pound, "I'ma miss you man."

"Dig it, I'm only a two hour plane ride, or phone call away. And besides, when the Tritons come to Atlanta, I'ma be all up in the house."

"You got that right dawg, you better be."

It was seven forty-five when we strolled into the Newark, New Jersey radio station. Stacy T was on the mic so we didn't get a chance to meet before the show. We went into the room facing Stacy T's studio and a glass separated us while the station people fitted us with headsets and microphones.

"Oh my God. Ladies, he's here. And what a sight to behold! He's just as fine in person as he is on TV and he's wearing his trademark Kangol. The color for today is white. His friend ain't bad either. What's up fellahs?"

I laughed at her outrageous personality, which seemed even more animated in person. She spoke whatever was on her mind. Tompy was enjoying himself, and I could tell, by the way he was trying to get his mack on, that he thought Stacy T as in Torez was the bomb. And yeah, she was fine. Tanned skin, pretty big eyes and black wavy hair, in a ponytail that hung past her waist. Stacy T had that bad girl, sexy thang going on and I bet she could back up the image she projected.

I was dressed in a pair of blue jeans, leather shoes with a belt to match, a blue and beige long sleeve shirt and a jean jacket and of course my Kangol turned backwards. We said our what ups to Stacy T and she started asking me the usual questions like how does it feel to be back home playing for the Tritons, among other things, then she opened the mic up to the callers.

Towards the end of the show she asked Tompy a few questions, then Stacy T *went there* and asked me if she could have my Kangol. My dad was the one who started me wearing those hats. Ever since I was a kid, he wore Kangol's. At age fifteen, I went to stay with him for my two-weeks during the summer and he let me have his white one. It was like this big deal to me because it was his favorite, which also turned out to be the one I was wearing that day. The hat was old as sin, but I took good care of it. I wore Kangol's because I like the way they look on me, but especially because they reminded me of my dad. But the public got a hold of it and kind of made it my trademark.

"Usually, after I'm finished loving a man, I'll ask him for his tee shirt so I could savor the memories." Stacy T laughed seductively, "You ever do that ladies? But since I can't go there, Hitman, can I have one of your famous Kangol hats?"

She put me on the spot, "Aww, babe this is my lucky hat."

"Come on Hitman, you gonna turn me down while my entire audience is listening?" Stacy begged in her womanly whine.

Contemplating it, I took off my hat and looked at it, "Naw, I can't part with it." Then I began unbuttoning my shirt and Stacy T's eyes got big and she let out a hoot.

"But I'll let you have my t-shirt." I finished unbuttoning my shirt and removed it along with the jacket.

"Stacy T hollered, "Oh my God! I wish this was television, The Hitman is taking off his shirt!"

Pulling the tee shirt over my head, my body was swollen like I had just finished working out. Everything was bulging, biceps, pectorals, and rippled abs, all wrapped up in midnight black skin and Stacy T was freaking *out*!

"Mandingo!" She yelled laughing, "Oh boy it's getting hot in here. That body! How much do you press?"

"Four-fitty," I boasted, balling my fist to my shoulder, popping a double bubble biceps for her.

"Well I only weigh one-thirty." Stacy T laughed, blushing herself silly. Tears were coming out of her eyes, "For all you women out there, if you were curious, The Hitman has an outy. And it's the cutest little thang you'd ever want to see."

I cracked up as I handed the t-shirt to one of the workers who ran it around to Stacy T. She continued to holler then she grabbed the shirt and put it up to her nose. Everyone in the studio was cracking up.

"Oh ladies, this is a smell to die for. What kind of cologne are you wearing?"

"Cool Water," I blushed as I put my clothes back on. "And to clarify, the *cute little thang* Stacy was talking about is my navel." I laughed, "I can't let nobody think the wrong thang, now. I have my rep to protect."

Everyone laughed.

"Don't worry, baby. We all know you packin' a load." Stacy T let her eyes deliberately fall on my crotch and couldn't take her eyes off of me. "On the real, though, Mrs. Cummings, you go girl. You have to be a heck of a woman to keep all this man satisfied. Thanks for letting me borrow your man this morning so I could have my way with him. And that does it for me today. I'll like to thank my special guest Duane "The Hitman" Cummings for blessing us with his company this morning and to his friend Tompy Seagrams. As for me I'm going straight home so I can slip into my new tee shirt. Until we meet again on WMSJ on your FM dial. I'm Stacy T and I'm out."

After the program, she turned off the mic and Tompy and I took off our headphones and went into Stacy T's studio. Stacy gave me a big hug like she knew me all of her life and kissed me smack dab on the lips. She had this big gym bag and started pulling out her "Duane The Hitman" memorabilia for me to autograph. Tompy was looking at Stacy like she was a tasty morsel. He was trying to push up on her, but she was all into me.

When I got home that afternoon, I asked Asia if she listened to the radio show. All she did was point to the stereo, "I taped it for you."

"Well what did you think?" I had to ask because she wasn't saying much and I was real curious. Asia really didn't listen to the radio all that much. Only when she was in the car or when I had it on would she actually listen, so when I was explaining to her about the Stacy T show she gave me the raised eyebrow look.

Asia walked up to me, hung her arms around my waist and said, "You're her dream, but you're my reality and as long as it stays like that I don't have a problem."

Yeah, that's my lady!

STOLEN MOMENT

Four o'clock in the morning, and it was pitch black in the room. I got out of bed and turned the buzzing alarm off. Asia woke up propping herself up on her elbows, "Duane, you don't have practice this morning."

"Yes I do babe, it's Wednesday." I thought maybe she was thinking today was Tuesday, the PFL's day off.

"I fell asleep last night before you got out of the shower and didn't get a chance to tell you. You got a call and the morning practice was canceled. They said to show up at two this afternoon."

I walked over and sat on the edge of the bed next to Asia. I bent over to kiss her on the forehead, "That's cool. I'm gonna go out for my run anyway since I'm up."

"Duane," Asia grabbed my arm just as I started to get up. "The kids are asleep, and we haven't spent any quality time alone in awhile. How about you cancel that run this morning, and you and I do something special?" She stroked my arm with her fingertips.

"Like what?"

"I've been so busy being mommy and taking care of everyone else, now Mommy needs Daddy to take care of her. Is that possible?"

The sound of her voice and the way she stroked my arm gave me an instant hard on. Leaning over kissing her lips, I was getting ready to take care of her, alright.

"Just a minute." Asia pushed me up, "I have something else in mind."

Sitting there with a full-grown erection, I stared strangely at her as she got out of the bed.

"I'll call you when I'm ready."

Asia went into the bathroom and closed the door. I leaned back in the bed stroking my nine inches with my eyes closed. I must have dozed off, 'cause I was awakened by Asia's voice calling my name. I got up and walked in the dark towards the bathroom. When I opened the door I was greeted by the flickering glow of candlelight. Asia had lit four candlesticks and placed them in their own wax along our marble double sink. The reflections of the candles in the mirror did the dance of seduction as my wife waited in the sunken Jacuzzi surrounded by bubbles. Visible only from her brown shoulders up, she looked so good I just had to stand there and check her out. The room smelled like wild jasmine.

"Are you gonna join me?" She smiled like she was enjoying the way I looked at her.

Stepping out of my draws I got into the warm water with Asia. She repositioned herself between my legs leaning her head back onto my shoulder.

"This is beautiful baby," I was loving the atmosphere she'd created.

"Thank you I'm glad you like it." She said softly. "Just a few candles."

We sat there in each other's arms talking about things going on in our lives, the family, what we were going to do today, where we wanted to go for vacation after the season was over, everything. I also talked to her about us becoming investors with the Gary Johnson sports clothing line.

In just a short couple of months of me wearing his clothes, Gary was getting all kinds of request for his merchandise. We were talking and he needed to get out of his storefront clothing mill and into a larger facility where he would be able to hire more employees to keep up with the demand. Asia thought it was a good idea and suggested that I call Tom Lester, my financial advisor to do some additional analysis.

Quality time was *hold me and let's communicate with each other* time. No sex time. Asia established that rule because she said I was mistaking intercourse for communication.

"This felt so good just being in your arms and talking Lovah. Thank you." She stepped out and grabbed a towel off of the rack.

As I stepped out and sat on the closed toilet drying myself, Asia grabbed my towel and pulled it away and let hers drop to the marble floor. "Girl, what's up with you?" I grimaced trying to stick to the rules.

"I'm not finished with you yet." Asia grabbed a small bottle of body oil from off the sink.

"Now that's what I'm talkin' 'bout." I said opening my legs ready to get busy, "Well come on then."

Asia took the bottle and held it over me. She dripped the oil drop by drop over my shoulders, down my back and all over my lap, and I was really diggin' it. She then stepped away from me into the candlelight holding the bottle so that the oil dripped down her neck, sliding between her breasts, down her stomach. She kept dripping it until it ran down past her navel and disappeared into her hairy bush. My heart was racing and I couldn't believe my conservative wife was doing this. Asia dropped the plastic bottle onto the tub squeezing her breasts as the oil seeped through her fingers. Slowly she ran her hands down her stomach, and up under her neck then teasingly between her legs. The candlelight glistened off of her greasy body. I lustfully watched thoroughly enjoying the seduction. With my fist gripped tightly around my nine I pumped it up and down. Asia continued rubbing, stroking and fondling her body, giving me an eyeful. At first she was putting on a show to get me hot, but I know my baby's noises. She started really getting off and I was loving it!

"Damn, Baby, ump. That shit is beautiful!" I couldn't take my eyes off of her, then we both started climaxing! That was a first for the both of us.

But still hungry for more, Asia straddled across my lap facing me. I gripped her soft behind and the friction from her rocking on me sent shock waves through my body. She moaned sucking and biting on my neck pumping harder. Once again I was ready for round two and Asia started riding me, grabbing at my shoulders and back, screaming, "Fuck me!"

Shit, I was *completely* turned on! Holding her tight, I gave it to her fast and strong until we fell limp in each other's arms. We held each other in a tight embrace, trying to catch our breath as we both floated back down to earth.

"I love you so much, Duane." Asia kissed me on the neck with what strength she had left then let her head rest on my shoulder.

"Love you too, girl." I said wiping the stinging sweat out of my eyes.

We got into the shower together taking turns washing each other's body. I took a towel and went into the bedroom. Asia blew out the candles and followed me. I had dried myself off then stretched naked across the bed. Asia turned on the light then dried herself off.

"Shit, girl. I think coach needs to cancel more practices. You blew my mind, I swear," I said looking at Asia in amazement.

She smiled, "Baby I be missin' you. It's not easy for me during the season to only see you for minutes during the day. I just wanted to make up for a little lost time."

"And that you did, Mama." I turned over on my stomach wrapping my arms snugly around the pillow. "I'm going back to sleep, catch me a couple more winks. You done wore me ite, girl!"

Asia laughed as she continued to lotion her body. She then dressed in a short white cotton nighty with a matching robe, and slipped her feet into her slippers.

"Duane, I'm thinking about pancakes for breakfast. How does that sound to you?"

"Sounds great babe, just wake me up when they're done." I was already half asleep.

"I'll do you one better. I'll bring them up to you."

Asia turned out the light and closed the door.

I had to be sleeping like twenty minutes when Asia's shrieking screams startled me awake. It was that kind of scream that you didn't answer with the question, *what*? It was that terrifying kind of scream that you never ever in your life wanted to hear. I jumped out of bed in a slumberous fog following the steady scream right into Piff Piff's room. Asia was bent over the bed shaking Epiphany. "Wake up baby." Not realizing that I was right behind her, Asia screamed out once again, "Duane! Duane!"

"What is it?!"

"Something's wrong with Epiphany!"

I still wasn't sure what she was talking about, but when I stepped in front of Asia and saw my daughter's face, the warm blood that ran through my veins felt like ice water.

Piff Piff had turned gray. It was obvious that she had stopped breathing. In high school I took a CPR class, but that was years ago and I had never performed it on anyone before. I grabbed my daughter off of the bed then put her on the floor. Tilting her head back, I pinched her little nose and blew air into her tiny mouth trying to resuscitate her but it wasn't working!

"Call 9-1-1!" I yelled out to Asia who was standing there trembling. "Asia!" Paralyzed with fear, she couldn't move. Hamilton Hospital was less than three blocks away, so I knew I could get Epiphany there faster than the ambulance could get here. I threw on a pair of trousers over my naked body, slid on my slippers and ran back into Piff Piff's room. I was trying hard not to lose my damn mind! I had to hold it together at least until I got her some help.

Asia was kneeling on the floor crying, cuddling her eighteen-month-old. I grabbed the comforter from off the bed, and almost had to pry Piff Piff from Asia's grip. Wrapping Epiphany in the blanket, I ran with her in my arms. From all the way downstairs I could hear Asia screaming for God's help.

By the time the garage door opened, I backed that Porsche out, doing forty miles per hour, then eighty all the way through the quiet residential neighborhood. Through the frosty October morning, I ran red lights, honking my horn and flashing the headlights all the way to the hospital. It wasn't quite seven o'clock yet, but already there was a light flow of traffic and a garbage truck was circling the street.

When I pulled in front of the emergency room, I put the car in neutral, jumped out, keys still in the ignition with the engine going, and ran inside with Epiphany, "Help me! Help me please! Help me!"

A nurse ran up to me, "What is it?"

"My baby! She's not breathing."

"Follow me!"

The both of us ran threw the swinging doors, yelling and they put Epiphany on a stretcher. Bare-chested, with my pants hanging off of my naked hips, I watched in horror as the doctors tried to revive my baby but she was just lying there not responding. "Please! Please!" I begged, "Wake up, goddammit!" I yelled, leaning over the doctor's shoulder as my fear turned to panic. And out of desperation I began to lose it, "Epiphany!" One of the emergency room nurses tried to assist me into the waiting area, but I shoved her to the side. "Epiphany!" I just knew if I called her she'd wake up for me, "Epiphany!" But the nurse pulled back, saying the doctors needed to be able to concentrate on my daughter and they couldn't do that with me in the room, so reluctantly I left.

Didn't even seem like five minutes later when the doctor who'd been working on my daughter came out. He placed his hand on my shoulder, "I'm sorry. We did all that we could. We just couldn't save her."

It took a few seconds, then the reality hit home. My baby was dead. Before I could even move, vomit poured from my mouth. Its rush burned my throat and the insides of my nostrils. I couldn't fucking breathe. An implosion of pain ripped through my body as I leaned over gasping for air. The vomit splattered on the floor, my arms were clasped around my head, and I cried hysterically as everything around me spun out of control. This shit just didn't make *any* sense! How?! Why?!

My mind went into a whole 'nother zone and it was like I either couldn't comprehend what was going on, or I was trying really hard not to believe it. I played with her and kissed her goodnight last night…now she's dead?! She was a healthy baby, she didn't even have a cold…nothing! No more holding her, and watching her grow. No more sweet kisses from that little mouth and no more squeaky little voice calling for her daddy. My little friend! My seed! Gone!

I was choked up. Only thing I could think of was to call Sylvia. I didn't tell her the whole story, just that Epiphany was sick. But I told her to call everyone and have them meet at my house, and *whatever* they had to do, *not* to let Asia use the phone or leave the house. Sylvia was freaking out over the phone wondering what was happening. Even though she didn't know that Epiphany was dead, she knew it was bad!

As I left out the hospital, the security guard handed me my keys and told me that they had moved my car to the lot around the corner. During the three-block walk, the October morning air was extremely cold on my bare skin. I was surprised that I could feel anything.

I just drove and drove, trying to get a grip before I had to confront my wife. I was still trying to digest what had happened myself! By the time that deep veiled fog somewhat lifted from my head, I was on Route 295 South, in Delaware just *driving*! Thoughts of Epiphany were all in my brain. Watching Asia push her into the world... I had never seen anything like that before and it was beautiful 'cause she was mine. I spotted an eighteen-wheeler about a hundred yards ahead of me. At a quarter-to-ten in the morning the highway was congested but sixty-five miles per hour was the flow. Seventy-eighty-eighty-five, I floored it weaving in and out of the lanes, trying to catch up with the truck.

It's a girl! Here dad, you get the honors of cutting the cord.

CLIP!

Waaa! Waaa! Waaa!

Thank you, Asia. Thank you for giving me my baby. The more I thought about Epiphany, my insides felt like they were swelling, ready to explode. The pressure was heavy. Using the back of my hand I wiped away the tears that had shattered my vision.

Driving up along side of the dirty white cab of the truck, I floored that Porsche then ripped the steering wheel to the right two car lengths ahead with nothing in between me and the truck but four seconds of space! *Give daddy kiss, Piff Piff... This daddy baby... Come on. Come on to daddy. Asia you missing it! She's walking! Get the camera!*

I lifted my foot off of the accelerator and slammed on the brakes and I heard the blare of the trucks horn. Count down: four—I just wanted to be crushed into nothingness along with the damn void that I had fallen into. Three—My mind flashed to Asia having to deal with Epiphany's death and with mine too. Her having to tell my son, that I took the easy way out. Two—I love them too much and I couldn't put her through that.

I ripped the wheel to the right jumping that Porsche into the next lane and the car to my right had to jump to the shoulder of the road to make room for me. One- The blare of the horns faded as the truck and the other car continued to speed up the highway as something even stronger inside of me told me to get off the highway and *pull over!* I wasn't much of a praying man, but I knew I needed help getting home in one piece.

When I finally got home four hours later, everyone's cars were there. Sylvia was standing outside smoking when I pulled up to the house. "Thank God you're here! Asia's going crazy in there and who can blame her, Duane! What's happening with Epiphany? When I called up to the hospital they said you left instructions not to give out any information. Daddy drove up there, and they *still* wouldn't give him any information!"

I was biting down on the side of my lip trying to keep myself composed because I could only tell the story once. I continued to walk into my house without answering her question and I knew I looked like shit.

"How's Epiphany?! I was waiting for you to come get me! What took you so long?!" Asia screamed. She looked even worse than I felt.

I looked at my Gramps who remained seated, then at Terry and Sylvia.

Wrenching my hands together, I walked over to my wife searching for the words. "She's in a better place now Asia." My eyes were fixed on her confused face.

"What better place? Where's Epiphany?"

"She's in heaven, baby."

"Heaven? Wha…no."

Whoever was standing behind me started crying.

"Baby, she's dead. The doctor said that she must have passed away sometime last night."

Then I heard someone shout, "Oh my God!"

"No, I checked on her last night, Duane! I check on them every night!" Asia stomped her feet throwing my arms in the air. My heart surged with adrenaline and my muscles started to spasm.

"Well, this morning then." I reached out to comfort her but she pushed me in the chest away from her.

"No! No!" she began to yell, "I want to see her! She needs me!"

"No, Asia, she's..."

"Where's my baby?!" She screamed.

"Asia, she's gone," I stretched my arms out to comfort her and once again she rejected me.

"No, you're lying!"

"Asia?" I stood there needing to hold her, needing her to hold me. Everyone in the room was crying. I needed Asia's arms around me 'cause I didn't know if I could get through this but instead Asia stormed upstairs to our bedroom and locked herself inside. I ran behind her banging on the door because besides needing her, I wanted to make sure that she was alright. When she wouldn't open it I began to kick it down. Gramps, who was standing at the top of the stairs, called to me. He said to give Asia some time.

Half an hour later Asia had still not come out of the room and that was making me bug even more. I needed to know what she was thinking…what she was doing. I had also been trying to contact Asia's parents, but they weren't home. I guess Pops must have had a doctor's appointment today or something. I left several messages for them to call soon as they got in.

My boy Tompy left his job and came right over after he got my call. I was in the kitchen, sitting at the table with Sylvia, Terry and Gramps. Gran was standing at the sink feeding DJ a bottle. We had to start making funeral arrangements but Piff Piff's body was still at the hospital's morgue. I was waiting for their call to give us the results of the autopsy. I didn't know what to do next. I couldn't think straight! Sylvia had her head down on the table. She couldn't stop crying. Terry rubbed her back trying to comfort her.

Tompy had gotten up to go to the bathroom, when I heard him yell into the kitchen, "Duane! Asia just ran out of the house!"

I jumped out of the chair nearly turning it over on Gran who was standing behind me. The tone of his voice meant that I needed to run. By the time I got out the door, I saw that Asia was in her bare feet, running full speed making her way down Honey Dew Lane and it was cold as shit outside.

I took off behind her, and I mean I was high stepping like I was on the football field. But even though I was running hard I still had to do a bit of hustling to catch up with her. I grabbed Asia by the arm and was able to restrain her as she struggled to break free. Then she got hysterical on me.

It was like forty degrees and hardly no one was outside. Just an old man walking his dog. He stopped to see what all the commotion was about.

"Come on back to the house. Asia, come on baby. Let's go back to the house," I was trying to guide her back down the street but Asia doubled over screaming and screaming with all of her might.

"Asia." Emotions rocked deep inside of me, "Come on baby, let's go home."

"Epiphanyyyy!" Asia screamed.

Terry and Tompy came running down the street to see if they could help out.

"Duane! Duane!" Asia continued to scream.

"I'm here baby," I said holding on to her. "Let's just go back to the house."

"Epiphany! Oh God, oh God. Nooo, not my baby. Nooo!" Asia continued to scream. I stood there holding her as tears flooded my own eyes. I wanted to help her. I wanted to give Asia her child back because no mother should have to go through this kind of pain. Then just like someone turned off the lights, she collapsed.

As Asia was going down I caught her then carried her to the house where we called the ambulance. She regained consciousness by the time they arrived, but she couldn't talk. She was in shock. At the hospital they gave her a prescription for tranquilizers to calm her down and make her sleep. Standing there at her hospital bed my only thoughts were, *Why God? Why have you forsaken us?*

Once the word got out, our home turned into a mad house. Florists, reporters and well-wishers, just everybody ringing the doorbell and stopping by. Zigna also stopped by the house in the midst of all the confusion and advised me to select two reporters and give them a short interview to thank my fans for their support. And have them send their money to an organization or charitable cause. I agreed. Zigna got on the phone and called the channel five news station, since it had the contract to cover the Tritons organization. We selected Michael Weddell for an exclusive in-home interview. Then she called WMSJ and asked for a number to get in touch with Stacy T to set up an interview. Michael and his cameraman were there within minutes. Sylvia and Zigna joined Michael and me in the formal living room and closed the door from all of the noise. I composed myself and gave a fifteen-minute interview.

"Michael, I want to thank you for allowing me to speak on this a very sad day for me and my family. I would like to thank everyone for their concern, sympathy and prayers for my family and me in our time of bereavement. My wife and I are holding up the best we can, given the circumstances. We ask that instead of the public sending us flowers and cards, which are all very much appreciated, to please send your donations to the Webster Avenue soup kitchen in our daughter's memory."

The next morning I called the Stacy T radio show at nine o'clock and was patched right in to her and we spoke on the air. She had callers call in and express their sympathy. I was moved. The interview lasted about seven minutes.

HOW LOW CAN YOU GO?

"Asia? Asia? Wake Up!"

As I slept I heard Duane walking heavily into the bedroom. He called for me to wake up, but I couldn't. My spirit, my will, my desire to do anything but lay there in a state of unconsciousness kept me still and unable to respond. I was lost! Internally, I was so lost trying to figure out why my baby had to die so suddenly, without warning. SIDS was the only explanation I got… Sudden Infant Death Syndrome.

I didn't know how to pull the pieces back together again. Seemed like everyone else had found a way to cope. Here it was a month and a half later and Duane had gone back to work, yet I couldn't even get through a couple hours if I wasn't totally medicated.

I tried, oh yes I did! Prayed about it. Told myself, *Okay, Asia. Today we're going to get up, get dressed and start cleaning this house. Then we're going to go out and maybe take a walk, or a drive… something.* Then I'd ask myself, why… for what? I could have driven from here to the ends of the earth and nothing would have brought my child back to life! My baby was dead and my soul was lost! As long as I stayed unconscious, I didn't have to deal with it.

I felt the covers being snatched away from my body and Duane's heavy hand slapping me roughly across the face. The violent sensation caused me to lose my breath and my heart pounded triple time against my chest.

"Get up right now, Asia!" He grabbed me by the arm and began to pull me out of bed.

My head started to throb and my body felt weighed down. It was that same kind of weight like when gravity kicks in as you step out of a pool of water.

"Duane?" I hollered trying to fight him off of me, "Stop!" Then I caught a glimpse of us struggling in the dresser mirror, and I looked horrible. Like no reflection of mine that I ever saw before. I knew I had lost some weight from the lack of an appetite, but the person in that mirror looked sickly. That really caught me by surprise.

"Look at you, you gonna get yourself together!" Duane shook me as I stood to my feet. I tried to fight him off of me, but I was no match for his strength. "We still have a son that you need to be a mother to. Get yourself together, we're going to bring him home tonight, you hear me, Asia? Tonight!"

I was steady trying to push Duane off of me. Couldn't he see that I was scared?! Didn't he understand that if I couldn't protect my daughter from dying that I really shouldn't be around my son? I just wanted him to leave me alone but he *wouldn't*! "Stop!"

Duane grabbed his T-shirt that I was wearing and ripped it down the front, right off of me. He pulled me into the bathroom, turned on the shower and shoved me inside. At that point I still don't think I was fully awake. I slid down into the corner, crying out loud while the steamy water projecting out of the showerhead drenched me. When I looked up, Duane was sitting on the edge of the bed with his head in his hands.

Crystal came by and cleaned the house for us last week. Scrubbed the bathrooms, washed the dishes and all of our dirty clothes. I still couldn't bring myself to forgive her even though Duane said that I shouldn't be so hard on her. She was supposed to be Epiphany's godmother. Not only did she break the trust that I had in our friendship, she missed out on the last couple of months of Epiphany's life. I don't know if I could ever forgive her for that. So what she came over here crying talking about she was sorry for the way she acted, and so what Duane bought into her sob story. She was supposed to be my sister-friend, nothing was supposed to come between us, now I don't see how anything could put back what she took away.

After I got out the shower, Duane was gone, but he had laid out something for me to wear. As I was getting dressed, Terry came upstairs and knocked on the door, "Asia, is it alright if I come in?" She opened the door, walked in and gave me a hug, "How you feeling today?"

I sat on the bed dressed in my underclothes, "This is the hardest shit I ever had to go through in my life." Still high from the medication, I tried to act as normal as possible but I couldn't fully open my eyes. My tongue felt numb, causing my speech to slur, "I miss her so much Terry. I want to hold her and feed her. I want to give her a bath." I laughed, "You know, sometimes I can hear her calling for me. Yes I can." Late at night when I'm sleep. I'd hear her little voice saying, *ma meee, ma meee.* I'd wake up and go into her room praying that she'd be there when I opened up the door. But the worse part was I couldn't seem to shake the picture of her all dressed up in the white lace dress and baby breath flowers in her hair as her body laid in that white coffin. That whole scene just stayed in my mind. "Now my baby's dead, laying in the ground rotting away. Now you tell me, what kind of shit is that?" As I talked my head felt light and I leaned up to catch myself from falling over. Just the thought of Epiphany filled me with grief, "What did I do to deserve this?" Tears formed in my eyes and I wiped them away with my hand.

"Asia, are you still taking those tranquilizers?" Terry looked at me strangely.

I don't know why her question bothered me, but it did. I pulled up my pants, "Yeah."

"How many do you take in a day?"

"I have no idea. When I feel it wearing off, I just take another one."

"Well do you know how many you took today?

"No." I didn't and it really wasn't any of her business anyway!

"No? Asia, you don't know how many you took today? Where's the bottle?"

"Terry, please, not now alright?!" My head started to pound even harder when I yelled at her and I closed my eyes tight to stop the throbbing pain.

She didn't' say another word, just got up and went downstairs.

After I got dressed and walked down the stairs Duane blurted out, "Where're the pills?!"

Not responding to his question, I rolled my eyes at Terry as I walked past them, and into the kitchen to pour myself a small glass of water from the purifier.

"Asia where're the fuckin' pills?! I want them now!" He demanded.

"There, in my purse. I'll give them to you when I'm finished."

Before I even swallowed a drop of water, Duane emptied my purse onto the table, rummaging through my things until he found the bottle. He walked over to the sink, flicked on the garbage disposal and dumped the pills down the drain.

I couldn't believe it! "Duane! What are you doing?" I tried desperately to retrieve the bottle from him, "I need those. You don't understand," I cried. What he didn't understand was that the hurt, guilt and pain was so much bigger than I was and I couldn't fight that monster sober, I needed help!

"No more of this shit, Asia! No more!" Duane pushed me out of his way and threw the empty bottle in the trash as I cried wondering what in the world was I going to do now?!

I fell asleep during the fifteen-minute ride to his grandmother's house. Duane woke me up after he parked the car. Once inside, I flopped down on Gran's couch without saying a word to anyone. I saw them as they traded looks with one another. Duane went into the bedroom and came back out with my three-month-old baby boy. DJ was asleep in his arm. He placed him on my lap and I choked up 'cause he was so beautiful. DJ felt like signs of spring. Like the green leaf of a flower bulb that pushes up in the dead of winter through the snow. As I held him I felt something in my soul flicker. With shade-covered eyes, I looked at my boy and couldn't remember how long it had been since I last held him. Still weary from the medication, I kissed him on the face and held him as tight as I could with my rubbery arms. His newborn scent filled my nostrils and I just sunk my nose in the crevice of his neck and inhaled. He smelled like life. I must have been holding him awkwardly because DJ started to cry and Gran rushed over and took him from me.

"Give her back the baby, Gran." Duane snapped.

"I just took him 'cause he needs to eat," she said defensively.

"Well, let her feed her own son!" Duane raised his voice at her. Something that he had never done before.

Offended, Gran went into the kitchen and Terry went after her.

When we arrived home that night, Duane was quiet. He didn't say much, but he was watching me close as I tended to DJ. I finally figured it out, it had been four weeks since I seen my son. That was also the last time I had breastfed him. By now I had stopped lactating. My breasts were no longer producing milk, and with all of the medication I was taking, I wouldn't have breastfed him anyway. I gave DJ a bath, a warm bottle then laid him down for the night.

When I went into our bedroom, Duane was on his back, fully clothed, snoring away, exhausted from the day's events. I called his name to make sure that he wouldn't awaken. When he didn't respond I crept downstairs into the kitchen and took the empty prescription bottle out of the trash. I called the twenty-four hour pharmacy and gave the pharmacist the prescription number. I put the empty bottle back in the trash, slipped out of the house and returned, praying that Duane hadn't awakened. Peeking into the bedroom, I saw that he was still snoring away. Then I checked on the baby as he slept in his crib. He was starting to stir so I changed his diaper and he went soundly back to sleep. I went into the master bath, and poured myself a glass of water, threw a tranquilizer down my throat and climbed in the bed next to Duane and went to sleep.

SEXUAL HEALING

Couldn't figure out why Asia still wasn't back to herself. She was still dragging listlessly around the house. Although she took great care of DJ, she couldn't do much of anything else. I asked her if she was still taking them tranquilizers and she swore to me that she wasn't. Not believing her because the pieces weren't fitting, I searched through her things but couldn't find any evidence.

It had been two months since Epiphany died and I was aching for some TLC. I needed Asia's love in the worst kind of way. Just wanted to be up inside of her getting my strength back. Couple of times I tried to get next to her but backed off, seeing that she still wasn't ready.

They say that the death of a child, either brought a couple closer together or tore them apart. All I know was I didn't want to lose Asia, but she was pushing me further and further away.

It was early afternoon on a Tuesday, my day off. Asia and I were in the family room watching television while DJ was in his automatic baby swing, rocking back and forth. We were on the couch and I had my arm around her as we talked. Asia wasn't wearing a bra and her nipples were poking against the thin shirt she was wearing. Just looking at them made my blood pulsate. I put my hand up under her shirt fondling her breast and my mouth literally began to water. I leaned over and started kissing and sucking on Asia's neck.

She squirmed away, giving me the *don't bother me* look. "Asia, come on. I'm hard baby girl," I whispered in her ear. Taking her hand, I placed it on my erection, and started kissing on her lips. Pressing Asia's hand hard against my nine inches, I started to grind and it was feeling good. I closed my eyes trying to get into a rhythm when she snatched her hand away from me, furious. "Duane?!"

I stood up, defiantly staring down at her. "Well, damnit, what do you want me to do?! I got needs!" I was physically spent and in need of having my hard-on inside of her soft, wet flesh. Asia looked at me and rolled her eyes like she could have cared less. Frustrated, I stormed out of the room and went downstairs into the basement to workout. I felt myself being pulled in by Asia's misery.

That night after she collapsed into a deep slumber, I went down to the family room and called Arizona. The room was dark and quiet. All the bullshit Sylvia was saying about Missy caring was playing on my tortured mind. About a week ago I went over to see how my mom was holding up and while we were eating she began telling me how Missy wanted me to get in touch with her. That she was worried about me. All I knew was I was *empty*, and needed to be filled up. Everything I knew how to give I had given Asia and she just sapped me completely dry and then some. I was still waiting for her to put her arms around me…just to acknowledge that I was hurting too. *I* needed somebody to be strong for *me*! "Hey, what's up baby."

"Duane?" Missy gasped in disbelief.

"Yeah, I heard you been askin' about me."

"Oh Duane. I was so hurt to hear about your daughter. How are you doing babe?" Sylvia was right, I thought. Missy sounded *good!* And it was nice having someone show me they were ready and *willing* to take care of my needs.

"I'm making it, you know. I'll be alright."

"I know she can't stand me, but how's Asia doing? I talked to your mother when I heard the news. She mentioned that Asia was taking it very hard."

"Asia's still not well, but I didn't call you to talk about her." I paused, unsure if I should go there or not but I was in need, "I miss you girl." After it was out I wanted to say it again.

"I miss you too, Pookie. When do you think you'll be back in the area?"

I thought to myself, *If things don't change around here, sooner than you think'* "Soon, real soon. Missy?"

"Yeah?"

I paused again thinking the same thought as before, *should I go there?* "What you wearing?" I spoke almost in a whisper.

"Umm." She purred not skipping a beat, "As a matter of fact I just stepped out of the shower and I was rubbing lotion all over myself when you called."

See, now that's what I'm talking about! I was visualizing Missy's soft body smeared with lotion. And for the next fifteen minutes we did things over the phone that would have made any operator, who might have been listening in, grab a cigarette. I didn't have nowhere near the satisfaction I would have had if I could have made love to my wife, but for tonight Missy's phone sex would just have to do.

"I love you, Duane."

"Yeah, I know," I whispered. "Missy?"

"Yeah?"

"Thanks."

"I said I love you. Whenever you need me, I'm always here for you remember that. No need to thank me."

"Night babe."

"Good night my love." Missy responded and hung up the phone.

For the rest of the night I stayed downstairs and watched television.

***

It was ugly football weather. Cold as a witch's tit and the snow was all over the field. Us Fighting Tritons were all decked out in our black and silver jerseys, and the stadium had a sold out crowd and they were chanting the Tritons' war song and I was pumped! The energy level was high as the opposing team's kicker punted the ball high in the air to began the battle.

Today was December 21 and the last game of the regular season and it was do or die. The winners would move on into the playoffs for the Champion Bowl and the losers would go home for a long and disappointing off-season! The Tritons were having an outstanding season of twelve and three and today I was praying for number thirteen under the wins column.

I was out of sync throughout the game. My mind kept flashing back to Asia, and I was wondering how she was doing. Wondering if I still had a marriage 'cause there was no way I could keep living under these conditions. My mind was fucked up for sure because I couldn't believe I almost hit her.

Three nights ago I walked in the house after working all damn day. I was out the house by six in the morning to be at the stadium on time. I had a full schedule of weight training, classroom time and field practice in full pads. After practice was through at three thirty I had just enough time to eat a quick dinner out and shoot on up to the mall with Gary Johnson to promote his sports gear. Around eight o'clock that night I walked through the door, tired. All I wanted to do was hold my son, take a hot shower, *maybe* make love to my wife if she'd let me, then go to sleep. But I didn't even get the chance to pull off my jacket before she gave me all this attitude.

"What's wrong with you?" I asked her.

She had the damn phone bill shaking it in her hand, "I want to know why the hell are you calling your girlfriend from my damn house in the wee hours of the morning?" She eyed me confrontationally.

I turned around without saying a word and walked back towards the door.

"You ain't even going to answer me?! I'm sick of you always making me wait to talk when I have issues. When you want to talk I have to sit there and deal with it when you say so and I want the same respect, Duane!"

Aggression was aggression, no matter whether it was on the football field or in the living room of my own house. On the field it was *kill* or be killed, at home however, I was the same person with the same instincts. That was why when things got heated between Asia and me, where *I* was on the defensive, I *always* left the house until I got my head right.

I threw my hands in the air, "Not tonight, okay. I'm not in the mood. I'll be at Sylvia's if you need me."

"No we're gonna talk about this now!" Asia was right behind me fuming but I kept on walking *quickly* to the door. And by now I was pissed because I was tired, I already knew I wasn't getting no loving, I was missing my daughter. I was fighting so damn hard just to keep myself from crumbling under the strain. Drama was the last thing I needed.

Just as my hand touched the knob and the door opened, Asia picked up the crystal ashtray that was sitting on the end table in our hallway and hurled it in my direction. "Answer me!" she shouted. I tried to move out of the way, but it bashed right into my shoulder then crashed to the floor, shattering into a thousand pieces.

It was like everything around me turned blood red. Stopping on a dime, I turned around and charged her. "What the *fuck is wrong with you*?! You must be out your goddamn mind?! If you *ever* do some shit like that again, you gonna wish you never had!" I had Asia hemmed up into the corner just screaming on her. It was like everything that had been bottled up inside of me was just being spewed all over her and it was a rush. Felt like a damn orgasm, but in reverse. Before I knew it I was standing over her with my fist clinched and she was bent over shielding herself. I didn't hit her but damn I wanted to, and that was some scary shit!

"This is why I tell you don't do this shit!" I paced around the room trying to get a grip on my emotions, "Asia? Asia I'm...I didn't mean..." The tension in the room was too much so I left. I loved my wife and never wanted to hurt her, but with the state of mind we were both in, I knew it would be best if I moved out 'cause I was at the end of my rope. So, the past three days I stayed at Sylvia's.

It was the fourth quarter with eighteen-second left on the clock and the Tritons were trailing by three points. Later for the team, *I* really needed this win! I swear I was hanging on by a fucking string. Seemed like everyday all I could do to keep from going insane was work my ass off. If I stopped for any length of time the grief would just swell up in me. So I ran from the grief. Knew it was going to catch up with me one of these days, but for now... for right now, I was ahead.

We were lined up on the opposing team's ten yard line. Our quarterback called, "Eighty-one zebra slant left on two!" That was my play. Squatting into position, I chewed down on my mouthpiece. My adrenaline was surging.

"Hike! Hike!" QB yelled and we all went in motion.

I ran across passing him as he handed the ball off to me. I secured the ball in my right arm, pushing defenders off with my left until my blockers came to the rescue giving me a presidential escort right on into the endzone for a thirty-four to thirty win. The stadium stood up and roared! I was elated and could taste that Champion Bowl in my near future. And I was so thankful that our season wasn't done yet!

As all of us, excited players and reporters stormed inside, I saw Asia waiting for me by the locker room entrance. She surprised me, because not only was I not expecting to see her, she had cut her hair real short. Shit kinda threw me! Asia had on a new outfit that I never seen before and she was wearing lipstick. Something she hadn't done in months. With sweat pouring down my face, I stepped over to the side, "Hey?" I was pumped from our victory, but didn't know what to expect from her.

"Hey yourself. I was wondering if I could steal you away for the night when you're finished here." Her big brown eyes were apologetic.

Relieved to see that she was alright I just stared at her then said, "It'll be my pleasure."

A calm almost relieved smile appeared on Asia's lips.

I ran my hand across her short hair. Felt like soft cotton and she had the cork screw curls in it like when we first got together three years ago. I really liked her long hair, but this was kind of cute too. "I'm going to be at least another hour. Why don't you go on in the lounge and relax until I get finished interviewing and showering." I looked down at her.

I could hear the noise in the locker room. Then one of my teammates peeked out, yelled, "Duane, they're calling for you, man!"

"Look, I got to go baby." I turned around to make my grand entrance when Asia stopped me.

"Duane."

When I looked back at her, she mouthed, "I love you."

Kissing my two fingers, I pointed them at her.

Exactly one hour later, I came walking into the lounge all freshened up and feeling good, sporting black trousers, a designer Gary Johnson, black, red and white pullover, loose fitting sweater, black Kangol and gold hoop earrings. "You ready?" I asked reaching for Asia's hand. She got up told the other Triton wives who were also waiting for their husbands, goodbye.

"Asia, call me and I'll give you that recipe," Phyllis said smiling.

"I'll do that." Asia said grabbing her purse and slung it over her shoulder.

"And Asia, it's good to see you back in the house again." Dana said.

Asia smiled and I knew she meant it when she replied, "Thanks. It feels good. I missed y'all."

"And we missed you too." Barbara added.

"Good game out there Hit!" Phyllis said, excited. I smiled at her winking my eye. Grabbing Asia's hand, we walked to the parking lot to her car. I left mine in the stadium's secured garage.

"So where are you taking me?"

"I booked us a suite at the Manhattan Regency. We have so much to talk about. I was thinking that a change of scenery might help."

Asia's Beamer emerged from the Lincoln Tunnel into New York. Once we arrived the valet took the keys. She took a night bag out of the back seat. When we walked into the Regency, Nat King Cole's voice crooned Christmas carols, and the lobby was decorated with a huge Christmas tree and lots of red and white Poinsettias. I was floored by Asia's planning and wondered what had caused this big turn around with her.

We checked in at the front desk, and rode the elevator up to the fifth floor. Our suite was decorated with lots of fresh flowers, a round bed, Jacuzzi, champagne, the works. When she turned around from closing the door, I wrapped my wife in my arms and it was the first time that I held her since Epiphany died. "I been needing this, baby," I whispered in her ear. For her to pay me some attention, to acknowledge my hurt…my pain…I been needing it. Our mouths met and I just took my time.

Asia went over to the closet and kicked off her shoes. I pulled off my sweater and undershirt, leaning my bare back on the chair getting comfortable. Asia poured us both a glass before she sat on the floor between my legs.

Looking up at me I could see that she was just as concerned about us as I was, "Baby, there's a lot we need to talk about."

"I know," I was ready to have this long overdue conversation.

"Sylvia came by last night. She really got me to thinking about a lot of things. I don't know why, but when she left, I knew I had to fight to get through this depression." One thing about sorrow, it had a way of making differences seem petty. Asia still wasn't one of Sylvia's favorite people, but Sylvia really took an interest in Asia's well-being. She'd go over and talk with her, and help out with DJ. It was messed up that it took something like this to make them bond, but I was glad that it was finally happening.

Asia paused, "I did something last night that I know you won't agree with, but I'm glad I did."

I looked at Asia for clarification, "What did you do?"

"I called Arizona. I spoke to Missy."

Asia studied my face and she didn't have to guess how I felt because I could feel the heat of anger building inside of me. I was thinking to myself, I know she didn't bring me all the way to New York to start no shit. "Why would you do that?" I grimaced.

"I don't know. I guess I wanted to tell her to leave you alone, and that you were my husband, and for her to get her own damn man. Something. After you left I was hurt…furious. I wanted to load all of my emotions onto someone, so I called the person that was threatening me."

"Asia…" I couldn't believe her. I moved Asia's elbow from off my leg so I could get up because I wasn't trying to hear this.

"Please, baby, let me finish," Asia said looking up at me. "Duane she told me that she loved you and that if I didn't want you that she would take you. And the way she sounded, I think she meant it."

Sitting back down, I was getting confused 'cause it didn't sound like Asia was angry or trying to make me mad. But I was real uncomfortable with her discussing Missy to me. "Why are you telling me all of this?"

"Because she told me something else too, something that I already knew. She told me that all you want is to be a good husband and father. Baby, I swear I already knew that, but soon as I hung the phone up it was like she had told me something that I was hearing for the first time. At that moment, I missed you so bad Duane, and I needed you and you weren't there. I was afraid that I had lost you."

I stroked my wife's cheek, "You know I'll never leave you Asia."

"No, I didn't know that Duane. I still don't know that."

"I'm here, baby ain't I?"

"Yes you are, but when I married Bryant, I thought that was going to be for forever. Duane, I always thought that our children would be with us always. I thought we would watch them grow up, go to school, then college, get married, have children of their own."

As I listened to Asia my heart began to get heavy.

"I know Piff Piff was only one-and-a-half, but I dreamt of the day when she would need my advice on what formula to feed her babies, and what brand clothes would be best to buy for them and all that stuff. See honey, I *knew* that my daughter and I would share those things one day, now she's gone and I'll never have that chance. Forever doesn't work for me." Asia put her head down on my thigh.

"You know what my grandmom said?" I stroked Asia's neck, "She said, 'And this too shall pass'. I know you're in pain baby, 'cause I'm in pain too. I miss Piff Piff's little fresh butt. I miss her smile and the way she used to point at DJ and say 'bae bee'." A distant smile came across my lips as I called up the visuals in my mind, "You remember the way she use to steal kisses from him?" I laughed almost to myself, "She was definitely daddy's heart. There wasn't anything on this earth that I wouldn't do for her, except one thing. I couldn't save her life. My little girl, our little girl, Asia. We brought her into this world together. But the one thing I couldn't do for her was save her life…I…tried." My voice started to stick in the back of my throat, but I remained composed. I held Asia's chin up so that I could look in her eyes, "Baby, it scared me to see you so out of it Asia. I thought that I was losing you too."

"Duane, *I* thought I was losing me. *I wanted to die.* Baby, I couldn't make the pain go away. I couldn't bear being awake thinking about her all the time. Knowing that her body is in some damn graveyard." Asia clenched her fist, "I still can't accept it. No." She shook her head, "I have to pretend that she is in the hospital, or with the family someplace, anything but dead." I squeezed Asia's shoulder to cue her to calm down, "Oh Duane, it hurts so much." She sighed.

All the grief that I'd been suppressing those last eight weeks was working its way to the surface and I was scared to let it go 'cause it was so big. "I think about her all of the time too. I know she's in heaven, but I wonder if up there she knows who we are…if she… misses… us." I hung my head down. My insides grieved and the tears started to flow from my tightly shut eyes. With *everything* in me, I missed my daughter! Asia got up on her knees hugging me around the neck. I wrapped my arms tightly around her and we cried together. They were healing tears.

"We have to make ourselves a promise." With tears running under my chin and liquid from my nose rimming onto my top lip, I cupped Asia's face looking deep into tear-filled eyes, "That we're gonna be strong and make it through this."

"How…I mean, how do we do that? How do we go on without her?" Asia studied my face for an answer.

I replied honestly, "I don't know. All I know is we have to."

I stood up, taking Asia in my arms, kissing her slow and deep. Our embrace was filled with love and apologies, promises and commitment to see this through, *together*. And I couldn't help but to think how close we came to ending it all.

Slow and easy I made love to my wife, reconnecting our bond, broken by grief. Asia moaned, as our bodies rocked like waves on a calm sea. Filling each other up on every level, physical, spiritual and emotional. We made love for hours, purging our souls clean, crying, consoling and loving the pain away.

SISTERS

The OB-GYN office was crowed with people. As patients left, new patients came in. I looked around as the expectant mothers and fathers waited snuggled together reading from the same "Parents" magazine. As I looked over at my sister, Terry pulled her distant glance away from the round belly of a woman who was sitting across the room, and she gave me a faint smile. I grabbed her hand, "You alright, girl?"

"Let's get out of here."

I couldn't quite read the emotions that were in her eyes. It was sort of a mixture of sadness, surrender, and solace all mixed into one. For the past two years Terry and Lawrence had been trying to have a baby. The first year they were trying naturally, then when nothing happened they got professional help. Lawrence's health came out fine, but Terry found that she wasn't ovulating regularly. At forty-two years old, the poor thing was premenopausal. Even though some women could have babies up into their late fifties, early sixties Terry just happened to be in the small percentile who's body began its change-of-life early. She and Lawrence had tried the rhythm method of taking Terry's temperature to find out when she *was* ovulating. She'd tried fertility pills *and* injections. Today she was due for another injection.

"Terry, are you sure you want to leave?"

She didn't say anything, just nodded her head, yes. I put my arms around her because I knew how much she wanted to have children. But I had always told my sister, that life was not something that she, or anyone else could plan down to the tee. And for Terry that was what she believed. She and Lawrence had been married now for fifteen years and if she wasn't so headstrong about having the house just-so, and their business just-so, and their finances just-so. I mean my goodness, they planned on having two children, Terry said a boy and a girl…and they even had the kids' college funds in the bank *waiting*. Only thing she needed was to add the kids into the equations and hocus pocus *a perfect world*. I knew I could be headstrong myself sometimes, but after I had Duane I knew that life was a roller coaster ride. It had ups and downs and the best you could do was learn how to ride. The sad thing about the whole situation was I really believed that Terry was so structurally driven because she didn't want to be like me.

After we left the doctor's office, we actually had a real nice day. Our first stop was to "IHOP" for their famous Rooty-Tooty Fresh and Fruity pancake breakfast. I got the peach pancakes and Terry got a big stack with blueberries. We both shared a large plate of scrambled eggs, sausage and bacon.

From there we drove downtown to check on the building that Duane had purchased for me that was in the process of being renovated. My business was already incorporated. It was a catering service and restaurant called "Fried Green Tomatoes" like the movie. I wanted a catchy name and Sylvia's was already taken by the lady in New York. I was really excited, but most of all Duane was excited for me because I was finally doing something just for me.

CHAMPION BOWL

I seen it unfolding in front of my eyes and held my breath for the entire ride. We finished first in our division then we went into the playoffs. Just like they were ducks in a shooting gallery we started picking off the playoff teams. And on January twenty-seventh, as if being smiled on from heaven the very last team that stood in our way, we knocked off with an embarrassing, for them that is, forty-six to eight win!

Our defensive unit was on the field while the rest of us players and Tritons personnel were on the sidelines jumping, hooping and hollering as the clock wound down the final seconds. Then over the P.A. system the announcer said, *"And the New Jersey Tritons will be headed to Atlanta, Georgia for this year's Champion Bowl!"*

I threw my hands in the air then dropped on my knees! FINALLY, after all these years I had a chance to play in the Champion Bowl. Some great players have played their entire careers, never to even play in this game of all games. As I knelt there on the sidelines about fifteen other teammates surrounded me on their knees. With bowed heads, we all held hands and Jessie Stanford led us in prayer as the television cameras zoomed in televising us to the nation.

Our conference was the first to finish the playoffs. Now we had to wait for the other conference to play so we could see who our competition would be. The two teams playing for the spot were Washington and Tennessee. We were hoping for Washington because we played them before and pretty much knew their playing style and were effective in stopping their plays.

A week before the Champion Bowl the Tritons flew down to Georgia to get ready. As our buses were pulling up to the nine-story hotel, mobs of people were outside screaming all excited. There were television cameras rolling, reporters anxiously waiting with their microphones and tape recorders in their hands, and of course…the groupie girls!

A lot of my teammates were flying their families down for the event at the end of the week, but for the first time, I was going at it alone. Sylvia, who usually loved these types of hyped up events, had her very first wedding to cater for the same weekend as the Champion Bowl. She was nervous as hell, but I told her to hang in there, give it a chance and to just try to enjoy herself. I knew she'd do fine. It was amazing how she took all of that drive and determination that she used to focus on me, and redirected it into her own business. Even though *sometimes* she would *still* forget that she wasn't my manager and try to give me her two cents. But instead of an everyday thing it only happened now every blue moon.

Asia was home with DJ. He came down with the flu so we decided it would be best for her to stay home with him. The one person who was here and we planned to meet up was Tompy. He came up to the hotel the same night we got in and came to a couple of the practices. Although it was February first and had only been four months since he moved down here, it seemed like forever since we kicked it together. He drove me around Atlanta, took me to the new Millennium office that he was heading up, and showed me his new place. It was real nice too, twice the size of his condo in Jersey.

I was surprised, but Coach Maxon had short not very intense practices during the week. He showed us some film, we ran a few drills, and mostly he did a lot of pep talking, trying to keep us focused and pumped. He told us, we already knew what to do, and we didn't come this far not to bring home the ring, and we understood!

Being that it was the last practice before our big day, I had all this nervous energy rushing through me. Had a lot on my mind, one thing in particular was Piff Piff because I still missed her like crazy. Me and one of my teammates, Mac, went walking the streets of downtown Atlanta looking for a tattoo pallor. Mac had over two dozen tattoos all over his body, he looked like a walking billboard, and to me that shit just didn't make any sense. Only thing I had on me was my Omega brand. When we did find one, Mac got a bulldog tattooed on his calf. I took my shirt off and jumped in the chair.

That night after I got out of the shower, I slowly peeled the bandage off of my left peck looking at the tattoo inside of the hotel's bathroom mirror. The word Epiphany was printed in fancy script inside of a heart. A head of a rose started the heart and the stem made the outline. At the bottom was a thorn with a droplet of blood. Staring at my reflection, I ran the tips of my fingers across the tattoo. Its image represented the beauty that my baby brought into my life, the everlasting pain I felt, and the permanent love I'd always have for her. "Now, you can sleep on Daddy's chest forever," I said closely inspecting the design in the mirror.

It was the night before the big game and I felt really good. I had just gotten off the phone with Asia, telling her about my tattoo. She said she couldn't wait to see it. We prayed over the phone so that everything would come together tomorrow. I didn't believe that God was a fan of one team or another, so I wasn't praying that we win or anything. I just wanted a blessing that we played our best. My relationship with God was becoming more of a focus in my mind these days. Gran gave me a copy of the "Footsteps" poem and I read it over and over. 'In your roughest time where you see only one set of footprints, that is when I carried you'. And I knew He *had* to be carrying me because I didn't know how else I would have made it *this far*.

I was in the bed drifting to sleep at around eleven o'clock when my roommate, Roy, sneaked in the hotel room with his arms around two ladies. One was a blonde, the other brunette. They didn't turn on the light as they walked through the room, but with the curtains open there was a fluorescent glow coming from the outside so I could still see through the dark.

They went over to Roy's bed whispering and laughing. Propped up on my elbows, I looked at him wondering if he was crazy breaking curfew. Roy pulled the brunette down on the bed with him and they started kissing and rolling playfully. The blonde looked at them having fun, then she looked at me and walked over to where I was laying in the bed with a sheet thrown over my mid section.

"Hi," she said seductively.

"Hey," I said checking her out, still propped on my elbows.

She took off her coat and neatly laid it on the floor, and sat on the edge of my bed. She was wearing a short brown suede mini skirt, black low cut top, jacket to match the skirt and brown suede high heels. I can't lie, she was something to look at. Tall, with long shapely legs, pretty face, and long golden hair, "I'm Jenny."

"And I'm getting ready to go to sleep." I replied kind of curt not believing that Roy would try this shit the night before the Champion Bowl.

"Roy said you would be in the bed," she flirted.

"Oh he did?" Turning, I looked over at Roy who was on top of his lady friend sucking her naked breasts, "Well, what else did he say?"

Jenny started giggling moving her crossed knee seductively up and down over her other. Then took her hand and lightly ran her finger across her pushed-up breasts. She ran her other hand across my arm. "He said that *maybe* you wanted to have a good time."

"A good time?" I repeated.

Jenny leaned over into my face. Her perfume was smelling a little too good, and her skin looked soft, smooth and inviting.

"You do know how to have a good time, don't you, huh?" She crooned, kissing me on the mouth. I stayed there propped up on my elbows. As she used her tongue to traced my lips, I caught a hard on.

Once again I looked over and Roy now had his head between his lady friend's legs, and she was in a state of euphoria. I liked Roy a whole lot because he was a fun person to hang around. Roy was always *the life of the party*, wherever he went. I also respected the man for his skills on the field, nobody played better. But as far as being a mature man, I thought he was a complete *idiot.* Outside of football, Roy had no respect for himself, and damn sure none for his wife or his family. He was loose and just didn't give a damn.

Jenny slid her hand under the sheet and rubbed my throbbing erection through my boxer-briefs. My heart pounded wildly as I breathed in deep at her touch. I just wanted to fuck the life out of her and I was so damn mad at Roy for putting me in this predicament. Lodged in the base of my abdomen was that damn pressure-sensation I got when I needed some sex, but I wasn't trying to go out like that. I had too much to lose! Grabbing Jenny's hand, I pulled it away from my jewels, sitting her up straight, "Whoa, baby," I said lightheaded from the lust, "I can't do this."

She looked puzzled, "What's wrong, don't you like me?"

With my erection about to burst through my draws, I got my ass out of the bed as not to get caught up 'cause temptation was *strong!* "That's not it, just that this..." I rubbed my nine inches, "...belong to someone else. Sorry baby."

I snatched my pants off the chair, put them on and slid on my leather slippers. I grabbed a pillow off of the bed, then left the room. Before I closed the door I glanced back at Roy who was now butt naked doing it doggy style to his lady friend.

Across the hall I went and knocked on the door.

Cheese answered, "You lost niggah?"

"*Hell yeah.* Roy got these two bitches in my room, man." I said disgusted.

"Word?" Cheese started laughing. Who would have guessed from the way he was riding me in the beginning of the season when I first became a Triton that he would become one of my closest friends on the squad?

Pissed, I walked into the room and threw my pillow on the couch, "Can a brothah crash here for the night?" Cheese was still laughing, shaking his head.

It was quiet in their room. Cheese was in his underwear with his big stomach hanging underneath his T-shirt. His roomy, Avery Watkins was quietly rapping on the phone, sitting on his bed with his legs crossed at the ankles. He and I acknowledged each other by throwing up the power sign.

The morning of the Champion Bowl, I woke up mad as hell because I hated sleeping on *any* couch. I was a bed man and the bigger the better. My back, neck, arms and legs were all cramped up. I was aching all over! Grabbing the pillow off of the couch, I told Big Cheese and Avery, who both were getting ready to go to breakfast then to the field, thanks for letting me crash. Then I stormed back to my room.

When I entered, Roy was sound asleep. Pissed, I took my size thirteen and kicked the mattress as hard as I could, startling Roy almost knocking him out of the bed.

He woke up staring daggers at me, his eyes red from the lack of sleep, "You got a problem, *partner*!"

"I ain't got no fuckin' problems long as you don't cross over into my space!" I shouted pounding into my chest.

"What the fuck you talking bout?!"

"You know what the fuck I'm talking bout. Don't be bringing no muthah fuckin' body up here for me. You keep that shit on your side of the room!"

Roy got up on the opposite side of the bed from where I was standing, "Fuck you man. Actin' all high and mighty."

Extending my arm towards Roy's face, I yelled, "I done warned your ass! I'ma embarrass you next time!"

"Fuck you!" Roy shouted

"No fuck you!"

There was a loud banging on the door, "Hey! Hey! What's going on in there? Open up the door."

I stood there for a few seconds in my aggressive stance looking at Roy, then I opened the door.

"Yo, y'all need to kill all this noise in here. White folks thinkin' we bout to turn this place ite." What a joke, Cheese, the prankster, was the voice of reason.

"We cool, we cool," I said getting a grip on my temper.

"Sure man?" Cheese put his hand on my shoulder. Staring at Roy I nodded my head.

"Rhains, you cool my man?" Cheese yelled.

"Yeah, man. I'm cool. Nothin' to it." Roy said bringing it down.

Coach Maxon marched down the hall and stuck his head through the door way, "What's all this shit?!"

Cheese, Roy and I all rolled our eyes up in the air and sighed.

"Nothing coach," I answered.

"Nothing?" Maxon repeated sarcastically. "Cummings, in the hallway." Maxon walked out with his hands in his pockets.

Gritting my teeth, I walked out of the room.

"What's going on?" Maxon looked dead in my eyes.

"Just a difference of opinion, nothing serious." I played the situation down.

"Rhains breaking team rules?" The coach said looking at me to confirm, "There are rumors he's breaking curfew and having women in the room. Would you know anything about that?"

"Coach, with all due respect. If you got a problem with Rhains, you should be taking this up with him." I stated matter of factly. I didn't appreciate him trying to stick me in the middle of that shit.

"You really disappoint me Cummings. I would expect that out of anyone of them, but you?" Maxon's beady little blue eyes closed even tighter, then he walked off down the hall.

Champion Bowl winners!!! We spanked Tennessee thirty to twenty-three and I felt complete. If I never played another day in my life, there was already such a sense of accomplishment because I had my first Champion Bowl ring!

Roy walked up to me, "We were unstoppable on the field."

"The Dynamic Duo. Good game, man" I said, then we grabbed each other's hand and embraced.

"Shit, kid. We tore it up out there!"

APRIL LOVE

It was a beautiful sunny day outside downtown Trenton and I was in the kitchen of "Fried Green Tomatoes" getting ready for the lunch crowd. My restaurant wasn't very large, just big enough to have a long buffet table, and comfortably seat thirty customers. I opened up at eleven and it was only nine forty-five, but the big Viking stove was already fired up. I was making a big pot of chicken soup, the soup for the day.

When I heard the chime of the front door I yelled from the kitchen, "We're not open yet!" Because I was running in and out getting things from my car, I had the door unlocked but I had the damn sign in the window big as day, which said closed.

"Yeah, but can a thirsty man have a glass of water?" The voice didn't sound familiar, so I dropped the spoon on the counter and went up front to see what was going on. When I got there, I couldn't believe my eyes.

"You still fine, girl."

"Eddie?"

"Hah, hah, hah!" He laughed from his belly with his arms stretched out, "Come here, girl."

I came from around that counter as fast as I could, and gave him a big ole hug! Eddie Henderson was the special teams coach for the Arizona Mavericks. When I would go to spend time with Duane in Arizona Eddie was always so nice to me. I knew he had a crush on me, but I wasn't paying that man any attention.

"Let me take a look at you." He said and I gave him a little spin. It was warm for April this year, so this morning I threw on my black thigh-high dress with the mini white polka dots, and my slip-in black clogs. My apron was over my dress.

And you know the hair and the nails were tight.

"Ump, ump, ump." Eddie had this smile on his face as he shook his head, "Give me some of that youth water."

Duane, smiling this wide smile, was standing behind Eddie.

"What are you doing here?" I said still in a state of shock.

"Had a pocket full of money..." he said tapping his pockets, "...some vacation time to spend, so I called up your son and decided to see what was happening in these neck-of-the-woods." Eddie stood about five feet-eleven, and his built was solid, even though at fifty-two years old his stomach was starting to round. And laid on top of his caramel lips was this thick black mustache that always seemed to catch my eye.

When I looked at Duane he wiggled his eyebrows still having that damn cheese grin on his face and I knew I had just been set up. And sure enough, my son made a swift and speedy exit.

"Eddie, you straight, 'cause I have to jet. I can swing back by in about an hour or so to pick you up."

"Ooh yeah, I'm straight." Singing the words like his heart was on wings, Eddie looked into my eyes.

"Sylviaaaa," Duane was tickled. He came over and kissed me on the cheek before he walked out the door, "I guess I'll catch you two later."

I smiled at Eddie, "Well since you're here and I have to get ready for my lunch crowd, I guess you better wash your hands, roll up your sleeves, and get to work."

"Whatever you say pretty lady."

For the whole five days that Eddie was in town we were together. He did stay with Duane and Asia the first night, but the other four days he stayed with me. He had never been to Atlantic City, so we drove out there for a night, but the rest of the time it was "Fried Green Tomatoes" during the day, and videos, wine, conversation and a whole lot of loving at night. Before he went back, Eddie gave me a round trip airline ticket and made me promise that I would come to see him before the season started in June. I promised him that I would.

FRIENDS, FORGIVENESS, AND FOREVER

In the solace of the lounge in my master bedroom, I sat on the floor with my tattered old photo album. I had dug it out of my hope chest because I had been thinking about Crystal and the good old times we used to share. The once clear plastic shield that covered the page had begun to yellow. And the sticky adhesive that held the pictures in place had turned dry and brittle allowing the pictures to fall about the page. I laughed out loud at Crystal and me in our younger days. At the clothes we wore thinking we were so fly, and now only to realize that we just looked so silly!

I had to admit that I was being a little hard on her. Neither one of us knew that Epiphany was going to pass and it wasn't fair of me to hold against her the fact that she wasn't there for us in the last month of Piff Piff's life. Crystal tried to offer the olive branch of friendship to me, but I wasn't ready to accept it. She came to the house, called, cried to Duane *and* my mother... and even though they told me that I should forgive her, it *still* wasn't in me. Guess I had too many things going on inside of me, but as time went on I began to miss the sisterhood that we once had.

Besides Duane, no one knew me like Crystal. Matter-of-fact there were things about me she knew, that Duane didn't know. There were experiences that she and I shared since the third grade; those were priceless. Like the time we were in the ninth grade and walked almost ten miles in knee-deep snow to Morrisville High School just so *she* could see her boyfriend play basketball. She was the only one in the world I would do something stupid like that for. And there was the time when my parents went down south for the week and left me home and Crystal convinced me to drive my dad's car damn near half way across the state to go clubbing. We got our training bras around the same time. We even got our very first periods on the same day. I called her excited to tell her my news, and she screamed, "Oh my God…me too!"

I loved Crystal, and I really needed my sister-friend back in my life. I just knew we had so many more priceless memories to make. I moved the photo album to the side, reached for the phone and dialed Crystal's house. When she picked it up I said, "Hey Crystal, remember that time we walked all the way to Morrisville in the snow…" We both laughed.

DOUBLE YOUR PLEASURE

3 Years Later

Ever since Epiphany's death four years ago, I hated hospitals…the sterile smell, the cold temperatures…it was all so fucking morbid…no matter how much they decorated and tried to cheer the place up. Asia was in the hospital bed steady pushing and after twenty-two minutes the baby's head started to crown. I was at the foot of the bed, propped up on my crutches watching in amazement. Asia had sweat all over her face as her hands tightly gripped the railings on both sides of the bed.

Within the last year so many things have happened, one of them being, Pop Walter lost his fight to cancer. He was a good man and I was so thankful that Asia was here with him in his last days. Mom Janie came to live with us shortly afterwards. Both Asia and I were concerned about her after her stroke. She's doing fine, though. Wasn't no major damage done, just her hands and feet get numb sometimes. We had her a bedroom built downstairs next to the family room. This way she didn't have to climb up and down the stairs.

To be honest, I wasn't quite sure how her living with us would change things around our house. Except for me not being able to walk downstairs in my draws everything's pretty much the same. She ain't no problem at all.

"This one got a lot of hair, Babe. A lot of hair." Asia pushed again and the head completely passed and the little one started wailing away. With the hospital gown pulled up and draped across Asia's huge belly, she gave another good push while looking at me. They gave her a spinal tap when she first went into labor, so she wasn't doing a whole bunch of hollering, but she was still moaning like she was in pain. As Asia bore down, Dr. Hampton pulled the baby girl out into the world. He suctioned her mouth talking baby talk to her then passed my daughter to the nurse. I hopped along side on my crutches while she lathered up the baby, washing, weighing, then fitting her with the ID band. I was so excited my heart was fluttering!

This season made my ninth year in the PFL, and as a player, it looked like it was going to be my last. While playing New England I was diving into the endzone when the opposing team's defensive lineman fell on me. My leg twisted underneath me and I tore my ACL. It was some painful shit! Felt like someone had poured gasoline on my leg and set it on fire. I had it operated on and I even been through the extensive therapy sessions, but something in my psyche just wasn't the same.

I'm thirty-one years old now and I just don't have that same desire to go out there and give my two hundred percent on the field. I don't know if it is a result of getting injured or if it was just my time to stop playing the game and go on to something else. Whatever the case, I always knew I wanted to go out on top. I wanted to retire from the PFL when my name, "The Hitman" still meant something. When my performance still commanded respect. Although I was almost certain that my career as a *player* was over, I was giving some serious thought to a new career as an assistant coach, preferably, an offensive line coach.

My attention went back to Asia when I heard her moaning trying to push out baby number two. Twins. I got to the edge of the bed just in time to see the head appear. Asia looked so tired. If I could have traded places with her, I would have. She continued pushing until the little boy was completely out. Then the second nurse came and took him to the sink to be cleaned up. Asia had puddles of sweat under her neck and her hair was completely shot! She looked like she went a couple of boxing rounds with Lenox Lewis. Man, standing there I felt *so high!* I loved my life…I loved my wife and I didn't know which one of my three loves in the room to pay attention to. Then the first nurse came over with my daughter all cleaned up and put her in my arms. I gently hopped on one foot along side of the bed to Asia and placed the baby in Asia's arms, "What's her name again?"

Asia smiled and reached for the baby, "Wonyae Allayah." Asia kissed our baby girl then the little boy started squealing.

We both looked over to where he was. I laughed full of pride, "Let me go and see what she doing to my man." With one crutch under my arm, I went and watched as the nurse shampooed and ID banded my boy. "Hey Walter Lee." I cooed, taking him in my arms for the first time. I already knew his name because we wanted to name him after Asia's dad.

About a year and a half-ago we started hinting around about expanding our family. I said hinting around because neither one of us was sure if the other was ready. Then finally one night while we were lying in the bed making love Asia told me she wanted to have a baby. From that point on she stopped taking her birth control…but when she came home and told me that she was having *twins*. I can't even explain how right that feeling was.

"Let me see him," Asia told me. I was extra careful as I hopped back to her bed. So she could look at the baby, I held him close to Asia and she must have kissed his face a hundred times. He turned his cheek like he didn't want her to stop. We compared our two babies. The little girl was fuller than her brother. She was sucking on the tips of three fingers like she was ready to eat.

"Oh Lord, how am I going to do this? Both of them must be hungry." Asia said like the reality of mothering twins had just set in.

The nurse walked over to Asia and patted her on the shoulder. "Don't worry. Everything is a system. While your son is calm and your daughter is obviously ready to nurse, you simply feed her first."

Asia started breast-feeding Wonyae then after a half hour, the nurse encouraged Asia to switch and start feeding Walter. I held my little princess, patting her back until she passed the gas that was in her system. "That was good Wonnie." Her new nickname.

The next day when we got home I was feeling real good about the family that Asia and I had created. The family had all just left from visiting the twins…*and* DJ…Asia had no problem reminding them that they can't leave him out. My mom and Aunt came up to the hospital last night, but they came back today with Lawrence and my grandparents. Crystal called and was on her way.

Asia was reclined on the sofa in the family room half a sleep while DJ sat at the computer reading. He reminded me so much of myself when I was a kid. DJ loved sports, he already knew how to handle a football and he was already playing tots basketball. And smart! At four years old Asia had him reading on a first grade level.

Mom Janie was in the kitchen cooking dinner. She loved to cook and I loved her cooking! Don't get me wrong, Asia had grown into quite a cook herself, but Mom just got that special touch.

I had to go to the store for some milk and juice so I grabbed my white Kangol to match my gray and white Gary Johnson sweat suit. That was something else I was proud of...the Gary Johnson line. It was now sold in the major department stores. I felt really good about helping a brother from around-the-way fulfill his dreams. Now he's mentoring some of the young talent coming out of Trenton. 'If you've been blessed...pass it on!' I didn't create the saying, but I try to live by it.

Asia was nodding, as the twins were asleep in their bassinet. I told DJ to grab his jacket and we took a ride down to the Supermarket. My left leg was still in a brace but it didn't bother me to drive. I walked around Acme Food Market with DJ beside me. He pushed the child-sized grocery cart as I dropped stuff into it. In the few minutes that we were in the store I had three people walk up to me for autographs and to see how I was making out, asking if I was going to return next season.

"Dad, can we get the Last Avenger cereal that they show on TV?" He asked me all wide-eyed as I was talking to one lady. Smiling politely, I handed her back her pen and paper then focused my attention on my son.

"Last Avenger? You mean to tell me that's a cereal now?"

"Yeah Dad, they have an action figure in every box. That's what they said on TV. It's cool!"

We walked towards the cereal aisle. While walking someone else called my name.

"Hey there Mr. Cummings."

I turned around, "Mr. Dansberry. How are you Sir?" I extended my hand for a gentleman's handshake. Mr. Dansberry was huge. He had to be like six-nine, around three hundred pounds. He used to be the principal at the school where Asia taught second grade. She told me that he was an excellent administrator, but the two of them never hit it off on a personal level. I only met him once or twice when I visited her class and he always seemed decent to me. I never had a problem with him.

"Quite alright, quite alright. And how's that lovely wife of yours?" He replied before DJ impatiently piped in.

"Dad can I go get the cereal?"

"Don't you see me talking?" I gestured towards Mr. Dansberry.

"Yeah...Excuse me, Dad!" DJ whined tugging on my shirt.

"What?" I looked at my son aggravated by his impatience.

"But can I go get the cereal pleeease?"

"Go head, but you come right back."

Sighing, I redirected my attention to Mr. Dansberry, "Asia's fine. We just had numbers three and four. Twins. They just got home this afternoon." I boasted proudly. Sometimes I still can't believe I'm actually married with three kids, four counting Epiphany.

"Well congratulations to the both of you." Mr. Dansberry gave a broad smile as he shook my hand, "Contrary to popular belief, I love children. Got three grandchildren myself." He laughed then nudged me with his elbow, "But I hear the rumors going around. I think the funniest one was about me eating a first grader for lunch." Mr. Dansberry held his round belly and laughed loud and hard, "Now that one really cracked me up. Say, how's the knee? Heard it was a career ending injury."

"Actually, I was told that I could return to the field next season, but Asia and I talked about it and I'm just going to hang up my cleats. I'm looking into PFL coaching positions. Already sent out the apps, now I'm just waiting for the responses."

DJ ran towards me with this big grin on his cute little face, holding the box of cereal in his hand and tossed it in the mini basket.

"I'm also going through a career change. I'm no longer at M.S. Jones Elementary. I'm now the Principal at Oliver Williams High." Mr. Dansberry shook his head, "What a mess, what a mess. I had to clean house. My first month there I expelled fifty students. During the course of a year I also had to replace over half of the teaching staff. Couldn't fire most of them, they just got relocated. They're somebody else's headache now. See Duane, a lot of people think that they can just come to work and half-ass teach." Mr. Dansberry covered his mouth, remembering that there were small ears around, "Pardon my French. But that's not how I run things. They come in, see a bunch of Black and Hispanic kids and think, what-the-hay, I can half-step and no one will notice. But that's where they're wrong. I notice. When I came into O.W.H., just like I did during my tenure at M.S. Jones, I demanded that the teachers consistently attended training sessions and seminars. Technology doesn't stop. New things are happening in this world every day. You have some teachers who received their degrees fifteen-twenty years ago and never went back to reeducate themselves on all the new stuff. Well that's not acceptable in my school. Everyone has to pull their weight. I even required the parents to interact with the students and faculty. I shook it up and got everyone involved. The lazy one's hollered, Mutiny!" Mr. Dansberry yelled, cracking himself up, "And they scattered faster than mice at a cat convention." Shaking his finger high in the air, he said, "But the cream remained behind, and I'm pretty darn pleased with the lot if I do say so myself. Say... we're in need of a Phys Ed teacher if you're interested? Thought about you when I saw you blow that thing out." Mr. Dansberry pointed at my knee.

I smiled, "I'll keep that in mind."

"Now you won't have no million dollar paydays, that's for sure. Far from it. But I could arrange to throw in some football coaching stuff. Our team stinks. They make the Bad News Bears look like winners." Mr. Dansberry laughed, "Well, I'm gonna let you go. Your wife must be waiting for you. Mine is waiting in the car. Says she hates to go places with me 'cause I always run into people, and I talk too much. Can you imagine that?" He slapped me on the shoulder, "You take care now. And tell Asia I said hello."

IT'S ALL GOOD

It was a boring Friday afternoon and I had been on the phone first with Crystal and then Terry. I guess we were all feeling that same restless vibe. Then Terry came up with the idea of a 'split second' get-together. But this time instead of the three of us girls getting together, she said, "Let's invite the fellahs and you guys bring the kids and I'm going to call Sylvia as well. I'll just throw something on the stove and we all can just have a nice time together." As Terry described her plans, I could feel the excitement building inside of me and *oooh*, I needed to get out of this house!

Duane was stretched out asleep on the floor in our family room. I went in, woke him up, and told him to get ready. He wasn't trying to hear it, but I wasn't trying to take no for an answer. I hadn't been anyplace since the twins were born and I was tired of sitting home. I got the kids all bundled up, gave mom Terry's phone number in case she needed to get in touch with us and we were out. She knew how to set the house alarm and she kept her MedAlert device on in case she was alone and couldn't get to the phone. One thing that she, Duane and I all agreed on is that we would all go about the business of our regular lives. She didn't want to be treated like a child with us fussing over her, and we *appreciated* the fact that we could still go out and enjoy ourselves as we always did.

By the time we got to Terry's house, Crystal and Allen were just driving up as well. She rushed over to Duane's Navigator and got Walt out of his baby seat while I got Wonnie. DJ ran out of the truck to catch up with Lil Allen who was already making his way to the house. And Although Lil Allen was eight years old and DJ was four, they were still best buddies.

When we got inside of the house it smelled so good. Terry was cooking her famous shrimp, okra and rice dish. And girl had the nerve to have two sweet potato pies on her kitchen counter ready to go in the oven.

"I thought you were just throwing something together real quick. Looks like you have gone all out if you ask me."

She laughed, well I figured, what the heck. It wasn't going to take that much longer to fix the good stuff, so why not just go ahead? Give me my baby." She said taking five-week-old Wonnie out of my arms and kissed her little face. Terry and Lawrence had a beautiful home. They lived in Lawrenceville Township, another suburb of Trenton and practically right around the corner from Sylvia. Matter-of-fact it was the same style house. Duane was right when he said Sylvia had expensive taste, because her house was laid! Every room was nothing short of fabulous. Looked like something out of a magazine. Terry's house on the other hand looked more lived in, but it was still nice.

"Hi Aunt Terry!" DJ yelled, wanting his rightful share of the attention.

"Hello big man." Terry stooped down for a kiss. DJ put his arms around her neck and gave her a big kiss right back. "Come here Lil Allen, where's Aunt Terry's kiss?"

Lil Allen looked like he wanted no parts of the kissing stuff, then Crystal popped him on the head, "Stop being so mannish, boy. Just like your daddy." Lil Allen frowned rubbing the spot where he got popped on the head, then he leaned into Terry's pucker and we all laughed at him.

Lawrence had his shoes off and feet propped up on the ottoman that sat in front of his chair. He was watching television, but when Duane and Allen walked into the room where he was, their loud voices and laughter resonated throughout the entire downstairs. And I tell you, it was something about men's laughter that just made it seem that all was right with the world so I just folded my arms and listened, until Terry broke my train of thought.

"I have a confession to make." She said, "I have some really good news of my own and that was one of the reasons that I wanted you guys to be here. Baby can you and the fellahs come in here for a minute?!" Terry waited for Lawrence,

Duane and Allen to come into the kitchen. I hadn't seen Allen in a couple of weeks and Crystal had told me that he had twisted his hair so they could begin to dread. I wasn't sure how it would look, but they actually looked nice on his tall thin frame. Terry had given Wonyae back to me and she was at the stove mixing the frying shrimp, okra and onions together and my mouth was watering for a big plate full. Lawrence walked over to her and kissed her lips while we all waited in anticipation. "Okay, you all know that Lawrence and I have been trying to adopt. And you all have met Meika and her brother Jamiere who have been visiting us for a few months now. Well we got a call last week that the court has severed all parental rights with their biological mother and they are going to be moving here with us next week until our adoption of them is final. I'm going to be a mama!" My heart jumped for joy at Terry's news. Crystal and I both squealed at the same time. Duane and Allen both went over and shook Lawrence's hand and we gave Terry a big hug and peck on the cheek.

Once Terry found out that she couldn't have a baby, she looked into adoption. Meika and Jamiere were the first children assigned to them…poor little things. They had been bounced from foster home to foster home as their biological mother battled with her drug addiction. Meika was a fragile little skinny thing. She was five years old and very timid. You could be in the same room with her for hours and not hear a peep out of her. Her brother Jamiere was seven and he was the protector out of the two. Just a baby himself, but he watched after Meika and would tell you quick what she could, or couldn't do. Hurt and disappointment was written all over those two kids, but Terry and Lawrence had so much love to give. If anyone could give those kids the life they deserved, they could.

Terry had asked me if I would babysit during the day and I had to tell her no. Gran wasn't feeling too strong these days so she couldn't watch the kids either. And Sylvia was busy. If she wasn't flying back and forth to Arizona to be with Eddie, she was at her café being miss entrepreneur.

My days were full with my three kids. Even when it was just DJ and me at home I always planned our week's adventures out in advance. I'd make breakfast, cook dinner and straighten up the house and I'd be done by noon. From noon on during the warm months, I'd take DJ to the park, drive to the beach, Sesame Place…something outdoorsy. During the cold months from noon on, we'd go to the library for story time, to the museum, or the planetarium. One of the reasons DJ loved to read and use the computer so much was because the library had a tot's computer learning center. They taught two-and-a-half to four year olds computer literacy. They started with shapes and colors, then moved up to words and numbers. It was really amazing all of the activities that were available during the daytime and I took full-advantage of them all.

Now that Mama lived with us and DJ was in preschool things were a little different, but not much. During the day, Mama went to the senior citizens day care and she loved it. Said they kept her feeling useful. The senior center had all types of activities. They took trips to Atlantic City to the casinos, out to Reading, Pennsylvania to the shopping mall discount outlets, and you know they played Bingo. But most of all it gave her a chance to socialize with other active people who were her age. So before the twins came I had free time to myself to do whatever I wanted for at least four hours a day. I've been pretty much house-bound since the twins were born, but soon as the weather breaks, I'm going to start my routine of finding day activities again. I already signed the twins up for the infant swimming program at the YWCA of Hamilton-Mercerville. They'll be six months old when the classes begin. That's how DJ learned to swim.

I told Terry that she had to really decide what was her priority…her career or raising a family. I had to make the same decision six years ago when Duane asked me to stop teaching. Terry and Crystal thought I had lost my mind, but it was one of the best things that I have done. I have had the chance to put my whole heart and soul into being a mother and wife, and I would not have had that opportunity if I had let their opinions influence my decision.

Do I miss teaching? Every now and then I do miss it, but what I do now fulfills me on an even deeper level. And I was blessed to have a husband who made it possible, 'cause I know there were *countless* women who would have loved to stay home with their kids but couldn't because they *had* to work to put food on the table, or to *help* put food on the table.

Every time DJ's nursery school bus dropped him off at our front door, and *I* was there to open it…I THANKED GOD! I had his little sandwich cut up in squares, a few cookies on the side and I was focused and ready to spend time with him. As Terry often reminded us…she and Lawrence have worked all their married life to be financially free to start their family. So it was not a matter of them *needing* her income to support their lifestyle. They already had options in place for them to make in regards of who was going to take care of their children. One of those options was for her to stay home.

Honestly, I didn't think she would choose to stay home. I thought that maybe she'd hire someone to watch the kids, but Lord when she announced that she was going to stay at home, and that she and Lawrence had already hired an office manager to take over her position at their real estate company, I couldn't believe it. But I was really proud of her for doing something that I knew had to be tough for her to do. Her being miss *I am woman hear me roar!*

After we all ate, Terry took me and Crystal upstairs to show us how they had two of their bedrooms decorated for Meika and Jamiere. And the rooms were beautiful. They had them painted in traditional colors, a soft pink for Meika, and this electric blue for Jamiere. In Jamiere's room they had the ceiling painted in some kind of sparkling paint and when you turned off the lights it glowed in the dark making it look like stars in the sky. It was so beautiful.

Around nine p.m. Sylvia came bopping in, and as soon as she walked through the door the whole party atmosphere turned up a notch. Me, Duane, Allen, Crystal, Lawrence and Terry were all at the dining room table playing Gin Rummy. Duane was sitting there bragging because he was winning this round. "Hey people!" Sylvia said beaming. She had called from the café half-an-hour ago to say that she was on her way after she made her nightly deposit at the bank.

"Hi Nana!" DJ shouted from the floor where he and Lil Allen were playing the video game Mario Brothers. Sylvia went over and gave him a hug, then she went to the couch where the twins were sleeping and gave them each a kiss. She joined us at the table and pulled up a chair between Duane and me. He leaned over and gave Sylvia a kiss on the cheek. She joined right in on the loud talking like she had been there the whole evening.

I didn't really know how to describe the relationship that Sylvia and I had. To me she was one of those people that as my mom would say, 'you feed with a long spoon'. Now we have been at a cease-fire for a while now, but there was still something about her that wouldn't let me put my guard down. Every time I did, she'd find a way to come in and strike. Like the other day we went over to her house and she *just happened* to have an invitation for Missy's graduation from medical school lying around. I cannot pick her friends or tell her what she should or should not have in her house, but she *knew* we were coming over! It was just little things like that that she continued to do that kept me off balance. Duane said that now I was the one keeping the mess going. He thought that *I* made too much out of what she did. Maybe he was right...maybe? Maybe I was just having a hard time letting go of our early days.

Even though I had my issues with Miss Sylvia, one thing I knew for sure was that she loved her grandkids! And DJ was crazy about some Sylvia. Every other word that came out of his mouth was, my Nana this, or my Nana that.

It was close to midnight and the card game was *still* going strong, but I was wiped out! I had taken the twins and went upstairs to Terry's guest room when I heard a light knock on the door and Sylvia peeked her head inside, "Asia, is it alright if I come in?"

The top of my shirt was pulled up because I was breastfeeding Wonyae while softly patting Walter on the back. He was stirring because he wanted to be fed. And I was doing everything I could not to fall asleep. Sylvia came over to the bed and sat down, "You need any help?" In the dimly lit room, she reached to pick Walter up.

"No, not that one." I said removing Wonyae from my breast, "If you can burp her. I can start feeding Walt."

Wonnie started wrestling like she didn't have enough to eat while Walt half-whimpered, half-whined as he waited patiently.

Sliding a towel over her shoulder, Sylvia reached for Wonyae. "I don't think she's finished eating."

"Oh, she's finished alright. I've been feeding her for the last thirty minutes. You know, they're twins, but they have such different personalities. Wonyae was baby A, the one who came out first and she's very aggressive and impatient. Walt, on the other hand, is a sweety." As I spoke, I slid my baby boy over to my breast kissing him on the head, "Duane says Wonyae reminds him of you."

Sylvia smiled at the thought. Wonyae let out a big belch, "That's Nana's baby." She held her granddaughter to her heart and got so filled up. "Sylvia are you alright?"

"Eddie asked me to marry him."

That was no surprise to me. Eddie was such a good man, and to see the two of them together, you could just tell that they were on the same page when it came to their feelings for each other. I mean, I have never seen Sylvia laugh so much as when she was around Eddie. And like Duane said, his mom had finally found her king. Eddie and Sylvia had been dating for four years now, so what I didn't get was what was the sad face for?

"Sylvia, that's wonderful. I know Duane is going to be so happy for you."

She looked at me for a few seconds without responding, then she finally said, "Asia you act like I don't know how you of all people feel about me."

I started to act like I didn't know what she was talking about, then decided I was through playing games with her. Apparently she was in the frame of mind to *be real* so I told her what was on my mind. "Sylvia, you can be a really decent person when you want to be, and you have a lot of qualities that I admire."

"But?"

"But, what makes us clash is that you feel you can talk to me anyway you want. And you have to stop controlling everything around you. Sylvia I know my husband loves you, but he's a grown man and needs you to respect him as one."

Wonyae started to wail, "Give her that pacifier," I pointed to the bottom of the bed.

"Not managing my son has given me a lot of time to think about things. It gave me a chance to step back and turn off my business mind and observe *his* life from afar. To *hear* what Duane had been saying…that he was *happy* and all that he wanted was for *me* to be *happy*. With Eddie, I finally realize what he's been talking about." Sylvia got quiet, "The hardest thing for me now is, if I give in to this happiness, I have to admit that I was wrong for driving Duane like I did."

"You were just doing what you thought was right. But now that you understand Duane has to make his own decisions, you shouldn't let that stand in your way of happiness, Sylvia. Eddie loves you, and that's all Duane ever wanted. And that is for you to have someone special in your life.

Through teary eyes Sylvia smiled, "I'm glad Duane married you."

My nipple popped out of Walt's mouth as I sat up in shock. "Excuse me!"

Rocking Wonyae in her arms, Sylvia laughed lightly, "Well you can't blame me for thinking what I did, I mean after all, you are a whole lot older than he is, you were married before *and* had a lot to gain from marrying my Duane."

"All of that is true and I thought about all of that too, but Sylvia, I was in love with Duane."

"Only time and events prove love, Asia. Duane was my boy and I was only concerned about him. You just wait until DJ and these two start dating. You'll find out quick what I'm talking about."

"Maybe." I said, "But what's with the change of heart?"

"My son is living the life I wish I could have given him as a child - a home with a mother *and* father. My mother always reminds me that Duane is a grown man. Let's just say that I accept the fact the I've raised him right and I know I have to let him go." Her tears began to roll once again as she kissed Wonyae on the head.

"Sylvia, it means *so* much to hear you being so honest," I was still stunned. "I'm sorry for staring at you all funny and everything, but…I've been waiting for a *long* time to hear you say these things."

"Really?" Now she looked stunned! "I thought you didn't care to hear anything I had to say." She laid a sleeping Wonyae down on the blanket next to me.

"I care, how could I not, Sylvia? Duane adores you and he has been so bummed out about our tense relationship. All he ever wanted was for us to be friends. My husband needs you in his life and that means I do too. What do you say we let the past stay in the past and you and I work at being family?"

"I would like that...I would like that very much."

TOO FAR AWAY FROM HOME

I arrived in Milwaukee at eight thirty-eight in the morning. There was a limo waiting to drive me to the Sheraton Hotel. My meeting with Mr. Tate was scheduled for ten-thirty. I did my usual thing that I always did when I went out of town...as soon as I put my bags down, I called Asia.

She was already up in the kitchen making breakfast, "How was your flight, baby?"

"It was alright, I fell asleep and when I opened my eyes I was here."

"Are you nervous?"

"Just a little, but nothing I can't handle." I had put a lot of time into learning the four teams that I submitted coaching applications to. Talked with everyone I played under who would give me the time to sit down and mentor me about the different aspects of being a team leader, coach and coordinator. So it was only a matter of waiting for the call so I could prepare a real tight presentation on how I could contribute to their team and make them a stronger unit. And my shit was tight. I knew I could do this.

"Duane, guess what?" Asia asked playfully.

"What?"

"Walt smiled today, and it wasn't gas. It was a real smile."

"Naw, for real?"

I heard Asia say in a baby voice, "Yes he did. Yes he did. Oh Duane he just did it again! I was tickling his little tummy and he opened his mouth like he wanted to laugh. Oh Duane." She sounded like she was just melting.

I laid across the hotel bed with the phone to my ear as Asia and I talked and laughed about our kids. She was telling me that this morning DJ tried to sneak out the house with his Last Avenger pajama top on under his coat to go to nursery school. We were both cracking up. Then I heard a knock on the door. It was the limo driver picking me up to go to my meeting.

Damn, I thought to myself! We were on the phone a whole hour and I hadn't even realized it. I didn't get a chance to change my clothes, go over my notes, nothing. I told Asia I loved her, hung up the phone then went into the bathroom and freshened up real quick. Brushed my teeth, rewashed my face, and put on my business clothes.

When I got to Mr. Tate's office he was there with four other gentlemen from the Milwaukee organization. As I was being interviewed, something inside of me didn't feel right. It was like my brain had switched to autopilot because consciously, I was hearing and responding to their questions, but subconsciously I was thinking about my life and asking, 'how much was enough?' Asking myself why was I even here in Milwaukee, who was I doing this for, and what did I have to prove? My heart began to fade with each question I posed to myself, because the answers didn't line up with me taking that job.

I was happy in New Jersey. My family was settled and things were really going well. It didn't make sense for me to uproot and relocate everyone here to start all over not knowing how things would actually workout. The Milwaukee management could love me, and I could spend the next fifteen to twenty years here, or they could hate me and let me go by next season.

Both my conscious and subconscious came together as I stood to my feet along with the other four men at the end of the meeting. From being so distracted, I didn't feel that I interviewed as well as I would have liked. I must have left a good impression with them anyway because they offered me the offensive line coordinating position.

Instead of jumping on the opportunity right then, I told Mr. Tate and the other men that I would give them my decision tomorrow. In doing so, I shocked everyone, including myself. They sort of looked around the room at each other, then Mr. Tate said, "Well, we'll all meet back here tomorrow at nine o'clock."

When I got back to the hotel room I dialed Sylvia. This was all she ever talked about…my post-PLF years and I knew if anyone had a dozen reasons why I should take this Milwaukee coaching job she would be the one!

"How's things in Milwaukee?"

"Cold." I laughed, "Naw, I'm just kidding. To be honest I don't know." I sat on the edge of the bed with my head down as I pressed the phone to my ear. My feelings were so sober yet conflicting. "I feel like I'm at crossroads, and if I turn left I have this great ass career, but not much time for anything else."

"What happens if you turn right?"

"If I turn right, I have Asia and the kids and time to do all the things that I envision for us. You know, a couple more babies…"

"A couple more babies?" Sylvia said laughing.

"Oh yeah, like two or three more…Disney World the whole nine. Only thing, if I'm not in football, I don't know where I'm supposed to be. I been doing this shit all my life."

"Duane it's obvious that your heart is telling you not to take that job. And if your heart is home with Asia and the kids, well that's where you need to be."

"That's it? That's all you have to say?"

"I have to admit that I've pushed a lot of my dreams onto you. I honestly thought I had your best interest at heart. But yes, that is *all* I have to say. This is your call. You do whatever you have to do 'cause I'm gonna love and be proud you no matter what."

For the first time in years…maybe even ever in all my adult years, Sylvia spoke to me like a mother concerned about her *son's* situation instead of a business manager going after the next big score.

I knew I was a man and had to do my own thing, but it felt good hearing her say that. For Sylvia to set me free and love me without conditions was an answer to my prayers. Her words unlocked the cage of control that she kept over me even after she stopped being my manager. Even though the flat out act of telling me what to do wasn't there, there was always the hinted. She'd give her two-cents and if I didn't act on it the way she intended there was always the mental backlash on her end. Then on my end there would be the guilt for bucking her system of doing things. All I ever wanted as an adult from my mother was the freedom to make my own choices and live with either the consequences or rewards of my *own* decisions. To be no longer be her *boy*, but a *man*... that just happened to be her son. And when Sylvia said that she would *love* me no matter what decision I made, I felt like a *complete* man!

I stayed up all night long thinking about the pros and cons of taking the job. Right before I drifted off to sleep, I decided not to accept Milwaukee's offer and the unrest that was inside of me chilled and I was at perfect peace.

The next morning I called Mr. Dansberry to see if he was actually serious about that Phys Ed position at the high school. He said he was and if I was interested the position was mine, so I secured the job.

Feeling like a new man, I walked into Mr. Tate's office and small-talked until the other men arrived, then I announced that I was very thankful for the opportunity of coaching that they had extended, but I had to turn down the offer.

"We're very sorry to hear that Duane. We had every confidence that you would have made a heck of a contribution to our organization. But if you don't mind my asking," Mr. Davenport the team's owner asked, "What made you decline?"

"Well Sir, I guess it's like this. After I blew my knee out, I wasn't sure what my next career move would be. Money's not a concern of mine any longer, thanks to my wife's insistence years ago that I stop wasting it. So I knew I didn't *have* to return back to the field to maintain my style of living. Once you get injured, you find out real quick how valuable your health is," I smirked. "I honestly believed that coaching for the PFL was the only logical choice for me to make, but now that I'm here, all I can think about is my family back in Jersey and what my kids are doing, *right at this moment.*" I stressed. "My grandpa's favorite saying is, that a man can only throw his loyalties into one ring at a time. If I had accepted this position, then it would only be right that I devote myself to being the best coach I could be and we all know that's an eighteen hour a day job, *and weekends too.* I have this incredibly sexy wife at home, we have a small boy and just had a brand new set of twins." I felt myself smiling, "I don't want to miss out on that. I don't *ever* want them to say I wasn't there for them. I'm just sorry I wasted your time...but I didn't realize this until I got here." I confessed honestly.

"Sounds to me like you are a very lucky man, Duane." Mr. Davenport said.

"Yes Sir, I am."

That afternoon as I flew back to New Jersey, I couldn't wait to get home. When I walked in the house at five, DJ was running around wild, Wonyae was wailing away and Asia was dressed in old gray cotton sweats with her hair all over her head looking a damn mess, but in the most beautiful kind of way. After I left the airport, I stopped to pick up a little something for everyone. I walked in with a big shopping bag and a single red rose.

Since she wasn't expecting me until the next day, Asia's eyes lit up. "Help!" she laughed, walking over to me with her arms stretched out, wrapping them snugly around my neck.

I was suited down in my gray Armani, looking fine, if I do say so myself. "You miss me, girl?" I wrapped my arms right back around her.

"Tremendously." she said and we kissed and she was feeling and tasting like home...as in, 'there's no place like!'

When DJ saw me he charged forward, calling my name. As I hugged him, it felt like I'd been away forever instead of just two days. Reaching down in my bag I gave him yet another action packed Last Avenger coloring book. Mom Janie walked up with Wonyae in her arms and I kissed Mom on the cheek and handed her the rose. She smiled while holding it to her nose.

I took Wonnie in my arms, "Daddy even got something for you." I pulled out a squeaky toy, kissed her head and gave her back to Mom Janie. Walt was in his bassinet asleep. I kissed his head and put his toy next to him. "Ma, you think you can handle them for a while? I need to grab my wife to myself."

She smiled, looking at me through the corner of her eye, "Go on na, and take your time."

Seductively, I looked at my wife, "You go on upstairs and get ready for me." I said winking my eye at Asia.

She squealed then ran upstairs.

I walked out into the garage and came back with a huge arrangement of flowers set in a Tiffany crystal vase, plus a bottle of Dom Perignon. I got two wine glasses from the kitchen cabinet, and my Boney James jazz CD from my music collection in the family room.

Mom was smiling at me as she cuddled Wonyae and watched me rushing around looking like a romantic fool with my arms full.

When I entered the room Asia was still in her sweats. She was making up the bed. The room was on the cluttered side, bordering junkie and Asia was stooping down tucking the sheet between the mattress, "Duane, I'm sorry about this mess. I was so busy today and I didn't know you were coming home tonight..." Finally, she looked up and saw the variety of flowers in my hand and she gasped, "Oh baby, they're beautiful." With her hair standing straight up on her head, Asia walked over to me and sunk her nose into the flowers.

I lifted the bottle of champagne for her to see.

Her eyes lit then softened, "Dom? Duane, did you get the coaching position?" She took the crystal vase from my hands and placed it on the table in our master bedroom's lounge.

I walked behind her and popped the CD in the player then pulled Asia close to me, "Baby girl, we have to talk." I knew how Asia felt about us discussing critical decisions that affected our family and I had made two without her input. One not accepting the Milwaukee position and two accepting the high school position with a boss that she disliked. I wasn't sure how she would handle my news.

"Talk about what, Duane?" Asia was confused, "Honey, obviously there's something to celebrate." She said pointing to the flowers and the champagne.

I just stared at her and let my eyes linger awhile. Ever since I was a kid and she worked at the concession stand at the movies, Asia was the girl of my dreams. Now she was my friend, my soul mate, the mother of my kids, and the one I *was* growing old with. At thirty-eight, she had some grays starting to sprout in her hair, and at thirty-two I had a few of my own. "Tonight, I'm celebrating you. I'm celebrating us...so I hope you understand what I've done."

"Wait a minute, Duane. What's going on?" She searched my eyes for an answer. "You didn't get the job, did you?"

My head dropped then I looked back at her, hoping that she wouldn't be too disappointed because we had both been psyched about me possibly coaching for the PFL, "How would that make you feel?"

"Baby, I'm here for you no matter what. I just know how much you wanted to it."

"I didn't get it."

"Ahh Lovah, I'm sorry, but it's their loss. They didn't know what they had." Asia comforted.

"Well actually, they did. Milwaukee offered me the position, *I* turned it down."

"You what?!" She looked at me like she couldn't believe her ears, "You trippin, right? You had me around here for four weeks on pins and needles. Stressed! They offered it to you and you turned it down? Why Duane?" Asia asked aggravated and pushed out of my embrace.

"You see babe, that's just it. Once I got to Milwaukee, my thinking got real clear. I was in Mr. Tate's office and we were going over my prospectus for the team and my ideas about how I wanted to put myself into the restructuring of their offense. Then they were talking about incorporating their options for the upcoming draft picks. Sitting there with them it became so clear that, yes, I could do it, *but...but* if I accepted it, then what time would I have left over when I came home? What kind of man would I be to you? What kind of father to our kids, you know? That's when I knew I couldn't accept the position."

Asia stopped then turned to face me and spoke softly, "I don't know what to say."

"You disappointed?"

"How could I be? You just gave up a lot for us." She walked over to me, wrapping herself back in my arms, "Baby, I am so blessed to have you." Asia kissed me on my Adam's apple, "So what now?"

"You're not going to believe this." Grinning, I grabbed Asia by the shoulders.

Her eyes sparkled just looking at mine.

"Have a seat." I said excited and popped the cork pouring us both a glass of Dom, "You're looking at the new Phys Ed teacher slash *head coach* for Oliver Williams High School."

Asia looked at me with her mouth hanging wide open, then she started laughing, "Baby, are you serious?! Lovah, that's great! How did that happen? When?"

"I saw your boy, Mr. Dansberry at Acme Food Market couple weeks ago. He mentioned the position in passing and when I was in Milwaukee, after it was clear I was not going to accept the job, I called him and followed up on it. He gave it to me on the spot." The more I thought about teaching at the high school, the more it felt right! I already had my degrees in physical education and nutrition, plus all the years I had in sports, I knew this was a good decision even though it wasn't glamorous.

"The Hitman" had served me well, but I was ready to leave all of that high profile lifestyle, hectic schedule stuff in the background. I wanted to fade into the PFL sunset and maybe in ten years have them feature me in a 'Sports Legends Where Are They Now' documentary or something.

My heart was just pounding over the excitement of becoming a teacher, "Asia, I have a lot to offer those young men. I look at this as my chance to really give back to the community some of the blessings and knowledge I've been given. I'm really feeling this, baby."

"Oh boy." Asia started laughing again, "The jerk is your boss now. And you know how much trouble he used to give me."

"Girl, shoot, *I'm* gonna be running things up at Oliver." Pointing at my chest with my thumb, I laughed, "And besides, I'll whoop his ass if he tries that shit with me girl." I grabbed Asia and started my tickle attack. She was laughing, trying to make her get away. She ran out of the lounge into the main part of the bedroom when I caught her and picked her up placing her on the bed. Dressed in my trousers, starched white shirt and tie, I straddled over top of her. It felt good bending my leg without that damn brace on it. It didn't feel good-as-new like the doctor said it would, but now three weeks with no constraints, it was getting stronger. Leaning so close that she could feel my breath on her lips I said, "You missed me, girl?"

"Yes, I missed you." She purred, "Can I practice blowing your whistle, Coach Cummings?" Asia teased me rolling over on top. She loosened my belt, unzipping my pants.

"Only if you squat and give me twenty on this afterwards." I said grinding my nine inches into her.

"I want an A in your class."

"Only if you deserve it, 'cause I ain't givin' nothin' away." I looked at my wife and I couldn't wait to feel her wet mouth around my dick, and when I did, my eyes rolled up in the back of my head. We been married almost six years and she *still* felt good to me!

As she removed her sweat pants and panties, I pulled my trouser down around my ankles looking at Asia, loving her brown skin now scarred with stretch marks from the three pregnancies. And even though she complained about them I told her I could read every mark just like an astrologer reads the stars. I knew which marks came from which babies and to me that was all a part of the sacrifice she made for *me*...for our family...to the generations that would come from the pregnancies that flawed her flawless brown skin. Her firm breasts, just like my PFL career had seen their prime come and go. No longer firm, they were now soft and lazily laid against her body. But they were more than sexy to me. My wife's breasts were nothing short of amazing! They nourished and sustained all of our babies during the first months of their lives, and I can't lie...I got me a drink or two my damn self. Long story short, stretch marks, saggy titties and fifteen extra pounds later my wife was beautiful and no other woman could *ever* turn me on more than Asia. No one could *ever* take her place in my life.

She got back on the bed straddling across me, teasing me with her body, then relieving me as she slid down slowly taking me all the way inside. Gripping her soft ass, rhythmically I worked her body into mine and she rode me until her back gave out. Then I rolled her over and made love to her.

Asia moaned as her fingernails scrapped gently across my back sending even more chills down my spine. Reaching up, I pulled Asia's gray sweatshirt over her head then unfastened her nursing bra. Her breasts were swelled with milk and I started licking across her nipples. She loosened my tie pulling it from around my neck then unbuttoned my shirt, struggling to get it off me. I kicked my trousers and draws from around my ankles to the floor then slid down Asia's body and began to lick her black pearl. Her fingers twisted in my hair as she took her time letting her love come down. As her breaths became rugged, Asia grabbed the pillow to her mouth to muffle her ecstasy.

While I gave it to her real good, I heard the rattling of the bedroom doorknob. Before I could say a word I snatched the comforter off the end of the bed and threw it across me and most of Asia, just before the door crashed open. Startled, Asia sat up in the bed with the cover pulled around her neck and I heard DJ's little voice.

"What you doin' Mommy?" he asked walking over to the bed.

My foot was hanging out of the bottom of the bed, then I pulled it up under the covers.

"Nothing, honey. Now why don't you go on back down stairs with grandmom? Mommy will be down in a second." Asia was holding the covers up to her neck.

"Why daddy under there?" He asked tapping on top of the cover where I was hiding between Asia's legs.

"We're just playing. Okay, now go on down stairs."

"Can I play with you and daddy."

"No honey..."

"DJ go down stairs, right now!" I had to say. With the way they were going Asia would have been talking to him half the night.

I heard him whimpering like I hurt his feelings then he walked out of the room.

"And close the door!" I yelled behind him.

Asia started cracking up after the door closed.

"Shit, it was getting hot under there, girl." I laughed, as I emerged from under the covers. We both looked at each other and started cracking up.

And so is life at the Cummings casa!

RETIREMENT DINNER

The crowd stood, applauding as the last speaker finished up his speech on the long list of Duane's accomplishments as an athlete, humanitarian, community leader, and as a man. We were at the Regency Hotel in the main ballroom and the place was filled to capacity with the media, family, and friends. Duane was sitting at the head of the table along with Coach Maxon, the owner of the New Jersey Tritons and the owner's wife along with their other distinguished guests.

Chandeliers hung from the ceiling and we sat at round tables draped in white linen. Even though it was only three o'clock in the afternoon, the main ballroom was dimly lit giving off the atmosphere of a evening affair.

Sitting at the first table along with Eddie and me was Asia, her mother, and the kids. DJ was looking so handsome in his little tuxedo that matched his dad's.

I did it! At forty-eight years old, I finally tied the knot. Eddie and I had a small but elegant garden wedding in my backyard. He still had three years left before he retires so we'll continue to live in both Arizona and New Jersey.

Tompy flew in for the event. Love was in the air because he was sporting his misses-to-be on his arm and he looked so happy with his life. They were seated at the next table with Terry, Lawrence and their two adopted children, Meika, and Jamiere. Terry said that Asia made taking care of kids look so easy, but I only had one and I could have told her that raising kids wasn't. She and Lawrence were getting adjusted to being parents. I think they were doing a good job. I told her that it was going to take some time for everything to settle and feel normal, but one thing they had in their favor, their two adopted children are good kids.

Duane's father Jericho and stepmom Marie drove in last night from

Maryland. Even though I made a mistake lying to him all those years ago, which resulted in my pregnancy with Duane, I was blessed to have made that mistake with him. Jericho had been such a perfect father for Duane and after thirty-two years, his eyes still lit up when he saw his son. And Duane's eyes definitely lit up when he saw his dad. I am eternally grateful to Jericho and Marie for the love they had given to my child, *and* for including me in their life as well.

"And without further ado…" the speaker said, "…I would like to introduce our man of the hour, Duane "The Hitman" Cummings."

Duane stood up to the podium dressed in his black tuxedo. He looked like he just stepped off of the cover of QG magazine.

Smoothing his dinner jacket against his chest, Duane placed a piece of paper in full view so he could read the speech he had prepared. After adjusting the microphone, he began to speak. First he addressed the panel and thanked them for their praise of his career, and kind words they said about him - the man, then he continued to speak.

"I feel so blessed and so complete tonight. There are so many people to whom I am grateful. God, who is my alpha and omega. I am deeply indebted to the Professional Football League for allowing me to have a forum to express myself athletically. For giving me the opportunity to see the world and affording me a chance to take care of my family in a manner that any man could only dream of. I stand here tonight grateful that this has happened to me." Duane took a sip of water from his glass. "Thanks to the Arizona Mavericks. Coach Barnes and Mrs. Helen Gratty, who flew in to help me celebrate this special occasion. I was drafted into the Mavericks organization right after college. This experience laid a solid foundation for my rise as a professional football player, and I thank you. The knowledge and skills that I learned in Arizona under Coach Barnes prepared me to become a *Fightin' Triton*!" Duane yelped, and his teammates began to roar, clapping and whistling. Then they got rowdy and began singing the Tritons' war song. Duane was grinning so hard I thought his face would freeze with that same smile on it.

"That's why I love it here." He raised his hand so they could calm down,

"But y'all got to let me finish this 'cause it's kinda warm up here." Duane put his finger in his collar, then he started reading once more. "I am grateful to be able to end my playing career as a Triton. As in Real Estate the key is location, location, location. I have spent four years here in Jersey. *Four years*, two Champion Bowls, and two rings later." And the crowd went wild again. "I want to thank my family, who have been there for me from the very start." Duane lifted up his retirement plaque, "I want to thank my mom for her endless love and support. Sylvia, this is for you." When my son said that, I had tears big as gumdrops falling from my eyes. I threw him a big kiss with both hands.

"My agent, Zigna Rodregues, who has become a part of my family. Love ya Zig." Duane pointed to Zigna in the audience. Nine wonderful years she's represented us. This was also Zigna's last year in the business. We attended her retirement dinner six weeks ago.

"To my dad, Jericho Austin, and his wife, Marie, love you guys." Duane spotted them and waved to them. "And tonight wouldn't mean a grain of salt if I failed to mention my loved ones who have passed on and whom I feel their presence every waking moment. Pop Heartly, this is also for you." Duane shook the plaque. Then he paused, biting his bottom lip and running his hand across his face, "To my daughter Epiphany, my first born, whose life was taken much, much, *much* too soon. My angel, all I can say is that daddy loves you and I'll never forget." Duane tapped his hand over her name engraved on his heart, "Which brings me to the last people on my list." Focusing his attention on Asia and their kids, Duane paused again, but this time with the most endearing smile on his face, "Order holds no preference or priority tonight. Asia Heartly Cummings, I thank you for being my wife. There's an old tired saying that goes, 'behind every great man, there is a great woman.' I would like to say that besides this great man stands an even greater woman. One of the greatest women God has created, and you're all mine." The crowd began to clap. "When we started dating seven years ago, I asked her what happens to a man who fills up on sweets if he has no substance. The answer to that question is, he will become weak and eventually whither away. I am thankful to you my dear for all of your love, forgiveness and support. You have always been the perfect balance of sweet and substance in my life. And I thank you for all our babies, Epiphany, Duane Jr., and our newest additions to the family, Walter and Wonyae." When Duane called out his kids' names DJ's face just lit up. He pointed his finger at Duane and started laughing out loud. Asia had to give him the eye to calm him down. DJ was too funny!

"To Gran, Gramps, Mom Janie, Aunt Terry, Lawrence, my two new little cousins, Meika and Jamiere." Duane stopped and waved at the two of them and just like DJ they both lit up as they waved back. "To Crystal, Allen, and my main man Tompy Seagrams. I love you all. And in conclusion, something I'm really excited about, in September, which is *only* three months away, I'll be starting my first year as physical education teacher and *head football coach* for Oliver Williams High. And I expect to see all you guys out there on the field supporting my team. Peace and love to everyone."

Duane stood back away from the podium and the audience all stood to their feet and applauded. Cameras flashed and the reporters swarmed around him taken by the news of his new average career. But he was such an extraordinary man…my son! His own man. Several weeks ago the rumors started circulating about him coaching at the local high school and there was this big debate about whether he was living up to his full potential. Whether he would be more effective as a college coach, or if he should have stayed in the PFL for a few more seasons. One reporter even had the *nerve* to say that Duane made a *soft* decision by retiring because he was *afraid* to get hit. Oooh, talking 'bout somebody getting hot! Duane told me not to even feed into all the chatter. He said that he made the decision and it was final. That was good enough for me.

I leaned over towards Asia, "He looks some kinda good up there doesn't he?" I said bursting with pride.

"He sure does." She replied and we both laughed grabbing each other's hand, basking in Duane's glory.

ABOUT THE AUTHOR

Undra E. Biggs is a native of Trenton, New Jersey. Her first novel published in 2000 is titled, *When You Look At Me*.

Undra is also a devoted wife and mother of two children: Miya and Alvin, Jr. To learn more about her endeavors, contact her at http://www.undraebiggs.com

www.ingramcontent.com/pod-product-compliance
Lightning Source LLC
Chambersburg PA
CBHW032040240626
47154CB00003B/1007